Dedalus European C

General Editor: Mike N

The Bells of Bruges

Georges Rodenbach

The Bells of Bruges

(Le Carillonneur)

translated by Mike Mitchell
and with an introduction by Nicholas Royle

Dedalus

Dedalus would like to thank The French Community of Belgium for its assistance in publishing this book.

Published in the UK by Dedalus Ltd, Langford Lodge,
24–26 St Judith's Lane, Sawtry, Cambs, PE28 5XE
email: info@dedalusbooks.com
www.dedalusbooks.com

ISBN 978 1 903517 54 3

Dedalus is distributed in the United States by SCB Distributors,
15608 South New Century Drive, Gardena, California 90248
email: info@scbdistributors.com   web site: www.scbdistributors.com

Dedalus is distributed in Australia by Peribo Pty Ltd,
58 Beaumont Road, Mount Kuring-gai, N.S.W. 2080
email: info@peribo.com.au

Dedalus is distributed in Canada by Disticor Direct-Book Division,
695 Westney Road South, Suite 14, Ajax, Ontario, LI6 6M9
email: ndalton@disticor.com
web site: www.disticordirect.com

First published in France in 1897
First published by Dedalus in 2007

Translation copyright © Mike Mitchell 2007
Introduction copyright © Nicholas Royle 2007

The right of Mike Mitchell to be indentified as the translator and the right of Nicholas Royle to be identified as the editor of this work have been asserted by them in accordance with the Copyright, Designs and Patent Act, 1988.

Printed in Finland by WS Bookwell
Typeset by RefineCatch Limited, Bungay, Suffolk

NICHOLAS ROYLE

Nicholas Royle is the author of five novels – *Counterparts, Saxophone Dreams, The Matter of the Heart, The Director's Cut* and *Antwerp* – and one short story collection, *Mortality*. A novella, *The Enigma of Departure*, is forthcoming. Widely published as a journalist, he has also edited twelve anthologies. He lives in Manchester with his wife and two children and lectures in creative writing at Manchester Metropolitan University.

MIKE MITCHELL

Mike Mitchell is one of Dedalus's editorial directors and is responsible for the Dedalus translation programme. His publications include *The Dedalus Book of Austrian Fantasy, Peter Hacks: Drama for a Socialist Society* and *Austria* in the *World Bibliographical Series*.

His translation of Rosendorfer's *Letters Back to Ancient China* won the 1998 Schlegel-Tieck Translation Prize after he had been shortlisted in previous years for his translations of *Stephanie* by Herbert Rosendorfer and *The Golem* by Gustav Meyrink. His translation of *Simplicissimus* was shortlisted for The Weidenfeld Translation Prize in 1999 and *The Other Side* by Alfred Kubin in 2000. He has translated the following books for Dedalus from German: five novels by Gustav Meyrink, four novels by Herbert Rosendorfer, three novels by Johann Grimmelshausen, two novels by Hermann Ungar, *The Great Bagarozy* by Helmut Krausser, *The Road to Darkness* by Paul Leppin and *The Other Side* by Alfred Kubin.

From French he has translated for Dedalus two novels by Mercedes Deambrosis and two novels by Georges Rodenbach.

I would like to thank Renée Birks for her willing help in sorting out some of Rodenbach's more abstruse expressions. Any remaining mistakes are, of course, all my own.

Mike Mitchell

INTRODUCTION

Bruges. Brugge. A museum piece, a town out of time. Known throughout the world by its French name, despite its being located in the half of Belgium that doesn't speak French – or not willingly. Indeed, this hauntingly beautiful, historic town is the provincial capital of West Flanders, yet most of the world calls it Bruges, not Brugge, harking back to a time when French was the dominant language, at least among the middle classes.

During the city's golden age, in the fifteenth century, Bruges was bustling with traders in wool, lace and diamonds, but when the Zwijn estuary began to silt up, trade moved 90 kilometres east to Antwerp. Bruges slowly died, then bravely geared up for its afterlife as a tourist attraction. British, French, German, American, Japanese – they all flock to Bruges.

Georges Rodenbach – Belgian novelist born Tournai 1855, died Paris 1898 – wrote the book on Bruges. It was he who pronounced the city dead. His 1892 novel *Bruges-la-Morte* painted an unforgettable picture of this strangely isolated, anachronistic town, cut off from the North Sea, geographically part of Flanders yet somehow separate, with its looping dead-end canals and winding narrow streets, its stepped gables and towering belfries. Pealing bells and crying gulls. A murder of crows around the Belfort, a train of jackdaws between the windmills and the ramparts. Sometimes you'll get a waft of the sea, often, but not exclusively, along the canals, even the occasional hint of the sewers, but if the town has a more pervasive smell it's a strangely sweet one. Waffles, perhaps, or chocolate. Continental cigarettes, patisserie.

You hear Bruges as much as smell it. The slap of rubber on stone as cars and, predominantly, bicycles negotiate the cobbled streets and leafy squares. The babble of the rabble, tourist hordes speaking in many tongues. The hoteliers and bartenders, ticket sellers and turnstile operators will answer you, it seems, in whatever language you use to address them, but if English is your mother tongue, don't try speaking to the Flemings in French. You might as well address a Geordie in Gaelic.

You don't *have to* take a trip to Bruges to get the most out of Rodenbach, but it certainly helps. They should stock him at the Eurostar terminal alongside the maps and guides. There's no better place to read *The Bells of Bruges* than perched on a parapet by the canal outside Gruuthuse Palace or sitting comfortably in De Garre with a glass of draught Gouden Draak, the colour and consistency of melted muscovado sugar.

It would be a considerable understatement to say that Rodenbach's 1892 work *Bruges-la-Morte* established the Belgian novelist as a writer with a sense of place. In it, the Flemish town becomes a character as important to the story as the principal *personnages*. The same is equally true of *Le Carillonneur* (1897), now translated into English for the first time as *The Bells of Bruges*.

Architect Joris Borluut wins a public contest to become the official town carillonneur. He is given the key to the belfry, and although happy to have won, feels a little like he has been given the key to his own tomb. Borluut is given to introspection and melancholy, and the people of Bruges, 'resigned to the town's decline, the stagnant canals, the grey streets', are described as having 'found a taste for the melancholy sweetness of resignation'. Yet when Borluut plays the carillon, they are revitalised – 'an ancient heroism still slumbered within the race, sparks resided in the inertia of the stones'. Thus are key elements of the narrative cleverly and subtly foretold in the first chapter – and likewise on into the second.

Borluut receives the congratulations of his friends – antiques dealer Van Hulle, lawyer and Flemish nationalist Farazyn, and painter Bartholomeus – at their regular weekly meeting at Van Hulle's house on Zwarteleertouwerstraat. Van Hulle's house is 'an ancient building with a double gable whose brick façade was storiated with a bas-relief above the door representing a ship, its sails billowing out like breasts'. No such house stands on Zwarteleertouwerstraat today, though many of those on the north-east side of the street are lovely old buildings with the distinctive stepped gables. Two houses in particular are studded with weathered faces of angels and sea-farers that peep out of the brickwork. 'The centuries were carrying out their dreary work of dilapidation, the posies withered, the faces eaten away by erosion, as if by leprosy.' Borluut's restoration of Van Hulle's façade brings him fame – 'Everyone went to see and admire the miracle of rejuvenation which still retained the essential oldness . . .' – and an end-less amount of further restoration work throughout the town, which, to Borluut, is a 'poem in stone, an illuminated reliquary'.

Van Hulle has two daughters – fiery, earthy Barbara and the more celestial, ethereal Godelieve. For Borluut, who falls in love with each daughter in turn, both are represented by particular bells in the bell-tower: Godelieve is embodied in 'the little bell whose pure song at that time was soaring, dominating every piece on the carillon', while Barbara is symbolised by the great Bell of Lust ('He had looked up into the bell as if he were looking up her dress').

The bells are not alone in being used as figurative symbols in Rodenbach's vision. The canals are useful, too: 'She stood between them like a canal between two stone embankments. The embankments are face to face, nevertheless apart and will never unite, but the waters mix their reflections, merge them, appear to join them together.'

Fittingly, the canals find further employment, standing in for a commodity rather more abstract. 'Her love, which he had thought superficial and ephemeral, persisted, reappearing here and there like the water of the canals in the town.'

Of course, Symbolism is not solely about representation. Through dialogue between Borluut and the painter, Bar-tholomeus, Rodenbach explores the life of objects. ' "I wanted to show that these objects are sensitive," ' says the artist, ' "suffer at the coming of night, faint at the departure of the last rays, which, by the way, also live in this room; they suffer as much, they fight against the darkness. There you have it. It's the life of things . . ." ' Borluut's own insights into Bartholomeus's character provide evidence of Rodenbach's deeper interest. 'His appeared to be a complex temperament. That was because he was close to the infinite. He naturally found mystical analogies, the eternal connections between things.' Thus Rodenbach approaches the essence of Symbolism. A religious parade taking place in the town of Veurne towards the end of the novel offers further opportunity to explore the subject. 'Indeed, all the symbols and emblems there were powerful, suggestive ways of putting things in a nutshell, allegories attesting to the Flemish sense of understanding the life of objects.'

The idea of objects having almost a life of their own is linked to Rodenbach's insistence that the town is more than just an assemblage of stone and brick, something inert and soulless. Borluut, not for the first time, becomes a mouthpiece for his creator's theories when he is carried away with enthusiasm for Bartholomeus's paintings. 'It was not so much painting as an apparition, as if the centuries-old walls had opened up and one could finally see *what the stones are dreaming.*'

Not only does the town reflect the emotions and inner lives of its inhabitants, but so too are the residents conditioned by the bricks and the stone and the hazy northern light and the water of the canals. Bartholomeus says: ' "The aesthetic quality of towns is essential. If, as has been said, every landscape is a frame of mind, then it is even more true of a townscape. The way the inhabitants think and feel corresponds to the town they live in." '

If the theory is revealed to be something of an *idée fixe*, it is not alone. The novel is a story, or several stories, of obsession. Van Hulle amasses a huge collection of clocks because he is obsessed by the idea of hearing them all strike the hour precisely at the same time, and indeed, as the hour rings out from the bell-tower. Farazyn is driven by his vision of the town reborn as the seaport of Bruges, while Bartholomeus devotes himself to painting.

Borluut is obsessed, at various times, by his love for Barbara, for Godelieve and for the town itself. The one place where he can indulge all three obsessions is in the belfry, the single most important location in the novel and an essential destination for all those visiting Bruges with a copy of this book in their pocket.

Viewed from across the Markt, the belfry or Belfort is a staggering sight. It looks almost organic, with its three distinct sections, each part growing out of the one before, like some kind of extravagant sprouting plant. And yet, at the same time, it could not be anything other than manmade and dizzyingly futuristic to boot: the world's first 88-metre Gothic telescopic tower.

It's an idea to go as early in the day as you can to avoid the crowds, although the experience of climbing the spiral steps retains an essential authenticity even when your progress is hindered by having to wait in doorways for people to pass. Climbing the tower, it's still possible to feel, as Godelieve does, like a captive: 'It was like an uphill exercise yard, a vertical prison.'

The carillon itself is played on a keyboard with pedals and large keys. In a small exhibit on the first landing, you can see the keyboard that would have been in use during the time when Rodenbach was writing.

A room closer to the top of the tower is dominated by the enormous brass cylinder, pierced and studded, responsible for playing the automatic carillon that precedes the striking of the hour. The mechanism may put you in mind of a large piano roll or a giant musical box, but in this room, where the wires for the bells are attached to the mechanism, Borluut felt 'he was seeing the anatomy of the tower. All its muscles, its sensory nerves were laid bare. The bell-tower extended its huge body upwards, downwards. But this was where its essential organs were gathered, its beating heart, the very heart of Flanders, whose pulsations among the ancient cogwheels the carillonneur was at that moment counting.'

When you reach the top of the bell-tower, having climbed 366 steps, you discover, as Godelieve does, that it is worth the effort. The views of the town are spectacular, even in the northern light ('a vibrant light such as you get in the north where a kind of grey gauze turns the sun to silver'), and it's easy to appreciate how coming up to the top of the tower makes Borluut feel high above the world, giving him the illusion of being distanced from ordinary mortals. 'It was his immediate refuge, wiping his mind clear, and he would hurry up to the top to wash his bleeding heart in the clean air, like washing it in the sea.'

Being right at the highest point in the town is one thing, but being up there when the carillon rings out over the canals and streets and stepped gables ('stairs to climb up to the land of dreams') is quite another, with the bells swinging right above your head, playing music as beautiful as it is deafening. You know that everyone within earshot is either looking in your direction or holding in their mind's eye an image of the tower. The personification of the belfry – 'Climbing it, Borluut was also raising himself up, becoming the belfry himself' – makes perect sense.

Reading *Bruges-la-Morte*, you might think the 1892 novel represents the last word on Bruges literature. Not only will no one else steal Rodenbach's crown, but he will be unlikely to surpass his own efforts should he attempt to do so. This fine translation of *Le Carillonneur* – an obsessive novel of obsession, an illuminating meditation on the nature of physical objects and human emotions – shows that he managed to do just that.

April 2007

PART ONE

DREAM

I

The Market Square in Bruges, usually deserted apart from the occasional passer-by, a straggle of poor children, a few priests or Beguines, had suddenly been enlivened by hesitant groups of people, gatherings forming dark blotches on the expanse of grey.

The contest for the office of town carillonneur had been set for the first Monday in October, the post having been made vacant by the death of old Baron de Vos, who had occupied it honourably for twenty years. It was to be filled that day, according to custom, by a public contest in which the townsfolk would decide the result by acclaiming the victor. That was why the Monday had been chosen, the weekday when all work ceased at noon, so that it shared something of the holiday mood of Sunday. Thus the choice could be truly popular and unanimous. Was it not right that the town carillonneur should be selected in that way? The carillon is, after all, the music of the people. Elsewhere, in the glittering capitals, public festivals are celebrated with fireworks, that magical offering that can thrill the very soul. Here, in the meditative land of Flanders, among the damp mists so antagonistic to the brilliance of fire, the carillon takes their place. It is a display of fireworks that one *hears*: flares, rockets, showers, a thousand sparks of sound which colour the air for visionary eyes alerted by hearing.

So a crowd was gathering. From all the nearby streets, from Wollestraat, from Vlamingstraat, parties were constantly coming to join the groups which had arrived earlier. On these shortened days of early autumn the sun was already starting to go down. It bathed the square in a golden light, all the softer for being the last of the day. The sombre building of the Draper's Hall, its severe rectangle, its mysterious walls apparently made from blocks of night, was glowing with a warm patina.

And the belfry, looming over all, rising higher than the roofs, was still basking in the full light of the setting sun, standing face to face with it. That made it look pink, above its black base, as if it were wearing make-up. The light was running, playing, flowing, moulding the pillars, the pointed arches of the windows, the pierced turrets, all the irregularities of stone; at other places it rippled in lithe sheets, like flags of luminous cloth, giving an appearance of fluid movement to the massive tower which usually rises in tiers of dark blocks where there are shadows, blood, wine lees and the dust of centuries . . . Now the setting sun was reflected in it as if in a pool; and the gold disc of the clock face half way up looked like a reflection of the sun itself.

The whole crowd had its eyes fixed on the clock face, waiting for the hour to strike, but calmly and in almost complete silence. A crowd is the sum of the faculty that predominates in each member and in everyone here the ability to remain silent is the greatest. And then, people are happy to stay quiet when they are waiting in expectation.

Yet the townsfolk, poor and rich alike, had hurried there to witness the contest. The windows were full of onlookers, as were the crowsteps that formed slender stairways flanking the gables of the Market Square, which seemed truly aquiver with splashes of colour. The gold lion of Bouchoute House glittered, while the old façade to which it clings spread out its four stories, its flushed brickwork. Across the square the Governor's Palace faced it with its stone lions, heraldic guardians of the old Flemish style, which had reproduced there a fine harmony of grey stone, sea-green leaded windows and slender pinnacles. At the top of the Gothic steps, beneath a crimson canopy, were the Governor of the Province and the aldermen of the town in their richly trimmed official dress, honouring with their presence this ceremony which is linked to those ancient memories of Flanders which are held most dear.

The hour of the contest was approaching.

The great bell kept on sounding its sonorous chimes. It was the Victory Bell, the bell of mourning, of glory, the Sunday bell which, cast in 1680, had resided up there since then and, like a great red heart, beat out the pulse of time in the clockwork of the tower. For an hour the great bell had been sending out its message to the four horizons, summoning. Abruptly the chimes slowed down, the intervals grew longer. A great silence. The hands on the clock face, which spend all day seeking then fleeing each other, were open at an obtuse angle. One or two minutes more and the hour of four would strike. Then, in the void left by the silence of the great bell, came the sound of a hesitant aubade, a chirping, the song of a nest awakening, scraps of melodic arpeggios.

The crowd listened. Some thought the contest had already started, but it was only the carillon operated mechanically by a copper cylinder lifting the hammers, working in the same way as a music box. The carillon can also be played by a keyboard and that was what the people would hear when the musicians joined battle.

While they were waiting, the mechanism of the carillon played the usual prelude to the striking of the hour: aerial embroidery, farewell garlands of sound thrown to departing time. Is that not the real purpose of the carillon? To create a little joy to offset the melancholy of an hour that is about to pass away?

Four strokes had just hammered the horizon, broad, deep-voiced strokes with distance between them, irrevocable, seeming to nail a cross in the air. Four o'clock! It was the hour set for the contest. Little swirls of impatience ran through the crowd . . .

Suddenly, at the balcony window of the Draper's Hall, just below the console sculpted with foliage and rams' heads on which the statue of the Virgin dreams, the very balcony from which the laws, ordinances, peace treaties and regulations of the commune were proclaimed, there appeared a herald clothed in purple who cried out through a megaphone and declared open the contest of carillonneurs in the town of Bruges, looking as if he were foretelling the future.

The crowd fell silent, furled its murmurings.

Only a few were aware of the precise details: that the municipal carillonneurs of Mechelen, Oudenaarde and Herenthals had entered, as well as others who might withdraw, not to mention unexpected participants, since it was possible to enter up to the last minute.

After the announcement from the balcony, the great bell rang out three times, like three strokes of the angelus, to announce the entry of one of the contestants into the lists.

Immediately the carillon started to play, a little confusedly at first. It was not the mechanical playing they had just heard, but free and full of caprice, they could sense a man's hand awakening the bells one by one, hustling them along, chiding, patting them, driving them on in front of him like a flock. They set off in reasonably good order, but a stampede followed, one bell seeming to fall, others running off or digging their heels in.

A second piece was better in its execution, but the choice was unfortunate. It was a hotchpotch of ordinary tunes cobbled together, a patchwork, music which seemed to be performing on a trapeze at the top of the tower.

The folk gathered below could not understand it at all and remained cool. When it stopped, isolated applause broke out for a minute, sounding like washerwomen beating clothes by the edge of the water.

After a short interval the three angelus strokes rang out again from the great bell. The second contestant was heard. He seemed to be better at handling the instrument, but he soon had the bells out of breath by trying to make them produce the roaring of the *Marseillaise* or the archaic dirge of *God Save the Queen*. The result was again mediocre and the crowd, disappointed, were starting to think they would never replace old Baron de Vos who, over so many years, had made the carillon sound as it ought to.

The next test piece was even more painful to listen to. The contestant had had the ill-advised idea of playing tunes from operetta and music hall in a sharp, staccato tempo. The bells skipped, screamed and stumbled, laughing as if they had been tickled and seeming slightly drunk and mad. It was as if they were lifting up their bronze skirts and lurching into an obscene cancan. At first the crowd was surprised, then angry at what their beloved ancient bells were being made to do. They felt it was a sacrilege. Cries of disapproval gusted up towards the bell-tower.

Two other contestants who were still to play were seized with fear and withdrew. The contest looked like being a failure. Would the appointment of the new carillonneur have to be postponed? Before they took that step, the herald was sent out again to ask if there was anyone else who wanted to compete.

As soon as the announcement was made, a shout was heard as there was a stir in the front rows of the crowd gathered outside the Draper's Hall. A moment later the old door creaked on its hinges. A man went in.

Uncertain, the crowd trembled, passing on vague rumours. No one knew anything. What was going to happen next? Was the contest finished? They weren't going to appoint any of the contestants who had already been heard, that much was certain. Might another appear? Everyone was asking questions, standing on tiptoe, jostling the people next to them, looking up at the balcony, at the belfry platforms, where they couldn't be sure whether it was human silhouettes that were moving or crows.

Soon the great bell was sounding out its three angelus strokes again, a warning, a traditional salute announcing a new carillonneur.

The crowd listened all the more closely for having waited and despaired, especially since this time the bells, ringing softly, demanded a deeper hush. The prelude was muted, a blend in which one could no longer distinguish bells alternating then coming together, it was a concert of bronze united, as if far off and very old. Music in a dream! It did not come from the tower, but from much farther away, from the depths of the sky, from the depths of time. This carillonneur had had the idea of playing some old Christmas carols, Flemish carols born of the race, mirrors in which it recognises itself. Like everything that has passed through the centuries, it was very solemn and a little sad. It was very old, and yet the children could understand it. It was very remote, very vague, as if happening on the borders of silence, and yet it was received by everyone, descended into everyone. Many eyes clouded over, without the people knowing whether it was from their own tears or from those fine, grey drops of sound falling into them . . .

The whole crowd of townsfolk was aquiver. By nature taciturn and pensive, it had sensed the obscure tissue of its dream unfolding in the air and appreciated its remaining unformulated.

When the series of old Christmas carols finished, the people remained silent for a moment, as if, in their thoughts, they had accompanied the bells back to eternity, those kindly grandams who had come to sing them stories of the past and tangled tales which everyone can complete in their own way . . .

Then there was a discharge of cries, a release of emotion, joy branching out, surging up to the higher tiers, climbing the tower like black ivy to bombard the new carillonneur.

He had become a contestant on the spur of the moment, by chance, at the last minute. Unhappy with the mediocre offerings of the contestants, he abruptly climbed the belfry to the glass chamber where he sometimes used to go to see his friend, old Baron de Vos. Was he the one who was going to replace him?

What now? He had to perform a second piece. The Christmas carols had been the little old ladies of the paths of history, Beguines kneeling beside the air. With them the people waiting below, far down below, had gone back to the times of their glory, to the graveyard of their past . . . Now they were ready for heroics.

The man wiped his forehead and sat down again at the keyboard, as intimidating as a church organ, with pedals for the big bells, while the little ones are activated by iron shafts rising from the keys – playing them is a craft, like weaving music!

The carillon rang out again. They heard the *Lion of Flanders*, an old folk song everyone knew, anonymous, like the tower itself, like everything that epitomises a race of people. The ancient bells were young again, proclaiming the valour and immortality of Flanders. It was truly the call of a lion from which, like the one in the Scriptures, there came forth sweetness. In the old days a stone heraldic lion used to top the belfry. With this song from the same age, it seemed about to return and emerge from the belfry as if coming out of its den. On the Market Square, in the last, fevered rays of the setting sun, the gold lion on Bouchoute House appeared to sparkle, to be alive, while the stone lions on the Governor's Palace opposite extended their shadow over the crowd. Flanders of the lion! It was the glorious cry of the guilds and corporations in their days of glory. They thought they had it firmly tucked away in the ironbound coffers where they kept the charters and privileges from the old princes in one of the rooms of the tower . . . And now the anthem had arisen once more: Flanders of the lion! A rhythmic song, like a people on the march, chanted, both warlike and human at the same time, like a face in a suit of armour.

The crowd listened, breathless. They could no longer say whether it was the carillon sounding, nor by what miracle the forty-nine bells in the tower had become as one: the song of a people in accord in which the silvery small bells, the swaying heavy bells and the ancient great bells truly seemed to be children, women in cloaks and heroic soldiers all returning to the town that had been thought dead. The crowd was not wrong about that and, as if they wanted to precede this procession of the past that the song embodied, they took up the noble anthem in their turn. It spread across the whole of the Market Square. Every mouth was singing. The song of the people rose up into the air to meet the song of the bells, and the soul of Flanders soared, like the sun between the sky and the sea.

For a moment, a sublime intoxication had lifted up this crowd of taciturn people who, accustomed to silence, resigned to the town's decline, the stagnant canals, the grey streets, had for a long time now found a taste for the melancholy sweetness of resignation. Yet an ancient heroism still slumbered within the race, sparks resided in the inertia of the stones. Suddenly the blood in every vein had started to flow more quickly. As soon as the music stopped, enthusiasm burst out, instant and universal, frenzied and wild. Shouts, cries, hands raised in a rolling sea of gestures above their heads, calls, uproar . . . The wonderful carillonneur! He was like a heaven-sent hero from a tale of chivalry, arriving last, unidentifiable in his armour, and winning the tournament. Who was he, this man who had emerged at the last minute, when they were already thinking the contest would end without a winner after the mediocre performance of the first carillonneurs? There were only a few, those closest to the bell-tower, who had been able to see him as he plunged into the doorway. No one had recognised him, no one had passed on his name.

Then the herald in his purple gown reappeared at the balcony window and cried, sonorous through his megaphone, 'Joris Borluut!' It was the name of the victor.

Joris Borluut . . . The name fell, came tumbling down from the tower onto the front rows of the audience, then ricocheted, flew, took wing, propelled from one to the next, from wave to wave, like a seagull over the sea.

A few minutes later the door to the Draper's Hall opened wide. It was the red herald preceding the man whose name at that moment was forming on everyone's lips. The herald parted the crowd, clearing a path for the victorious carillonneur to the steps of the Palace where the town authorities, who would invest him with his office, were standing.

Everyone drew back, as if in the presence of someone greater than them, as they do before the Bishop when he carries the relic of the Holy Blood in the procession.

Joris Borluut! And the name continued to soar round the Market Square, rebounding, knocking against the façades, thrown up to the windows, even up to the gables, thrown back endlessly, already familiar to everyone, as if it had written itself on the blank air.

Meanwhile the victor had reached the top of the Gothic steps, where he was congratulated by the Governor and the aldermen, who endorsed the people's unanimous choice by signing the document appointing him town carillonneur. Then they handed him, as the prize for his victory and the sign of his office, a key decorated with ironwork and brass ornamentation, a ceremonial key, like a bishop's crozier. It was the key to the bell-tower which, from now on, he would have the privilege of entering at will, as if he lived there or were master of it.

But the victor, as he received this picturesque gift, suddenly fell prey to the melancholy that follows any celebration. He felt alone and troubled by something indefinable. It was as if he had just accepted the key to his tomb.

II

At around nine o'clock on the evening of the contest Borluut went, as he did every Monday, to visit his friend, the old antiques dealer van Hulle. His house, in the Zwarte-Leer-touwersstraat, was an ancient building with a double gable whose brick façade was embellished with a bas-relief above the door representing a ship, its sails billowing out like breasts. Once it had been the seat of the Corporation of Boatmen and the date of 1578 in a cartouche testified to its noble antiquity. The door, the locks, the leaded windows, every-thing had been knowledgeably restored in the old styles, while the brickwork had been uncovered and repointed with, here and there, the patina of the ages left intact on the stones. It was Borluut who had carried out this invaluable restoration for his friend when he was making his début, so to speak, hardly out of the academy where he had studied architecture. It was a public lesson, a lesson in beauty given to all those who possessed old homes and were letting them crumble away irreparably or were demolishing them to build ordinary modern houses.

Van Hulle, for his part, was proud of his home with its face from bygone days. It was exactly what was needed to go with his old furniture, his antique curios, he being less of an antiques dealer than a collector, only selling items if he was offered a good price and if it suited him. He did things as his fancy took him and had every right to do so, since he was well-to-do. He lived in the house with his two daughters, having been a widower for a long time. It was only by chance that he had gradually became an antiques dealer. It started with his love of the old things from the local area which he accumulated; earthenware jugs in deep indigo which were used for beer; glass-fronted display cupboards holding a Madonna in painted wood, dressed in silk and Brussels lace; jewels, necklaces, feather archery targets of the guilds from the fifteenth century; chests with curved sides of the Flemish Renaissance – all the flotsam, unblemished or scarred, of the past few centuries, anything that bore witness to the former wealth of his homeland. But he had bought things less to sell them on again in the way of business than out of love for Flanders and of old Flemish way of life.

Kindred souls recognise each other quickly in the middle of a crowd and come together. In any one age there is never a soul which is one of a kind, however exceptional the person may be. Every ideal must be realised, every thought formulated, which is why Fate makes sure it has several that are in accord, so that at least one will be realised. There are always a number of souls sown at the same time, so that the indispensable lily shall flower in one at least.

The old antiques dealer was a Fleming passionately attached to his Flanders. As was Borluut, who, through his craft of architecture had come to study and to love this unique city of Bruges, which in its entirety seemed a poem in stone, an illuminated reliquary. Borluut had dedicated himself to it, embellishing it, restoring it to all its purity of style; from the very beginning he had seen that as his vocation, his mission. It was not surprising, therefore, that he should meet van Hulle and strike up a friendship with him. Others soon joined them: Farazyn, a lawyer who would be the spokesman for the Movement, and Bartholomeus, a painter and devotee of Flemish art. Thus it was the single ideal that gave rise to their weekly meetings, which now took place every Monday evening, at van Hulle's house. They came together to talk about Flanders, as if something had changed for the land, or were impending; they recounted their memories, enthusiasms, projects. Thinking the same way made them feel they shared a secret. It filled them with joy and excitement, as if they were in a conspiracy. Solitary men with time on their hands letting themselves get carried away, giving themselves the illusion of action, of playing a role in this grey life. Deluding themselves with words and fantasies. Yet their patriotism, for all that it was naive, was ardent; each in his own way dreamt of giving Flanders, of giving Bruges, a new beauty.

27

That evening there was rejoicing at van Hulle's because of Borluut's triumph. It had been an afternoon of art and glory when the town seemed reborn. It was the old Bruges, with the townsfolk gathered in the public square, at the foot of the bell-tower, the shadow of which was huge enough to contain them entirely. When Borluut arrived at the antiques dealer's house, his friends clasped his hands and embraced him in a silent show of emotion. He had done well for Flanders. For they had all understood the reason for his unexpected intervention . . .

'Yes,' Borluut said, 'when I heard them playing their modern tunes and their oompah-oompahs on the carillon, I was extremely unhappy. I trembled at the very thought that one of them might be appointed, that he would be officially allowed to pour his vile music down from the belfry, soiling our canals with it, our churches, our faces. I immediately had the idea of taking part in order to keep the others out. I was familiar with the carillon, having played it occasionally, when I went to see old Baron de Vos. And then, when you know how to play the organ . . . I really don't know how I did it. I was mad, inspired, carried away . . .

'The best part,' said Bartholomeus, 'was playing our old Christmas carols. It brought tears to my eyes, it was so sweet, so sweet, so far away, so far away . . . Sometimes men should hear their nursemaid's songs again like that.'

Farazyn said, 'All the people were moved because, as you say, it was the voice of their past. Oh, the good people of Flanders, what energy is still hidden inside them! It will burst forth the moment they reawaken. Our land will rise again the more its old language is restored.'

Then Farazyn began to get carried away and elaborated a vast plan of renewal and autonomy: 'Flemish must be the language spoken in Flanders, not only among the people, but in parliament, in court; all deeds, all official documents, street names, coins, stamps, everything should be in Flemish because we are in Flanders, because French is the language of France and their domination is over.'

Van Hulle listened without saying anything, silent as usual, though a brief blaze flared up intermittently in his dull eyes. He found these clarion calls disturbing; he would have preferred a quieter, more intimate patriotism: Bruges venerated in a cult, like a dead woman around whose tomb a few friends gather.

'Yes,' Bartholomeus objected, 'but how can we expunge all the conquerors?'

'There were no conquerors,' was Farazyn's riposte. 'Restore Flemish here and the race will be renewed, whole again, as it was in the Middle Ages. Even Spain itself could not affect its spirit. It did leave something behind, but only in the blood. Its conquest was rape and the only result was children in Flanders with its dark hair and amber complexion . . . You still see some like that even today.'

As he spoke, Farazyn turned round towards one of van Hulle's daughters. Everyone smiled. Barbara was, indeed, an example of this alien kind, her hair a violent brown, her lips red as a chilli in her darkish complexion, while her eyes were still those of the original race, the colour of the water in the canals.

She was listening to the discussion with slightly feverish interest, filling up the stoneware mugs with beer, while her sister, Godelieve, indifferent, her mind elsewhere one would have said, accompanied the noisy discussion with the purr of her lacemaking pillow.

The painter looked at them. 'True,' he said, 'one is Flanders, the other is Spain.'

'But they have the same soul,' Farazyn countered. 'Everyone in Flanders is the same. Spain never touched the soul . . . What did it leave us: a few street names, such as Spanjaardstraat in Bruges, some inn signs and, here and there, a Spanish House with a gabled façade, sea-green windowpanes and a flight of steps from which death often came down. And that's all. Bruges has remained intact, I tell you. It's not like Antwerp, which wasn't raped by its conquerors, but loved them. Bruges is the Flemish soul entire; Antwerp is the Flemish soul occupied by the Spanish. Bruges is the Flemish soul that has remained in the shade; Antwerp is the Flemish soul sitting in the alien sun. From that point onward Antwerp was more Spanish than Flemish and remains so today. Its bombast, its arrogance, its colour, its pomp are Spanish. Even its hearses,' he concluded, 'covered in gold like reliquaries.'

'Besides,' Bartholomeus added, 'you only have to compare their painters. Bruges had Memling, who is an angel; Antwerp had Rubens, who is an ambassador.'

Borluut backed them up. 'And their towers!' he exclaimed. 'Nothing tells you more about a people than their towers. They are made in its image and in its likeness. Now the bell-tower of Saint Saviour's in Bruges is austere, one could call it a citadel of God. It has never wanted to express anything other than faith, its blocks of stone placed one on top of the other like acts of faith. The Antwerp tower, on the other hand, is airy, decorated with open-work, stylish and a little Spanish, too, with the stone mantilla draped over its skyline –'

Bartholomeus broke in with a pertinent remark: 'No matter what you may say about Spain, it is fortunate for the whole of Flanders, from the sea to the Scheldt, even for Antwerp, which it corrupted to a certain extent, that the Spanish came, despite the Inquisition, the autos-da-fé, the red-hot pincers, the blood and the tears that flowed. Spain kept Flanders for Catholicism. It saved us from the Reformation because, without Spain, Flanders would have become Protestant like Zealand, Utrecht, all of the Netherlands, and if that had happened, Flanders would not have been Flanders!'

'Agreed,' said Farazyn, 'but today all these convents represent a different danger. We have religious orders here as nowhere else in the world: Capuchins, Discalced Carmelites, Dominicans, seminarists, without counting the secular clergy; and so many orders for women: Beguines, Poor Clares, Carmelites, Redemptorists, Sisters of Saint Andrew, Sisters of Charity, Little Sisters of the Poor, the Dames anglaises, the Black Sisters of Bethel . . . That is what in part explains why there are ten thousand more women in the population here, something you don't get in any other town in the world. Chastity means sterility, and the corollary of these ten thousand nuns is our ten thousand poor supported by the Welfare

Board. That is not the way for Bruges to reverse its decline and become great again.'

Borluut spoke, his voice solemn. It gave one the feeling that what he was about to say was very important to him, a matter close to his heart.

'Is that not what makes it great?' he retorted to his friend. 'Its beauty resides in its silence, and its glory in now only belonging to a few priests and poor people, that is to say to those who are purest because they have renounced the world. Its higher destiny is to be something which has outlived its time.'

'No!' Farazyn retorted. 'It would be better to bring it back to life. Life is the only thing that matters, one must always seek life, love life!'

Borluut resumed his argument in urgent, persuasive tones: 'Can one not also love death, love sorrow? The beauty of sorrow is superior to the beauty of life. It is the beauty of Bruges. Great glory that has gone! One last, fixed smile! Everything around us has withdrawn within itself: the waters are still, the houses closed, the bells whisper in the mist. That is the secret of its charm. Why want it to become like all the rest? It is unique. Walking through Bruges is like walking through memories . . .'

Everyone was silent. It was late. Borluut's impassioned evocation had touched their hearts. His voice had been as a bell sounding out an irreversible conclusion. And now it was as if it had left its wake in the room, the echo of a sound that was advancing and refusing to stop. It seemed as if the town, having been evoked, had poured all its silence into them. Even Barbara and Godelieve, rising to fill the empty mugs one last time, did not dare make any noise and softened their steps.

Each of them made his way home wrapped in thought, in contentment at an evening in which they had shared together their love of Bruges. They had talked of the town as if they were talking of a religion.

III

In the morning two days later Borluut set off for the belfry. It was his duty, henceforward, to sound the carillon on Sundays, Wednesdays and Saturdays, as well as on feast days, from eleven o'clock to midday.

As he approached the tower, the thought going through his mind was: to withdraw *high above the world*. Was that not what he could do now, what he would be doing from that day onwards when he climbed up there? For a long time, ever since he had been visiting old Baron de Vos in the bell-tower, he had had vague dreams of this life as a lookout, of its intoxicating solitude, like that of a lighthouse keeper. That was the reason, the real reason, for his haste to take part in the contest. He could admit it to himself now. It had not been solely due to his artistic sensitivity, to his affection for the town, nor to his desire to stop the silence and neglect, which were its beauty, being polluted by sacrilegious music. He had also immediately sensed the enchantment of being the sole possessor, so to speak, of the high belfry, of being able to ascend there whenever he liked, to look down on the world of men, to live as if on the threshold of infinity.

High above the world! He repeated the mysterious phrase to himself, a fluid phrase which seemed to soar itself, straight up into the air, then descend in steps to the heavy syllables of the *world* below ... *High above the world!* At an equal distance between God and the earth. To have something of eternity while still remaining human so as to savour, thrill and feel through his senses, through his flesh, through his memories, through love, desire, pride, dream. *The world:* so much that was sad, evil, impure; *high above:* an ascension, taking flight to a Delphian tripod, a magical refuge in the air where all the ills of the world would melt away and die, as if the atmosphere were too pure for them.

So there he would make his abode, on the edge of the sky,

the shepherd of the bells, living like the birds, so far from the city and men, on a level with the clouds . . .

After he had crossed the courtyard of the Draper's Hall, he reached the doorway to the inner buildings. The key he had been given drew a metallic screech from the lock, as if it were being forced by a sword and wounded. The door had opened; it closed of its own accord, as if responding instinctively to the invisible hand of the shadows. Immediately everything was dark once more, silent, and Borluut started to climb the stairs.

At first his feet stumbled; now and then he missed his footing, some steps being uneven, worn down like the coping round a well. How many generations had flowed along here, as tireless as water! How many feet had trodden the steps over the centuries to result in such wear! The stone staircase twisted round in short curves, tortuous, coiling round on itself like a snake, like the tendrils of a withered vine. He stormed up the tower as if he were storming a rampart. Now and then an arrow-slit, a fissure in the masonry, let in some leaden daylight, a thin gash on the face of the gloom. Darkness distorts everything if it is only partial: you start to think the walls are moving, waving shrouds; a shadow on the ceiling is a beast crouching, ready to pounce . . .

The spiral staircase suddenly narrows, swirls like a stream drying up. Can he still get through up there, or is he going to be crushed against the sides? All at once the darkness increased. Borluut felt he had already climbed more than a hundred steps, but he had not thought to count. By now his pace had adjusted to a rhythmical tread, instinctively shortened to adapt to the stone steps. But plunging into impenetrable darkness disoriented his senses. Borluut no longer knew in which direction he was going, whether forwards or backwards, whether up or down. Unable to see himself, it was in vain that he tried to determine which way his steps were taking him. He had the feeling he was descending, making his way down a subterranean staircase, in a deep mine, far from the light of day, through motionless landscapes of coal, and that he was going to come to a lake . . .

So Borluut stopped, slightly disconcerted at these fancies induced by the darkness. But he still seemed to be going up. Despite the fact that his legs were still, it felt as if the stairs were undulating, carrying him on, as if it were the steps that were ascending one by one beneath his feet.

Above all no noise, except his own echo as a transient in the tower. And, barely audible, sometimes a bat, disturbed by the unaccustomed steps, unfolding its wings in the void and shivering in their soft velvet. But quickly silence returned, as far as a tower can ever be silent, can ever hush that vague rustling, that crumbling of something in the hourglass of time that it is, where the dust of centuries trickles down, speck by speck.

On the various floors Borluut came across bare, empty rooms; like granaries of silence.

He was still climbing. Now the stairs brightened; pure, white light came in through openings, the castellated platforms, the pierced architecture, and flowed over the steps, breaking in foaming waves, setting them suddenly ablaze.

Borluut was seized with joy, as at a truce, at convalescence, at being set free after the limbo of the dungeons. He had found himself again. He had ceased to be one with the night, absorbed by it. At last he could see himself. He felt intoxicated by being, by walking. A sudden, sharp wind ran over his skin. The abrupt flood of brightness gave him the feeling of moonlight on his face. Now he was ascending more quickly, as if the air were rarified, making his exertion freer, breathing easier. Gripped by a feverish urge to climb, he felt like running up the stone stairs. People often talk of the attraction of the abyss. There is also the *abyss above*. Borluut was still going up; he would have liked to keep on going up for ever, melancholy at the thought that the stairway was doubtless going to stop and that at the end, on the edge of the air, he would still yearn to continue, go farther, higher.

At that moment an immense clamour flowed in, pouring along the narrow stairway. It was the wind, groaning all the time, ceaselessly going up, going down the steps; the sorrow of the wind which moans in the same voice in the trees, in sails, in towers. The sorrow of the wind which contains all other sorrows within it. In its shrill cries one can hear those of children; in its laments women's grief; in its fury the hoarse sob of a man repulsed, broken. The wind that Borluut could hear was, it is true, a definite reminder of the earth, although very faint already. Up there it was nothing more than the semblance of complaints, faded voices, echoes of sorrows that were all too human and ashamed. The wind came from below. The only reason it was so afflicted was because it had passed through the town. But the grief it had taken on down there and which, reaching the top of the tower with the wind, groaned out loud, began to dissolve, to metamorphose from sorrow into melancholy and from tears into drops of rain.

Borluut felt this wind was truly the symbol of the new life he was entering upon, the life of a lookout, high above everything, vaguely dreamt of, attained by chance. For him as well, all his troubles would melt away within his soul, as the laments melted away in the wind.

He was still climbing. Here and there doors opened revealing vast rooms, dormitories with heavy joists where bells were sleeping. A vague feeling stirred within Borluut as he went over to them. They were not entirely at rest, just as virgins are never completely at rest. Their sleep was visited by dreams. He felt as if they were about to move, stretch, moan like sleepwalkers. The incessant murmuring among the bells! A noise that persists, like the sound of the sea in shells! They never empty themselves entirely. Sound forming like beads of sweat! A condensation of music on the bronze . . .

As he went on and up, more bells appeared everywhere, aligned, appearing to kneel, in the same robes, living together in the tower as if in a convent. There were tall ones, slim ones, old ones in faded dress, young ones who were the novices who had replaced some ancients – every aspect of cloistered humanity which retains its variety beneath the uniformity of the Rule. A convent of bells in which most had been there since the foundation. It was in 1743 that the new carillon of forty-nine bells had been cast and hung in the belfry by Joris Dumery, replacing that of 1299. But Borluut was taken by the fancy that some of the original bells had survived, mingling with the new ones. However that may be, the same bronze had been recast to make the new bells, so that it was the old metal from the thirteenth century which continued its anonymous concert.

Borluut was already beginning to feel at home. He went to have a closer look at the bells that were going to live in dutiful submission to his authority. He wanted to get to know them. One by one he questioned them, called them by their name, inquired about their history. Sometimes the metal had a silvery patina, the marbling of a breakwater pounded by the tide, a complicated tattoo, bloody encrustations of rust and patches of verdigris like a dusting of pollen from resedas. Among this enchanting chemistry Borluut found, here and there, a date, like a jewel pinned on, Latin inscriptions winding round, and the names of godfathers and godmothers who had entrusted their memory to the new-born bell.

Touched and charmed by all these discoveries, Borluut was hurrying from one attraction to the next. The wind, stronger than ever at that height, suddenly turned violent and roared, but with a voice that was all its own now, beyond all human comparison, the voice of a force, an element whose only parallel was the voice of the sea.

Borluut sensed that he was approaching the battlemented platform of the belfry, where the stairway emerges at a staging post before continuing to the top of the tower. There, ensconced in one of the corners of the platform, is the carillonneur's cabin, an ethereal dwelling, a glass chamber with six wide windows opening onto the empty air. He had to fight his way there. The wind was blowing more and more furiously, aggressively, like the torrent from a floodgate, in vast separate sheets, vicious bursts, tumbling masses, plunging weights, suddenly gathering, as compact as a wall. Borluut made his way forward, rejoicing in the struggle, as if the plundering wind, carrying off his hat and undoing his clothes, were trying to divest him of the world below and carry him, free and naked, into the healthy air of the high place.

Finally he reached the little aerial abode. A welcoming inn

at journey's end! Warmth and silence! Borluut recognised it, nothing had been disturbed since the time when he sometimes used to come and visit Baron de Vos, the old master carillonneur, without suspecting that one day he would succeed him. Now he saw everything in sharper detail, since this confined space was already his and he, in his turn, was going to spend many future hours there. He was somewhat moved at the thought. He was going to live *high above the world!* And, as if in confirmation, he glimpsed the immense landscape through the high windows, the town lying there, down below, at the bottom, in an abyss. He didn't dare look . . . He would feel dizzy . . . He had to get his eyes used to looking from the vantage point he had reached, which seemed like the edge of infinity.

Closer to him he surveyed the keyboard of the carillon with its yellowed ivory, its pedals, its articulated iron rods rising from the keys towards the clappers of the bells. Facing him, he discovered a small clock, very small, looking strange in the immensity of the tower, producing its sound of the humble regularity of life, that pulse of things which is the envy of the human heart. He wondered whether the little clock was in time with the huge clock of the tower. It was right next to it, like a mouse living in the cage of a lion.

The hands on the small clock-face were about to show eleven o'clock. Immediately Borluut heard a rumbling, the uproar of a disturbed nest, the sound of a garden billowing in the wind when a storm is getting up.

It was a prolonged vibration, the prelude to the carillon which plays automatically before the hour strikes, operated by a brass cylinder pierced by square holes, like a piece of lace. Borluut, interested in the mechanism, rushed to the room where all the wires of the bells met the cylinder. He watched it, studied it. He felt he was seeing the anatomy of the tower. All its muscles, its sensory nerves were laid bare. The bell-tower extended its huge body upwards, downwards. But this was where its essential organs were gathered, its beating heart, the very heart of Flanders, whose pulsations among the ancient cogwheels the carillonneur was at that moment counting.

The music swelled, blurred because he was too close. However, it was still as joyous as the dawn. The sound swept over all the octaves, like the light over all the fields. A little bell trilled like a lark and others responded with the awakening of all the birds. A bass bell was the deep lowing of the cattle. Borluut listened, part of this rural wakening, already familiar with this pastoral music, as if it were that of his own beasts in his own fields. What bliss to be alive! With Nature everlasting! But the idyll had scarcely been sung than the great bell sounded, absorbing the festive airs of the carillon: solemn, tolling the death of the hour, eleven strokes, immense, slow, each distant from the next, as if to show that one feels alone when one is dying . . .

Eleven o'clock. It was the moment for Borluut to begin his official function. He went back to the cabin with the keyboard and sat down at it. However, being new and having taken up the position by chance, he had not had time to prepare other tunes, so had decided to play once more the old Christmas carols he had used in the contest. He played them with fine nuances, the tips of his fingers tingling with emotion, with a slightly feverish joy, entirely absorbed in his playing now that there were no comings and going round him, as there had been on the evening of the contest. Immense silence. He heard his little carols wending their way through the air, tripping over the church spires, walking along the roofs, going into the houses. Were people already welcoming them? What a difference from the other day when the whole crowd had taken them to their hearts as they descended. That that should have happened was like an incredible dream. It would never happen again. Was he – at least at that moment – causing someone to raise their eyes to the heavens as he played? Was he sending consolation to some soul in torment, melancholy to some too happy heart betrayed by its rapture?

To play like this, above the crowd, was to produce a work of art. What point was there in wanting to know if it moved people, carried them away, delighted them or made them comfortable? To set it blossoming should be sufficient. It will always spread, go elsewhere, fulfil a destiny of which we know almost nothing. Our glory is always outside us and is accomplished so far from us.

This was the reflection that went through Borluut's mind. He accepted it. It was not for others that he was playing. The sole reason he had, on the spur of the moment, taken part in the contest for the position of carillonneur was to create beauty, because at that point he believed he was the only one capable of giving the town a carillon in accord with it, with the same antique charm and melancholy. Thus Bruges retained its perfect harmony. And since he was contributing to it, he was truly creating beauty. But he had not conquered the tower solely to create beauty, it was also, and above all, for himself, to isolate himself, to spend his time in a worthy occupation, to leave men and to live *high above the world*.

His reward was therefore immediate.

Borluut felt he was happy, thrilled at the last swing of the bells which were his own dreams, the whispering urns into which all his soul poured.

IV

Dead towns are the Cathedrals of Silence. They, too, have their gargoyles, singular figures, exaggerated, dubious, set in high profile. They stand out from the mass of grey, which takes all it has in the way of character, its twitchings of stagnant life from them. Some have been distorted by solitude, others grimace with a directionless fervour; here there are masks of cherished lust, there faces ceaselessly sculpted and furrowed by mysticism. Human gargoyles, the only figures of interest in this monotonous population.

The old antiques dealer, van Hulle, was one of these strange types, living a retired life in his ancient house in Zwarte-Leer-touwersstraat with his two daughters, Barbara and Godelieve. At first he had been enthusiastic about the Flemish Movement, had brought together all the militant patriots, Bartholomeus, Borluut, Farazyn, who came to his house every Monday to get worked up over their hopes for the town. Memorable evenings when they conspired together, but *to preserve* the beauty of Bruges!

Since then van Hulle had cooled down. He still invited his friends, listened to them talk as before, full of ambitious projects, but without joining in himself. He had been seized by another obsession: he had started to collect clocks. It had come about in a most unexpected way.

His occupation of antiques dealer predisposed him to it. He had spent his whole life searching for rare curios, old pieces of furniture, Flemish relics, but having grown old and tired – and rich into the bargain – he started to neglect his business, only selling occasional pieces to some rich stranger who happened to be passing through the town.

Then he fell ill. It was a long illness followed by an equally long convalescence: time passing slowly, days never ending, divided into so many minutes he had to count and thus, so to speak, measure out one by one! He felt alone, prey to the tedium, the dreariness of time, especially at the approach of twilight which, during those late-autumn days, came in through the windows, settling on the furniture with a leaden pallor, sending the mirrors into mourning at light's farewell . . .

Sometimes van Hulle would ask, 'What time is it?'

'Five o'clock.'

And he thought of the time stretching out before him that he would have to live through before the night, when he could drift along in a deep sleep which shortens the stages.

Five o'clock! And suddenly he heard the hour strike from the belfry, among the last notes of the little bells of the carillon, in the solemn tones of an officiating priest calming his choirboys. And he compared the hour struck from the bell-tower with that shown on the face of his clock, a little Empire clock on the mantelpiece with four tiny columns of white marble supporting a low pediment with sinuous, swan-necked ornamentation of gilded bronze. In the enforced inactivity of illness, empty of life and thought, he gradually got into the habit of concerning himself with the time. He worried about his clock as if it were another person. He regarded it as a friend. It was the clock that taught him patience, that provided a distraction with the interplay of its hands, the noise of its mechanism. It told him of the approach of the better moments, when he had his light meals. The clock face obsessed him. Other people, when they are ill, unconsciously count with their eyes the posies on the wallpaper, the flowers on the curtains. He did calculations on the clock. He searched it for the day of his return to full health, which was there already, but indistinct among so many other days. He looked to see what time it was, he checked the time, because often there was a discrepancy between his clock and the clock in the tower.

Van Hulle retained this preoccupation with the *exact time* after he had recovered. Whenever he went out he regulated his watch, which he had not wound up at all during his illness, by the clock on the bell-tower, almost feeling annoyed if he found it was slightly fast or the tiniest bit slow. The fixed points in his life – meals, going to bed, getting up, always at set times – had to fit in with these minute details.

'Oh look,' he would say, vexed, 'I'm five minutes behind time.'

Henceforward he made sure that his watch and the clocks in his home always agreed, not only the little Empire clock with the swan-necked bronze ornamentation, but also the kitchen clock, with red tulips painted on the face, which his old servant Pharaïlde used when going about her household tasks.

On one of his convalescent strolls – it was a Friday, market day – he was dawdling among the stalls on the Market Square when by chance he saw a slightly odd Flemish clock which attracted his attention. It was half hidden, almost buried beneath the mishmash of bric-a-brac littering the cobbles.

They sell everything in that market: linen, cotton goods, iron objects, agricultural implements, toys, antiques. A gaudy jumble, like a clear-out of the centuries. The goods are piled up, strewn haphazardly over the ground, still covered in accumulated dust, as if part of the inventory of the house, long closed, of someone who has gone away. Everything is old, oxidised, rusted, faded; it would be ugly were it not for the intermittent northern sun abruptly igniting shafts of light amid the shade, the russet golds of Rembrandt. It was among these ruins, this graveyard of things, that van Hulle discovered an unexpected piece of jetsam, the Flemish clock which he immediately desired. It consisted of a long oak cupboard with carved panels which the years had given a warm patina, a shimmering glaze, and of a marvellous metal face: pewter and copper imaginatively, delicately engraved: first of all the date – 1700 – and, all around, a wild cosmography with the sun shining, a crescent moon tapering like a gondola, stars with little lambs' heads grazing, moving towards the numbers of the hours, looking as if they wanted to nibble them.

It was this ancient clock that had initiated van Hulle's obsession. Other clocks, large and small, followed.

He had bought them at sales, from antiques dealers and goldsmiths. Without intending, he had started a genuine collection and he concerned himself with it more and more until it was his sole preoccupation.

The only man who is truly happy is a man who has an *idée fixe*. It takes up his every minute, fills any empty spaces in his thought, sneaks unexpected pleasures into his boredom, gives direction to his idle hours, again and again enlivens the stagnant waters of existence with a surging current. Van Hulle had found a means of giving passion to his life, more than the secret meetings of the past, the merely formal conspiracies, all the vain enthusiasm for the restitution of Flanders, so poorly defined and so far off.

Now he enjoyed immediate gratification, a pleasure that was personal and continuous. In the middle of this sombre town, living the uneventful life of a widower in which every day was the same colour, as grey as the air of Bruges, what a sudden change this new life was, always on the alert, on the lookout for some find! And then the strokes of good fortune a collector enjoys! The unexpected discovery that will increase his hoard! van Hulle already had some specialist knowledge. He had studied, sought, compared. At first glance he would assess the period the clocks came from. He diagnosed their age, sifted the authentic ones from the reproductions, judged the beauty of style, was familiar with certain signatures, elucidating them like works of art. He soon had a whole series of different clocks, put together little by little.

He travelled to the neighbouring towns to increase his stock, he followed the house-clearance sales where, sometimes, after a person had died, one could find rare, strange examples which had been in old families since time immemorial. His collection became important. He had specimens of all types: Louis XV and Louis XVI clocks with fretwork rosewood panels covered in marquetry, inlaid *galant* scenes making the panelling as dainty as a fan; mythological, idyllic, warlike clocks; clocks of biscuit-ware, of costly and fragile china, Sèvres or Dresden, where time laughed among the flowers; Moorish, Norman and Flemish clocks with oak or mahogany cases and chimes that whistled like a blackbird or creaked like the chain of a well. Then some curiosities: marine water-clocks in which drops of water are seconds. Finally a whole assortment of little bracket clocks, of silver display watches as delicate and detailed as jewels.

Whenever he had made a new purchase, he hurried to set it up in the vast room on the first floor where he kept his collection. And the new arrival immediately added its buzz, as of a metal bee, to that of its fellows in that room, mysterious as the hive of Time.

Van Hulle was happy. He still dreamt of other types of clock which he did not have.

Is this not the collector's exquisite pleasure, that his desire should know no bounds, should reach out into the infinite, should never know full possession which disappoints by its very completeness. O what joy to be able to *postpone the fulfilment of desire* to infinity! Van Hulle spent whole days in his clock museum. His great anxiety was that someone might enter, while he was out, on some pretext or other, and disturb the weights, brush against the chains, break one of his rarest acquisitions.

Fortunately his daughter Godelieve kept a close watch. She alone was charged with the task of watching over them and removing the dust, of putting them back with fingers rendered calm by prudence, light as a wing as she aired and dusted. Barbara, her elder sister with the Spanish complexion, the lips red as a chilli, could be moody and irascible. The merest trifle and she could lose her temper, sulk, fly into a rage. Van Hulle recognised in her all the temperament of her mother, who had died young from a nervous disorder. Nevertheless he loved her, for her moods were followed by moments of tenderness, tokens of affection lavished abruptly, without transition, a storm wind suddenly slackening, humming, caressing the flowers.

The younger sister Godelieve, on the other hand, enfolded him in an unvarying affection delightful in its monotony. It represented the security of something unchanging, something fixed. He found her as obliging as a mirror. He saw himself in her because she resembled him. It was his own face, the same eyes the colour of the canals, those water-laden northern eyes, and also the same slightly aquiline nose, the same immense, flat forehead, a smooth façade, a temple wall letting nothing appear, apart from a little light, of the calm celebrations of her mind. But above all it was her soul, the same gentle, mystic nature, absorbed in musings, reclusive and taciturn, as if given to unravelling skeins of thoughts, swirling mists. They often spent hours in the same room without talking, happy to be together, enjoying the silence. They did not have the sense of being distinct from each other.

She was truly *his flesh*. You could say that she continued him, that she was an extension of him outside himself. As soon as he wanted something, she did it straight away, just as he would have done it himself. He felt her to be the hands and feet of his own will. And truly, literally, *he saw with her eyes*.

Living in unison! The daily miracle of being two, yet being as one. And so the old antiques dealer trembled at the thought that Godelieve might one day marry, might leave him! It would truly be like losing a limb, something of himself would go far away. Afterwards he would feel as if he were maimed.

He thought about it frequently, already jealously guarding against it. His initial fear was that one of the firebrand patriots he welcomed into his home on Monday evenings might fall in love with Godelieve. Was it not imprudent to entertain them there? Was that not to invite his own misfortune? Joris Borluut was still young, Farazyn too. But they appeared to be confirmed bachelors, like Bartholomeus who, as if the better to secure himself against marriage, had gone to live within the Beguinage, where he had set up his studio in one of the abandoned convent houses. He was, so to speak, wedded to his art. And the others, were they not married to the Town, devoted to making it beautiful, to adorning it like a woman? They had no room for a new passion. And when they visited him in the evening they were too carried away with furthering the Movement, with setting the flags flying within themselves, too full of plans and hopes to pay any attention to the little silent maiden beside them that was Godelieve. The sound of her lace-making pillow, like the murmur of prayers, was hardly calculated to satisfy those turbulent souls who hoped to hear the lion of Flanders roar anew.

Thus van Hulle set his mind at rest. Godelieve was safe. As for Barbara, with the fierceness of her beauty, the colour of her lips promising a ripe fruit, she might well arouse some man one day. Oh, if only she, Barbara, could get married! With what joy he would give his consent! It would mean an end to the perpetual alarms: capricious moods, sudden tantrums because of trifles, protests, outbursts and fits of despair during which the whole house seemed to be foundering.

It was a hope at the thought of which van Hulle trembled: to live with Godelieve alone! Only with her, for ever, until the end. A life that was uniformly quiet, at peace, calm, a life in which she would make no other sound in the silence than the monotonous tick-tock of her heart, in which she would be just one more clock in his museum of clocks, a little human clock, the tranquil face of Time.

V

It could be said that Borluut was in love with the town.

But we only have one heart for all our loves, consequently his love was somewhat like the affection one feels for a woman, the devotion one entertains for a work of art, for a religion. He loved Bruges for its beauty and, like a lover, he would have loved it the more, the more beautiful it was. His passion had nothing to do with the local patriotism which unites those living in a town through habits, shared tastes, alliances, parochial pride. On the contrary, Borluut was almost solitary, kept himself apart, mingled little with the slow-witted inhabitants. Even out in the streets he scarcely saw the passers-by. As a solitary wanderer, he began to favour the canals, the weeping trees, the tunnel bridges, the bells he could sense in the air, the old walls of the old districts. Instead of living beings, his interest focused on things. The town took on a personality, became almost human. He loved it, wished to embellish it, to adorn its beauty, a beauty mysterious in its sadness. And, above all, so unostentatious. Other towns are showy, amassing palaces, terraced gardens, fine geometrical monuments. Here everything was muted, nuanced. Storiated architecture, façades like reliquaries, stepped gables, trefoil doors and windows, ridges crowned with finials, mouldings, gargoyles, bas-reliefs – incessant surprises making the town into a kind of complex landscape of stone.

It was a mixture of Gothic and Renaissance, that sinuous transition which suddenly draws out forms that are too rigid and too bare in supple, flowing lines. It was if an unexpected spring had sprouted on the walls, as if they had been tran-substantiated by a dream – all at once there were faces and bunches of flowers on them.

This blossoming on the façades had lasted until the present, blackened by the ravages of time, abiding but already blurred.

The centuries were carrying out their dreary work of

dilapidation, the posies withered, the faces eaten away by erosion, as if by leprosy. Blocked-up windows were sightless eyes. A ruinous gable, shored up, looked as if it were hobbling towards eternity on crutches. A bas-relief was already decomposing like a corpse. They needed to take action, make haste, embalm the dead town, dress the wounds of the sculptures, heal the sick windows, give succour to the ageing walls. From the very beginning Borluut had felt this vocation, had felt drawn to architecture, but not as a profession, not with the idea of building, of making a success of it, a fortune. As soon as he entered the Academy, in the initial fervour of his studies, there was but one thought on his mind: to employ them for the town, and solely for the town, not for himself. What would be the use of aiming at glory for himself, of dreaming of a great monument he would build and that would bear his name for centuries? Contemporary architecture was of necessity mediocre. Borluut often thought of the disrepute, the decadence into which his art had fallen, deluding itself with archaism and reproduction.

And his conclusion was always the same: it is not the individual who is to blame, it is the crowd. It is the crowd that constructs monuments. A man himself can only build private houses, which are therefore a product of the individual imagination, the expression of a personal dream. Cathedrals, belfries, palaces, on the other hand, have been built by the crowd. They are in its image and in its likeness. But for that the crowd must have a collective soul, must vibrate in unison. It is what happened with the Parthenon, which is the work of a people at one in art, and with the churches, which are the work of a people at one in their faith. Then the monument is born of the land itself; it is in fact the people that has created, conceived, fertilised it in the belly of the land and all the architects do is act as midwives to the soil. Today the crowd as such no longer exists. It is no longer united, so that it cannot engender a monument. A stock exchange, maybe, because there it would be unanimous in its base instinct for gold. But what kind of architecture – or any other art – would it be that built *against* the ideal.

From this reasoning Borluut immediately concluded that there was nothing to desire, nothing to realise for himself. But what a noble aim it would be to devote himself to the town and, not being able to endow it with an impossible masterpiece, to restore the excellent architectural monuments of the past in which it abounded. It was urgently needed. Elsewhere people had waited too long, had allowed weary stones, old houses, noble palaces to waste away, hastening to turn into ruins, which represent for them the calm of the tomb.

It was a delicate task, too, for the danger was twofold: on the one hand not to restore would mean losing precious vestiges which are a town's armorial bearings, the past ennobling the present; on the other hand there was the danger of restoring too much, rejuvenating, replacing stone with stone to the point where the house or the monument had lost everything of its survival through the centuries, was nothing but a sham, a deceiving copy, the wax mask of a mummy, substituted instead of its authentic face moulded by the centuries.

Borluut's concern above all was to preserve as much as possible.

In was in this manner that he had restored, as his first commission, the façade of van Hulle's house, retaining the fine patina time had spread over the walls and leaving the eroded sculptures as they were, as if they had retreated into the stone. Another would have had them carved afresh. Borluut did not touch them. It gave them the charm of unfinished work. He also took care not to scrape or polish anything, retaining the old appearance, the faded colours, the rust, the original locks and tiles.

At once the restoration of van Hulle's house determined his future. Everyone went to see and admire the miracle of rejuvenation which still retained the essential oldness, and they all wanted to save their houses from death.

Soon Borluut had all the old façades to restore.

There were incomparable ones scattered round the streets. Some, in Korte Ridderstraat for example, had retained to the present the old fashion of wooden gables, authentic models of the ones you can see painted along the quay of a frozen harbour in the portraits of Pieter Pourbus which are in the Museum. Others had survived from times that were more recent but no less picturesque, with a similar gable making a nun's cornet above these ancient dames with their air of Beguines kneeling by the side of the canals. Ornamentation, festoons, carvings, cartouches, bas-reliefs, countless surprises among the sculptures – and the tones of the façades weathered by time and rain, the pinks of fading twilight, smoky blues, misty greys, a richness of mildew, brickwork ripened by the years, the hues of a ruddy or anaemic complexion.

Borluut restored them, treating them with care, accentuating the fine fragments, filling in the ruined parts, healing over the abrasions.

This renewal of the ancient dames, the old Beguines, brightened up the streets. It was Borluut who had freed them from their approaching death, preserved them for what might be a long future. His reputation grew with every day, especially after the magistrates, following his triumph in the contest of carillonneurs and in recognition of what the town owed him already, named him municipal architect. Thus he was involved in official works, since the movement for restoration which he had set off had become general, had spread to the public monuments.

After the Town Hall and the Records Office, where polychrome decoration and new gold tints had, as it were, clothed the nudity of the brickwork in shimmering fabrics and jewels, they had decided to renovate the Gruuthuse Palace. Borluut set to work, restoring the brick façade with its open-work balustrade, its dormer windows with their flowery ornaments and finials, its fifteenth-century gables with the coat of arms of the master of the house who had given refuge to the king of England there, when he had been driven out by the party of the Red Rose. The old palace was reborn, saved from the clutches of death; it suddenly seemed to live, to smile in that remarkable district of Bruges where it would alleviate the sharp thrusts, right beside it, of the Church of Our Lady, which leaps up, block by block, to assault the air, setting out its piers, its platforms, its naves, its flying buttresses as drawbridges to the sky. An infinite accumulation of masonry, piled up, interlocking, from which the tower suddenly bursts forth like a cry.

At least the Gruuthuse Palace beside it, with its more ornate and pleasing antiquity, would, when its restoration was completed, do something to relieve the fierceness of this edifice. Now that the town had developed a passion for its improvements, the people were waiting impatiently for the work on it to be finished. They had come to realise it was their duty to preserve the town from falling into ruin, to consolidate its sagging beauty. A feeling for art descended, suddenly, like a Pentecostal fire illuminating every mind. The town authorities had their monuments restored, private individuals their homes, the clergy their churches. Thus fate sometimes sends us a reminder, a magic sign everyone obeys unconsciously, unwittingly. In Bruges the impulse was unanimous. Everyone collaborated in the creation of beauty, contributed to the town which thus, as a whole, became a work of art.

In this enthusiasm, which soon became general, Borluut, who had set it off, was the only one whose ardour had cooled a little. It was since the time when he had been appointed town carillonneur, since he had started going up the bell-tower. His pleasure in the restorations he had undertaken, in his researches among the plans and archives, was diminished. He was more interested in playing the carillon than in his drawings and designs. And, moreover, he was finding his work more difficult. When he came down from the belfry, he needed time to recover, to empty his hearing of the roar of the wind up there, which persisted in his ear like the sound of the sea in shells. His whole being was in turmoil. He could not hear properly, had to search for words, was astonished at the sound of his own voice, stumbled on the paving stones. The people in the streets got in his way. He was still flying with the clouds.

Even when he had himself once more under control, there

was still something inside him which affected him, modified his ideas and views. Things which had previously filled him with enthusiasm now left him unmoved, almost indifferent. For a while he was no longer himself.

Whenever he descended from the bell-tower, it was as if he had been there to forget, a little, how to live.

VI

When he climbed the tower, Borluut did not spend just the minimum time there, the hour prescribed for the carillon. He liked to linger, taking a gentle stroll around, during which he discovered new bells, the biggest ones that he had not examined during the first times he had been up there. Above all, the great bell, which was hung at the top of the belfry, an immense urn, venerable with age, founded in 1680 by Melchior de Haze and signed with his name. Looking inside it was like looking into an abyss. It gave one the feeling of standing on the edge of a cliff falling away sheer into the sea. It seemed as if a whole flock of sheep could have drowned in it. It was impossible to see to the bottom.

He discovered another bell, huge as well, but not plain and bare. Its metal sides were covered in scenes, bas-reliefs spreading their greenish lace over the bronze dress. Its casting mould must have been as complicated as the plate for an etching. From a distance Borluut could make out figures, hazy scenes, but the bell was too high above to make out precisely what they represented. Seized with curiosity, he found a pair of stepladders and climbed up until he was close to them. The bronze was a wild orgy, a drunken, obscene carnival; naked satyrs and women were swirling round the bell, its curve giving movement to their saraband.

At intervals couples had tumbled to the ground, piling up, body against body, mouth to mouth, flesh mingling in the fury of desire. The bronze picked out, emphasised the details . . . The vine of sin with its feverish fancies, clinging, thrusting up, falling back down the sides – and the breasts plundered like bunches of grapes!

Here and there, away from the rest, on a curve of the bell far from the stampede of the dance, were lovers silently enjoying their love like a fruit. They looked as if they were each, through the other, discovering their naked flesh, which was not yet ripe for sensual pleasure. These idyllic retreats apart, Sex was everywhere triumphant, howling, cynical. What a surprise to find this bell here, the Vase of Lust among all the others, its sisters who were silent, without memories and without bad dreams. Borluut's astonishment intensified when he found a Latin inscription round the inside, saying: *Ill^{mus} ac R^{mus} D. F. de Baillencourt Episc. Antw. me Dei Genitricis Omine et Nomine consecravit Anno 1629.* It was the bell he had been told about, an Antwerp bell that used to belong to the Cathedral of the Holy Virgin and had been presented to the town of Bruges. The bell that was full of sin bore the name of the Virgin, it had hung in a church, sounded the holy offices and been consecrated by a bishop! Typical of Antwerp and its school of art . . .

The animal enjoyment of the flesh. You could call it the ideal of Rubens, the ideal of Jordaens cast in bronze, capturing those vile moments of the race: the explosion of instinct, the fury of the orgy, the season of love, which in Flanders appears in fits, rare and torrid like the sun. But this vision belonged more to Antwerp than to Flanders. Borluut thought of the virginal imaginings of the artists of Bruges with their mysticism . . .

This bell, then, was the Foreigner. Despite that, it attracted him, haunted him with carnal visions. There were women in the bronze sprawled out in provocative postures, bending their bodies, ecstasy highlighted on their faces. Some were proffering mouths wide open like a wine glass, others held out their hair like a trap. Everywhere the mute appeal of debauchery, temptation, all the more disturbing for being indistinct, embraces as if glimpsed in the dark and filled out, made worse by the imagination. Everything that was on the bell immediately engraved itself on Borluut's mind which, in its turn, pictured lascivious revels. He started conjuring up women he had seen in those postures, he recalled former lovers, variations of rapture. Then, without knowing why, he started to think of van Hulle's daughters, or at least of Barbara. Godelieve seemed too chaste, she was one of the bells from another chamber in the tower, the bell with the black robe of a Beguine who has taken her vows. Barbara, on the other hand, was the Bell of Lust, her dress covered in all the sins and, underneath, he saw her naked body. He imagined the gleaming skin she must have, she a kind of foreigner as well with her Spanish heritage . . .

The obscene bell had drawn him into some dubious daydreams! Was it certain that he was going to fall in love with Barbara? What was certain was that he felt a violent desire for her. And when he returned to the glass chamber he searched, in the town spread out before him, for the tiny spot where she lived and moved, where she was perhaps even thinking of him. He took his bearings, his eye followed the line of the canals until it reached Zwarte-Leertouwersstraat, so narrow, imperceptible, like a thin strand of seaweed among the haphazard waves of the roofs. Without doubt she would be there. Haunted by her image, the carillonneur went back down into the world.

VII

Borluut no longer seemed to know what was going on inside him. Every time he came back down from the bell-tower he felt disturbed, and the feeling persisted, his mind was in turmoil, his willpower paralysed. He needed to find himself. He felt he was adrift. His head was teeming with clouds. The carillon continued to ring in his mind, immersing him in a shower of sound before which all the other noises of the world faded. It was above all in matters of the heart that his confusion increased. For quite some time now Borluut had been aware that he did not continue his assiduous attendance at van Hulle's Monday evenings simply for the pleasure of seeing van Hulle himself and Bartholomeus and Farazyn and the other supporters of the Flemish Movement, of getting carried away with them in the great hopes they had for their land. The love of the town was not the only element in that pleasure any more. Another love had wormed its way in. Van Hulle's two daughters were there at the soirées, different, but both attractive in their way. Their presence radiated a feeling of gentleness slipped in between the harsh, bellicose utterances, like a sachet of herbs between the sheets. No one took any notice of them. Bartholomeus and the others appeared to be confirmed bachelors anyway. Still, their charm had an effect . . .

Now Borluut tried to work out how this had happened to him. Passion flows like a river and it is very difficult to go back to its source. It began imperceptibly. He felt happier every Monday and looked forward to the evening. Once at van Hulle's, he took to speaking above all for the young women, trying to be eloquent in order to please them, expressing the opinions he assumed they shared. He looked for signs of approval in their faces. Soon, as he walked home at dead of night, through the empty streets, he felt they were there beside him, and his obsession remained as he fell asleep, continuing even in his dreams. At other times, after having accompanied his friends to their homes, he would return to van Hulle's house, waiting at some window that was still lit, to see the black silhouette, already half undressed, of Godelieve or Barbara. Nocturnal fever! A shadow in breathless poise, trying to become one with the shadow, with the darkened façade opposite, in order to catch some glimpse, to anticipate in some small way the intimate closeness of the wedding night. Borluut watched, went away, came back. Especially on certain evenings when he felt there had been a response to his inner turmoil, a shared agitation. It was above all Godelieve that he dreamt of seeing on the screen of the blind, Godelieve who seemed the more tightly enclosed in her dresses.

She was so impenetrable! True, she would smile a little when he turned towards her, when he spoke. But it was an indefinable smile, he couldn't say whether it was happy or sad, at a memory or some secret joy, perhaps simply a crease that had become fixed, an inherited expression, the echo of some happiness one of her forebears had felt.

Her whole being gave the impression of a gentle maiden from the past. She was the original Flanders type, still intact. Fair-haired puberty like the Virgins we see in the paintings of van Eyck and Memling. Honey-coloured hair undulating, unfastened, in calm ripples; the forehead rising to a pointed arch, a church wall, the masonry smooth and bare, with the two monochrome stained-glass windows of the eyes.

At first Joris had felt attracted to her . . . Now, without knowing how it had come about, Barbara was the object of his daydreams. He was haunted by her tragic beauty. She had a strange complexion, with a sulphurous flush, as if from some inner storm. At times her too-red lips made Godelieve's pink lips seem insipid. But he had liked Godelieve, still liked her. She was a pretty little virgin – and very Flemish, in harmony with his ideal of Bruges and his exclusive pride in their race. Barbara appeared as a foreigner, true, but the aroma she exuded, the promise of sensual delights! That was why he had turned away from Godelieve. He no longer knew what he really felt. It was the belfry that was to blame. It had happened since he had seen the Bell of Lust, instantly, as he faced all that sin in high relief, the couplings as if embroidered on the bell, the breasts like bunches of grapes, the wine-harvest of Hell! He had started to conjure up the image of Barbara in his mind. He had looked up into the bell as if he were looking up her dress. He had been overwhelmed with carnal desire. And that desire, born high up in the bell-tower, had remained with him when he came back down to the ground. Whilst his initial emotion reasserted itself when he saw the two sisters, reawakened by the graceful arch of Godelieve's countenance, his belfry desire would immediately rear up again, tumultuous, demanding. An inextricable conflict of emotions! It seemed as if the house and the bell-tower were pulling him in opposite directions. In van Hulle's home he loved only Godelieve, she matched the old objects so well, was like an old portrait herself; and he thought of the calm she would bring to his life, if he were to marry her, with the mystery of her eternal smile, which seemed to remain fixed so as not to disturb the silence at all. In the belfry, on the other hand, he loved only Barbara, tormented by desire, by a curiosity to know her, to know her love, doubtless because of the obscene bell, the dark bedchamber into which he plunged with her, possessed her, enjoying all the sins represented in the bronze . . .

Borluut would have liked to know, to be clear about what was happening to him.

Since he had started going up the tower, life had become a mystery to him. The alternatives were making him very unhappy. He tried to pull himself together, to think things through.

Oh, how wretched I am, he thought. Things are so badly arranged. The elements that we have of our destiny are so tenuous, it's difficult to recognise them. We only have a small detail, the colour of a pair of eyes, of someone's hair. He, for example, had always been looking for eyes the colour of the water in the canals – and Barbara and Godelieve both had them. But what face, what lips, what hair, what body, above all what mind was he to choose to go with those eyes? In short, we only know enough to mislead ourselves. The known element, which we have by instinct, by some vague indication, is like a key fate has thrown us. So we start looking for the house to which the key belongs, the house that will contain our happiness. Unfortunately, there is not just the one door the key will fit. We search – nothing but fumbling, groping in the dark! Futile gestures to stop the horizon as it passes. Then we enter one, at random. Most often we're wrong, it's not the house of our happiness. There's a slight similarity. Sometimes we think there are worse places we could have gone into. But we also think we could, as surely happens to some people, have entered the one, unique, special house, the house of our happiness. And our awareness that it does exist somewhere is enough to give us an aversion to the one where we live. However, mostly we resign ourselves to it.

Therefore, Borluut concluded, since we know nothing, there is no point in choosing. After all, it is Fate which does it for us. Our free will is an illusion. Thus the inescapable conclusion of his analysis was that he felt that if he had been free, he would have continued to prefer Godelieve, but Fate was driving him to desire Barbara and, in the end, she was the one he would marry.

VIII

Oh, the vanity of plans! Our lives proceed regardless. All the things we work out in such minute detail slip away from us at the last moment, or change.

You are following the highroad through the forest of events, where it is always evening. You catch a glimpse of a small light, at the end, which you think is the right inn to stay at. Then, suddenly, you branch off, you take a path, a short cut, which leads to other lighted windows. Everything turns out differently. And almost always it is the Woman who guides our steps, leading us into a maze according to the lines of her hand. Her whim alone, the state of her nerves on a particular morning or evening, determines our happiness or unhappiness.

The whole of Joris's life was decided in one minute. He thought he was in a state of indecision with no way out. One glance from Barbara and everything was resolved, beyond recall. One Monday evening he arrived early for van Hulle's weekly soirée. Was he distracted, had he forgotten what time it was or was it premeditated so that, arriving first, he would be alone and could enjoy all the more the closeness, the familiarity? That day he had dreamt of Barbara more than ever, was haunted by her. It was like a signal, a premonition of the approach of something decisive. When he had been shown into the usual drawing-room, he found Barbara there, setting out glasses and teacups. She was alone, looking preoccupied. At first Joris was slightly embarrassed, but also delighted at the prospect of a tête-à-tête. As if to ascertain that it would be prolonged, he asked, 'And your father?'

'Oh, he's very busy today. He's rearranging his clock museum. The servants are never allowed to enter. He's been shut in there all day, together with Godelieve.'

'And you?'

'Me? Oh, I've been alone, as always. They hardly need me . . .'

Barbara gave a deep sigh.

'What's wrong?' Joris asked, suddenly seized by a vague agitation, a tenderness full of pity at seeing her so forlorn, holding back her tears.

She did not reply, remaining impenetrable.

'Tell me. What's wrong?' Joris asked again, his voice almost trembling with emotion.

Now Barbara vented her feelings in an angry, vehement outburst, the words coming in spurts, like a spring that has been too constricted:

'It's . . . it's my life that's wrong. I would like . . . to change my life.'

And she described her monotonous young girl's life. Her father, she claimed, did not love her. All his affection was directed towards her younger sister, who resembled him. They were always making arrangements from which she was excluded. Little kindnesses, intimate gestures, tokens of affection . . . And always in agreement . . . Always together . . . They spent whole days side by side in the clock museum – her father working at his bench, taking clock mechanisms to bits, the way he was always doing; Godelieve beside him, with her lace-making pillow – and from time to time they would look up from their work and smile at each other. Such mawkishness was not for her . . . that was why neither her father nor her sister loved her. She was like an intruder in her own home.

Once more the tears were about to fall. 'Oh yes, I would like to change my life,' she repeated.

Joris was moved to see her so forlorn. She looked beautiful like that, the more beautiful for her loss of composure, with her eyes cut like diamonds by the teardrops welling up.

Joris's emotions were in turmoil. He suddenly felt an immense desire that she should be happy, and that she should owe her happiness to him. Her lips, onto which a few tears had rolled down, were a moist flower, suffering, offering themselves . . .

Soon Joris could see nothing but those tempting, haunting lips. They had been with him for such a long time now, as if they had a life of their own, a single flower that could be gathered separately in the garden of her flesh. That is the way it is, we always fall in love because of a detail, a nuance. It is a marker we set up for ourselves in the midst of the confusion, in the infinite space of love. The greatest passions come from such little causes. What makes us fall in love? Hair of a particular colour, the tone of a voice, a beauty spot which disturbs us and hints at others, an expression in the eyes, a contour of the hands, a certain palpitation of the nose, which quivers as if it were always facing the sea. Joris loved Barbara because of her lips which, at that moment, were trembling from the evocation of her unhappiness, were more lustrous because of the tears that had flowed, like a flower in too much rain.

Barbara fell silent. She had perceived Joris's inner turmoil, the wavering inside him. So she gave him a decisive look, her two eyes spearing into his, a look which signalled acquiescence.

At the same time her mouth, as if ripening all at once, changed from a flower into a fruit, with a promise of its succulent flesh. Joris, sensing the iron hand of Fate, had gone up to her.

'You would like to change your life?' he said, after a pause. His voice was hesitant, panting a little, as if he had been running, precisely in time with the rhythm of his pulse, with the beating of his heart, of which he could hear every single palpitation.

'Oh yes,' said Barbara, not taking her eyes off him.

'Well, that would be easy,' Joris went on.

Barbara did not reply. She had lowered her eyes, slightly embarrassed, anxious, realising that the decisive moment had come. Despite her dark complexion, she had suddenly gone pale, making her lips seem even more red.

Her pose was one of consent.

It was more than Joris could bear. Words were beyond him. Suddenly, pressing up against her, he took her hands, holding them to her body, and, on an impulse, in a moment of wild recklessness, without knowing why, he yielded to the temptation of those lips and flung his lips onto them, eating them, partaking of their sacrament . . . Eucharist of love with a red host! Was it not truly a real presence? In that moment he possessed her entirely in the species of her lips in which she was subsumed and transubstantiated.

A few moments later van Hulle and Godelieve came in together, having finally finished ordering and meticulously removing the dust from the clocks in the museum. They were not at all surprised to find Joris with Barbara. He was one of the regular visitors to the house. Anyway, van Hulle's mind was still preoccupied with the work he had done during the day, with the changes he had carried out; for a collector, to move items is almost like acquiring them anew. He did not notice anything, nor did Godelieve, whose eyes, as always, seemed fixed on more distant spheres, her thoughts else- where. Borluut threw out some non-committal remarks, stock phrases, empty words, which floated aimlessly round the room . . . What an effort it was to return to normal life after having plunged all of a sudden into the depths of love!

Then Borluut was beset by the sense of a strange confusion, such as he felt when he came back down from the belfry. He was stumbling over words as he stumbled on the paving stones. He felt the way one does returning from a voyage, slightly abnormal, with a sense of solitude inside oneself, of infinity. Was entering into love like entering the tower? But love seemed like a tower with steps made of light . . . He felt he had taken leave of the world, had climbed up very high, was once more *high above the world*. A dizzying ascent, a couple mounting the stairs together to seek their souls as he had sought the bells. The whole of the evening Borluut remained distracted, bemused, sad at having come back down to earth.

During the days that followed the thought of Barbara con- tinued to haunt him. He realised that something definitive, unforgettable had happened. What was the point of going over things again and again, hesitating, examining his feelings? It is the flesh which, all of a sudden, decides everything. An unknown force had thrown him onto the young woman's lips. And there had been no lack of prior warning from Fate. It was her lips by which he had felt obsessed, refreshed and scorched, as if they were both flower and flame. All at once her lips had granted him communion and now love resided in those lips, as God resides in the host. There was no going back. There was no way of undoing it. It had only lasted a moment, but that moment was bound to eternity.

From that point on Borluut felt committed. To renounce her would be a sacrilege, a blackguardly profanation of those consecrated lips. He already thought of Barbara as his fiancée, his wife. His conscience did not resort to subterfuge to avoid his obligation, even though no decisive words of love, no promise nor vow, had passed between them on the evening of the kiss. No matter! The kiss itself was sufficient. In placing his lips on those lips of red wax Joris had imprinted on them the seal of a pact that was as irrevocable as it was tacit.

And anyway, the thought of withdrawing had not occurred to him for one minute. His mind was made up. He went to see van Hulle.

'I have come to see you, my friend, on a serious matter . . .'

'What a tone of voice! What is it, this serious matter?'

Borluut felt embarrassed. He had worked out a plan for this conversation; at that moment he forgot it completely. He was overcome with emotion and became sentimental.

'We've been friends for a long time now.'

'Yes, for five years,' said van Hulle, 'the date is on the house, the date of its restoration – and of the start of our friendship.'

It provided an opening and Borluut seized it. 'Well, would you like us to be even better friends, even closer to each other?'

Van Hulle stared at him, eyes wide, not understanding.

'Yes,' Borluut went on. 'You have two daughters . . .'

Immediately the expression on van Hulle's face changed; his eyes blazed up briefly. 'Oh, no! . . . Let's talk about something else,' he went on hurriedly, as if something was causing him deep distress.

'I'm sorry, but –' Borluut said.

Without letting him explain, van Hulle went on, getting more and more worked up. 'There's no point . . . I beg you . . . Anyway, Godelieve wouldn't think of it . . . Godelieve will never marry . . . She wants to stay with me . . . At least wait until I'm dead . . .'

His features contorted in an expression of anguish, of deep distress. Unaware of his surroundings, letting himself go as if he were alone, he started to moan, to pour out his feelings aloud: 'It was bound to happen! It was inevitable. Love is contagious. But my dear Godelieve had kept her love for you well hidden. I was the only one who knew. I was the only one to whom she confided it, at that point she had not even admitted it to herself. We tell each other everything. But she had renounced her love, she had forgotten it, for me, to stay with me, so as not to leave me all alone in my old age, to keep me from dying, because I would die straight away without her. And now it's you, you love her, you've come to tell me. She'll know, she'll see. What will become of me? Oh, no, no, don't take Godelieve away from me.'

The old antiquary was imploring him, hands clasped, breathing heavily because of the danger he felt was imminent, repeating the name of Godelieve over and over again, like a miser the value of a treasure he is about to lose.

Borluut was stunned by this revelation, by the passion of paternal affection revealed in the heartrending cries. Van Hulle had spoken so quickly, the words pouring out like a spring bursting forth, he had given himself up so completely to his distress, had so instantly become deaf to everything around that he gave Borluut no time to think and interject to bring the conversation back to the matter in hand.

A lull gave him the opportunity to break in quickly. 'But it's Barbara I'm in love with. She's the one whose hand I've come to ask in marriage.'

At that van Hulle, rescued from the peril he had thought was about to engulf him, threw himself at Joris, as if he had gone mad, and clasped him to his breast, crying and laughing at the same time, resting his head on his friend's shoulder, as if the excess of happiness were more than he could bear. And he repeated the same words over and over again, mechanically, like a man in a trance:

'Oh yes . . . oh yes! It's not Godelieve . . . it's not Godelieve . . .'

He calmed down a little. So this wasn't about Godelieve. What a relief! Of course. Of course he agreed. He would be delighted to let him have her.

'May she make you happy, you who really deserve it. But how could I have known?' van Hulle became very thoughtful. He turned to Borluut again. 'So you didn't know?' he asked, seeming hardly able to believe that things were as they were. 'You didn't guess that Godelieve was in love with you, last year? She suffered so much, poor girl. She sacrificed herself for me. Now it's over . . . But Barbara now, does she love you in return? Has she told you?'

Borluut nodded.

The old antiquary was astounded. How could it have happened? The two sisters had both fallen in love with Borluut, one after the other. Though it wasn't surprising, all things considered. They didn't meet many young men, spending all their time at home, with no mother. And Borluut was attractive, he had been successful, a fine career was in prospect, his name was well known. Fortunately everything had turned out for the best. Barbara was the only one who had aroused his feelings and he was going to marry her. Van Hulle was still slightly concerned. As long as she did not make Borluut unhappy with her capricious and irascible temperament, the tangle of nerves that would suddenly tighten inside her, confusing all her thoughts and feelings – Borluut, that fine fellow whom he already loved like a son. But van Hulle's scruples did not last long. 'All that will disappear with love, or pass as she gets older,' he told himself, quickly regaining his habitual serenity, his agitation calmed, exultant, rejoicing in the thought that Godelieve was left to him, dearer than ever, like a convalescent recovering from his fear of losing her, which had for a moment thrown him into a panic.

'Above all,' van Hulle advised, 'never say anything about this to Godelieve – nor to Barbara, either. We must keep this to ourselves. As if I had not told you anything, as if nothing had . . .'

Borluut paid no further attention to his confidences. All young girls had these passing fancies for men they came into contact with. Preliminary sketches of their future happiness, models in clay before the great statue of love which would take up their life and sit on their tomb. Besides, he was completely committed to Barbara. He felt bound to her. Brushing her lips with his had created an eternal obligation. Now her mouth seemed to him like an open wound, the point where they had come together, where, for a moment, they had been as one and which was now left bleeding, painful, as if something had been torn away.

He was delighted with what had been done. His obsession with her continued. She was truly beautiful, and she aroused his desire. An aroma of ripe flesh, a freshness like the juice of a fruit, persisted in his mouth from those lips of which he had eaten and drunk. He longed to taste them again, to possess them entirely . . .

Now he realised that all the time it had been Barbara, and Barbara alone, whom he had desired when an as yet indefinable charm had drawn him to van Hulle's, bathing the Monday evenings in a halo of light, something to look forward to in the grey monotony of the week. Now that the old man had confided in him, he understood. He had never lusted after Godelieve, but she had caused him some agitation, despite himself, because she had secretly been in love with him and love can influence, can affect others. For a time he had been between the two sisters, as if he were being pulled in opposite directions by two mysterious forces. In that moment he was not master of himself. When Godelieve renounced her love, he had become himself again. And his will, now released, had chosen Barbara. He loved her! He was in raptures as they poured out their hearts, as they gazed into each other's eyes, as their hands met in those first touches in which we possess each other in a small way.

The marriage had been announced and was close at hand.

Joris frequently came to van Hulle's house. Barbara was transfigured by joy. At last she was going to change her life, be happy. Sometimes they went out together. Joris took her to the Museum to see Memling's great triptych which contains a picture of St. Barbara, her patron saint, because in her hand she was holding a tower. Was it not an allegory of the two of them? He had often thought of it when their love was just beginning. The tower was him, since he lived there, since he was its music, that is its presence, its consciousness. And Barbara was going to carry all that, to take it up in her slender hand, as St. Barbara in the triptych holds in her palm a tiny gold bell-tower, which relies on her and would break if she should take it into her mind to change her gesture.

Joris went into ecstasies over the picture. He looked at Barbara tenderly. 'My tower is in your hand and my heart is in the tower.'

Barbara smiled. Joris showed her the donors on the wings: old Willem Moreel, burgomaster of Bruges, and his wife, Barbara de Vlaenderbergh, with all their children, five sons and eleven daughters, set out in rows, with their different-sized heads overlapping like the tiles on a roof. A House of Happiness, made with faces! An edifying example of the ancient families of Flanders!

Borluut gave himself up to reverie, to dreams of a similar line of descendants which might perhaps come from them to increase the race.

Thus love had restored him to the world. Loving Barbara, he loved the town less, its obsolescence, its silence.

Now, even when he climbed the tower at the regular times set for the carillon, he no longer had his previous sense of rising up high and far away, of leaving his self and the town behind, of ascending *high above the world*. He took the world, *his* world, with him, up to the top. No longer did he drift in the sky, with the clouds. From the battlemented platform of the bell-tower he watched the town, observed the passers-by with interest, thought of Barbara, called to mind her dark complexion, her haunting aroma, above all her too-red lips. Down below, the roofs were piled up, red as well. He compared them. The faded tiles had weathered into the last pinks of twilight, the crimsons of old banners. There were feverish reds and bleached reds, reds of clotted light, reds of rust and of wounds, but all fixed, defunct, lifeless.

It was like a graveyard of reds, far below, above the grey town. So then Joris would search until he believed he could see, right at the bottom, the only living, blooming red, the red of Barbara's lips, the burning chilli red that made all the tiles look pale.

IX

One day Borluut had some great news for Bartholomeus, good news that would fill the painter with joy. One of the aldermen had come to tell him that the Town Council had finally approved a commission for his friend, an important work for which he had been waiting for years: a large-scale series of pictures to decorate the walls of the Council Chamber in the Town Hall. For Bartholomeus it was the realisation of a long-cherished dream, to use the talent for decoration which he felt he possessed and which it pained him to leave idle. He would finally be able to release onto the walls the splendid processions he held captive within him.

Borluut set off for the precinct of the Beguinage where Bartholomeus lived. An impulse had taken the painter there, a feeling that the solitude and silence would be good for his work. The Beguinage of Bruges was in a state of decline, was slowly being abandoned. There were only some fifteen Beguines left, a constantly depleting flock around the Grand Mistress. They only occupied a few of the houses – their shutters green and white, their façades rain-coloured – but it was impossible to tell which were empty and which not because the windows of both were equally sparkling and so discreet, contenting themselves simply with reflecting the elms in the raised strips of grass and the chapel opposite, with being faithful mirrors of the precinct.

So for lack of Beguines, some dwellings were let out to lay people, mostly old. Bartholomeus had had the idea of setting up his studio there. The little whitewashed chamber was a true monk's cell. He had no need of a big room since, having been unable to find any commissions for large decorative pieces, he had perforce to confine himself to pictures that would fit on an easel, small-scale canvases he worked over slowly, with infinite pains, bringing them to harmonious perfection, simply for the pleasure of the task itself. He was

70

not concerned with selling them, nor did he paint to please others. He had a small private income, enough on which to live frugally, and he was happy with that. Working in the Beguinage was very fruitful. The windows let in a perfect light, a vibrant light such as you get in the north where a kind of grey gauze turns the sun to silver. And such solitude, such quiet.

Bartholomeus's work was accompanied by the sound of the occasional canticle chanted punctually at lauds by the choir of Beguines. He would come across them as they returned, one by one, to their little houses with the air of sheep returning to the fold. He had studied and caught on paper some of their postures, their cautious gestures, their Gothic walk, the calm flight, white wings spread, of their cornets, and above all the folds, like organ pipes, of their black robes. He had dreamt of being the painter of the Beguines and, lying in wait behind his windows, eyes always on the alert, had painted a few pictures inspired by them and accumulated numerous drawings and sketches. Then he had turned away from them, finding that art still too exclusively bound to the forms of the material world. He looked within himself, looked elsewhere.

Now the news Borluut brought had once more turned his ideal, turned his life upside down.

'Well? Are you pleased?' his friend asked seeing his indifferent reaction.

'Several years ago I would have been pleased,' the painter replied. 'Now I've been thinking along other lines.'

'But your main talent was for large-scale paintings, you said. You declared that decoration was the supreme form of painting.'

'Perhaps. But there are more interesting kinds of painting.'

Then Bartholomeus went over to the corners of the Beguines' former visiting-room with its light-coloured walls, which he used as his studio, rummaged among canvases and framed pictures, all of which were turned to the wall, made a choice, hesitated, then took one out and put it on the easel.

'There!' he said. 'Some objects in a distinctive light. It's an arrangement by a window in an October twilight.'

Borluut looked at the picture and was gradually won over to the point where it touched him. It was something other than a piece of painting, something more. Looking at it, one forgot about techniques and, anyway, they were all combined: charcoal with colour highlights, a skilful chemistry of pastels and pencils, of dust and mysterious cross-hatching. It was evening in the picture. As if shadow and silence had been put under glass.

Bartholomeus went on, 'I wanted to show that these objects are sensitive, suffer at the coming of night, faint at the departure of the last rays, which, by the way, also live in this room; they suffer as much, they fight against the darkness. There you have it. It's the life of things, if you like. The French would call it a *nature morte*, a picture of inanimate objects. That is not what I'm trying to show. Flemish puts it better: a still life.'

The painter showed him another work. It was a figure, not very large, a priestess-like woman dressed in an ageless garment with, around her, a slenderness of columns, a blossoming of capitals.

'This,' said Bartholomeus, 'is Architecture. See, she's making the gesture of *measuring the sky*. It's for the tower that is going to rise up there and which she is pondering.'

'It is admirable, truly admirable,' Borluut declared in solemn, impassioned tones. 'But how few will understand you, with that kind of art.'

'Nevertheless,' said Bartholomeus, 'it is along those lines that I will paint the pictures for the town. The essential thing is to create beauty. First and foremost I work for myself. What is the point of making things others like if you dislike them yourself? It would be like a reprobate having the reputation of being virtuous. Would it make him feel any the less remorseful? The main thing for inner contentment is to be in a state of grace. And there is an artistic state of grace, for art is a kind of religion. It has to be loved for itself, for the intoxication and consolation it offers because it is the most noble means of forgetting the world and conquering death.'

Borluut listened to the painter holding forth, moved by his calm, sonorous voice, which seemed to come from outside time. His wiry black beard jutted out, tapering. Thin and pale, he had one of those profiles burning with the fever of a monk in the act of adoration. The studio around him, the Beguines' former visiting-room, really did seem like a monastic cell. No luxury. On the walls simply a few scraps of old chasubles, pieces of stoles he had hung up out of a taste for faded tones and also to suggest to himself ancient cathedrals, abolished processions; then reproductions of those Flemish Primitives who, at once meticulous and visionary, were his masters: the altarpieces and triptychs of van Eyck and Memling with nothing but Annunciations, Adorations, Virgins, Christ Childs, angels with rainbow wings, saints playing the organ or the psaltery. And these ancient liturgical silks, these mystical images increased the impression surrounding Bartholomeus of a monkish cell and of an art-religion.

'Besides,' Bartholomeus concluded, 'I have always seen the artist in this way, as a kind of priest, a priest of the ideal who must also make a vow of poverty, of chastity . . .'

Smiling, he added, 'Haven't I remained a bachelor?'

'You have done well,' Borluut said, suddenly filled with concern.

'What! You approve? And you've just got married?'

'Yes and no.'

'You're not happy?'

'One is never as happy as one thought one would be.'

'That is to say you imagined Barbara was an angel and she's turned out to be a woman. They're all more or less temperamental, quick-tempered. Barbara more than any, I would think. She's Spanish, isn't she? What's left of the old blood of the conquest, Catholic and violent, domineering and inquisitorial, takes a certain pleasure in making people suffer. You had no idea, did you? Yet it was obvious. She never even managed to get on with her father and you know how easygoing he is. Don't you keep your eyes open? You don't see things very clearly, do you? At one point I thought of putting you on your guard, but you were already in love with her . . .'

'Yes, I loved her, and I love her still,' Borluut said. 'I love her in a strange way, in the only way it's possible to love that kind of woman. It's very difficult to analyse, and very variable. She's so changeable herself. Transports of delight, moments of abandon, a yielding, purring tenderness which wraps itself round you, words simply flowing, lips playful – then, the slightest little thing, a word misinterpreted, a delay, a mild criticism, an irritating gesture and disaster strikes. Everything goes blurred, nerves tense and let fly stupid, cruel words, perhaps unintentionally.'

Borluut stopped, suddenly confused, surprised at his confession, at having said too much. That morning there had been another scene with Barbara, more acrimonious than previous ones, which had filled him with concern about the future. It was so soon after their marriage. Had he perhaps exaggerated? He had spoken under the influence of one very recent experience. All in all, the alarms were rare, a few rainy days in the three months of their life together. It was doubtless inevitable, a law of nature really. Borluut reassured himself, recalled Barbara, her dark beauty, her lips that were so dear to him. He had gone too far in complaining about her. Bartholomeus was to blame for setting him off down that slippery slope. The painter had always been hostile to Barbara, anyway. Who knows, perhaps at some point he had been smitten with her and maybe she had spurned him? Borluut was annoyed at the way he had analysed Barbara and had encouraged him to join in maligning her. He was annoyed with Bartholomeus for the way he had confided in him, feeling he had somehow been tricked into it. He was annoyed with himself.

As he made his way back to his house on the Dijver, along the canals, beside the calm waters, Borluut felt his regret, his remorse at having divulged his worries, grow at the sight of the noble swans, sealed-in snow, which, prisoners of the canals, prey to the rain, the sadness of the bells, the shadow of the gables, have the modesty to remain silent and only complain, with a voice that is almost human, when they are about to die . . .

X

After Barbara's marriage van Hulle had given up dealing in antiques. He got rid of his old furniture and curios, keeping only the most precious for himself and his home. He reckoned his private income was sufficient to stop having to put up with the disturbance of connoisseurs, visitors to the town who came to his home, looked round, picked up this or that object, holding it with tingling fingertips – that exquisite sensual pleasure of collectors, who are a *tactile* species – and, more often than not, left without purchasing anything. He was growing old and wanted peace and quiet, at most to continue to entertain Borluut, Bartholomeus and the rest on Monday evenings; but that was just out of habit, he was no longer interested in the Flemish Movement, which he felt had lost its purity and been taken over by the politicians.

Besides that, his secret – and principal – reason for retiring was to devote himself entirely to his *idée fixe*, his collection which was becoming ever larger and more complicated. Van Hulle's concern was no longer simply to have beautiful clocks or rare timepieces; his feelings for them were not simply those one has for inanimate objects. True, their outward appearance was still important, their craftsmanship, their mechanisms, their value as works of art, but the fact that he had collected so many was for a different reason entirely. It was a result of his strange preoccupation with *the exact time*. It was no longer enough for him that they were interesting. He was irritated by the differences in time they showed. Above all when they struck the hours and the quarters. One, very old, was deranged and got confused in keeping count of the passage of time, which it had been doing for so long. Others were behind, little Empire clocks with children's voices almost, as if they had not quite grown up. In short, the clocks were always at variance. They seemed to be running after each other, calling out, getting lost, looking for each other at all the changing crossroads of time.

It annoyed van Hulle that they were never in unison. Living together, is it not better to do things together? He would have liked to see them all go the same, that is think the same, think as he did, show the same time, without deviation, from the signal he had given. But this accord was a miracle that had so far seemed impossible.

One might as well hope that all the stones in the sea, which had come from different parts of the horizon and been pushed along by unequal tides, should be identical in volume. Still, he tried. He had taken instruction from a clockmaker and now he was familiar with the wheels, the springs, the delicate teeth and pinions, the jewelled bearings, the chains, all the nerves and muscles, the whole anatomy of this creature of steel and gold whose regular pulse marks out the life of time. He had bought the necessary tools, files, fine saws, tiny instruments with which to dismantle, polish, regulate, correct and cure these delicate, impressionable organisms. Perhaps with observation, patience and meticulousness, putting this one back and bringing that one forward, giving each one the assistance its weakness demanded, he would one day realise his obsessive dream, his *idée fixe* which had become more precisely defined: finally to see them all in unison, to hear them all, if only once, strike the hour at the same time, while that same hour rang out from the bell-tower. To achieve his ideal of having *unified time!*

Van Hulle's mania persisted, he did not become the least disheartened. He spent whole days in his clock museum, trying to adjust them so they were the same, absorbed in his dream of them showing the identical time, absorbed in the pleasure of his engrossing forays into clock-repairing. Sitting at his bench, his eyeglass over his eye, he observed the working of the springs, the little ailments of the wheels, the germs that were the fine motes of dust. For him it was as fascinating as conducting experiments in a laboratory.

Oh the joy of an *idée fixe!* The contentment of a life taken up with some ideal, any ideal! A gentle trap to catch the infinite, like the sun in a piece of mirror in a child's hand.

The peace and quiet of a house filled with a single dream!

Van Hulle was happy, especially after the departure of Barbara, whose moods and bickering resulted in shrill cries that rent the solitude in which the only sound to be heard was the regular heartbeat of the clocks.

And Godelieve's heartbeat too. It was so calm! And so in unison with his own, van Hulle thought. That was what had unconsciously led him to dream of the agreement of his clocks. It ought to be achievable for mechanical clockwork, for the passive life of objects since, with Godelieve, he had achieved the much more complicated and mysterious accord of two human beings.

Even their occupations seemed to be parallel. While he was sorting out the mysterious threads of time, all the gold wires inside the clocks, Godelieve, who was staying at home more and more, was arranging the no less fine and intricate white threads of her lace-making pillow.

She, too, was bringing them together, combining the innumerable threads in a precise whole – the lace veil which, having become very pious, she had promised to the Virgin in a glass case at the corner of the street where they lived. It would take a long time to finish, but she had the time in her empty life, which already had something of that of an old maid. She was gradually accumulating pieces: a flower, rosettes, an emblem, scattered fragments of the dedicated veil. Was that not also a kind of collection, of successive designs, before the completion of the whole veil?

Resemblance. Identity! A life together, in which one was the other, simultaneously and alternately. One said what the other was thinking. One saw with the other's eyes. They understood each other without having to speak. From spending their whole time together, they had become like facing mirrors, each reflecting objects to the other. Van Hulle loved Godelieve with a jealous affection. In the past it had caused him pain, almost physical pain, to think that a man might love her, might embrace her. But above all she was, for him, his own self-awareness. He felt that without her he would be nothing but a dead body.

XI

High above the world! The feeling returned as Borluut climbed the bell-tower again to play the carillon. He had had to endure further scenes with Barbara, brought on by trifles, sudden fits of anger, her every nerve instantly on the alert as her features contorted. Only her too-red lips remained, redder than ever in a face white with rage. And from them came harsh words, hasty, absurd, bombarding him like stones. Every time, Borluut held his breath, terrified at the outburst which at any moment, he sensed, could lead to the worst. And he came out of these alarms distraught, even physically exhausted, as if he had been struggling against the elements, against the wind in the dark.

Now, as he climbed the tower since it was one of the days appointed for the carillon, he felt as if he were gradually leaving behind him his troubles, his life in the world below. The events of the morning were already so far away! Space distances us from things in the same way as time does. Every step on the dark stairs was the same as a year in time. At each step a little more of his distress fell away from him, remaining fixed, like his house and similarly growing smaller as he moved farther away, already almost indistinguishable in the mass of the town.

High above the world. Yes, truly. What was the importance of his house now, so minuscule already, glimpsed through the trees on the bank of the Dijver, sending its pale reflection onto the canal, which could no longer be made out. Barbara, too, cast such a short shadow in the world down there. It was all petty, shallow. Little by little he shed his memories, all the human baggage which hampered his ascent.

Soon the air of the high place was blowing in through the gaps in the masonry, the open bays, where the wind flowed like water round the arches of a bridge. Borluut felt refreshed, fanned by this sea-breeze coming from the beaches of the sky.

It seemed to be sweeping up dead leaves inside him. New paths, leading elsewhere, appeared in his soul; fresh clearings were revealed. Finally he found himself.

Total oblivion as a prelude to taking possession of one's self! He was like the first man on the first day to whom nothing has yet happened. The delights of metamorphosis. He owed them to the tall tower, to the summit he had gained where the battlemented platform was ready for him, a refuge in the infinite.

From that height he could no longer see the world, he no longer understood it. Yes, each time he was seized with vertigo, with a desire to lose his footing, to throw himself off, but not towards the ground, into the abyss with its spirals of belfries and roofs over the depths of the town below. It was the *abyss above* of which he felt the pull.

He was more and more bewildered.

Everything was becoming blurred – before his eyes, inside his head – because of the fierce wind, the boundless space with nothing to hold on to, the clouds he had come too close to, which long continued to journey on inside him. The delights of sojourning among the summits have their price.

At once Borluut was vaguely aware of this. Bartholomeus's remark, the day when he had made the mistake of confiding in him about Barbara, had already been disquieting, a warning about what was happening to him: 'You don't see things very clearly, do you?'

Now the painter's words came back to mind, haunting him like an appeal, a regret. No, he had not seen things clearly, and that was why he felt eternally sad and unhappy. He never guessed anything, never suspected anyone, looked without seeing, was incapable of making an analysis, of gauging his words, of assessing people he came across. Borluut thought it was the tower that was to blame. Every time he came down again, back to the town, he was lost, could neither see nor think straight.

It was as if he had seen the world, and continued to see it, from the perspective of eternity. That was the source of all his woes. Another man would have guessed, would have perceived Barbara's dark temperament, her unhealthy state at the mercy of nerves to which her life was for ever bound. And even now another man would be able to deal with it, impose himself, find the right tone to adopt, the words that pacified, the looks that mastered or calmed her. A more level-headed man, who saw things more clearly, would have found a way through this maze of nerves.

He remained dismayed, alarmed and, what was worse, clumsy; all he could do was suffer in silence, bemoan his lot, drift along on his own. At least he had the tower; he never failed to go there in his distress. It was his immediate refuge, wiping his mind clear, and he would hurry up to the top to wash his bleeding heart in the clean air, like washing it in the sea.

Thus the tower was both disease and cure. It rendered him unfit for the world and it remedied the hurts inflicted by the world.

On that day too Borluut immediately felt once more at peace, recovered from his recent troubles. Solitude was balm to his soul – the nearest clouds were teased out like lint.

Once he had reached the top, he looked down on the town at his feet. Such repose, such tranquility, what a lesson in calmness! Seeing it, he was ashamed of his troubled existence. He renounced the love that brought him misery for the love of the town. It took hold of him again, suffusing his entire being as it had done during the first days of the Flemish Movement. How beautiful Bruges still was, seen from above, with its belfries, its pinnacles, its stepped gables like stairs to climb up to the land of dreams, to return to the great days of yesteryear. Among the roofs were canals fanned by the trees, quiet streets with a few women making their way in cloaks, swinging like silent bells. Lethargic peace! The sweetness of renunciation! A queen in exile, the widow of History whose only desire, basically, was to carve her own tomb. Borluut had made his contribution. Remembering it, joy returned, and pride. Among the age-old agglomeration of the town he searched out, counted the ancient houses, the rare façades to which he had, so to speak, given back a face. Without him, the town would be in ruins – or repudiated in favour of a modern town.

He had saved it with his skilful restorations. Thus brought to perfection, it would never disappear, it could make its way down the centuries. He was the one who had performed this miracle, which few people realised, even and above all Barbara who, being his wife, should have been proud of him instead of subjecting him at any moment to such harsh and scornful treatment.

He was, after all, a great artist in his own field. In Bruges he had carried out a work which was anonymous and brought no glory, but was seen as admirable once it had been understood. He was the embalmer of the town. Being dead, it would have decomposed, disintegrated. He had mummified it in the bandages of its inert waters, its regular columns of smoke, with the gilding and polychrome decoration on the façades like gold and unguents on nails and teeth; and the lily of Memling across the corpse, like the ancient lotus on the virgins of Egypt.

It was thanks to him that the town stood triumphant and beautiful in the adornment of death. In that garb it would be eternal, no less than the mummies themselves, eternally in funeral finery, which has nothing sad about it, since it has transformed death into a work of art.

Borluut got carried away, rapt in his solitary dream. What were the disappointments of love, a woman's tantrums, the woes which, only moments ago, still clung to him as he climbed the tower?

'None of that,' he said to himself, 'is worth bothering with.'

He thought it better to ignore such fleeting trifles when one had undertaken an enterprise such as his, which was still to be completed, but of which future generations would speak.

Pride intoxicated him with its red wine. He saw himself as great, dominating the town as if the tower were his legitimate pedestal.

At that moment the hour fixed for the carillon sounded.

Borluut sat down at the keyboard and set the bells ringing. Immediately the tower started to sing. It sang the joy, the pride of Borluut, who was master of his own self again. On a simple reed-pipe the first musician, the primordial shepherd, told of the intoxication of living, his happiness in love, his sorrow at being deceived, his griefs, his fear of the dark which his fingers, lifted off the holes, tempered a little by the light they let in. In the same way the carillonneur in the stone flute of the tall bell-tower played himself. A tremendous confession! His whole being rang out in the music; from the tune he was playing one could tell whether it was dark or light in his soul.

This time it was songs of renewal – a forest awakening, the quivering of leaves after rain, the horn with the hunt at daybreak. The bells hopped and skipped, running after each other, gathering together then scattering, a colourful, spirited pack. Borluut, light at heart, kept their clamour under control, his hands trembling as if there were a scent of game on the wind. He dreamt of plunder, of conquering the future; he felt strong, triumphant and as his hands struck the keyboard it was with the feeling of a tamer of wild beasts forcing apart the teeth of a vanquished animal.

Borluut was heartened, virile, far removed from his suffering, from himself, so much changed already. He felt as if he were on a voyage, having left after some sorrow or disaster which was gradually fading, vanishing from within him. Little by little the memory returned, the thought that he would have to go back to the house where he had suffered. Oh, if only the voyage could last for ever, and forgetfulness with it. On such days the carillonneur stayed in the bell-tower for a long time, even after he had finished playing. That day, too, he lingered, pacing up and down the platforms, daydreaming in the glass chamber, which the landscape decorated with its distant tapestries, walking round the rooms, the dormitories of the bells. Good, faithful bells, obedient to his call. He stroked them, called them by their names. They were friends whose consolation he could rely on. Others had doubtless confided greater sadness, greater disillusionment to them.

Being acquainted with the world, they always had comfort to offer, good counsel. Oh, how good it was to spend his time there with them. Borluut had almost forgotten the present; he was of an age with the bells and the pain he had suffered had happened a long time, perhaps centuries, ago . . .

But one can never wholly escape one's self. After the mirages produced by illusion and delusion, reality reappears and the least chance can restore it in its entirety. It is the sorrowful awakening, the greatest heartache to find, at dawn, – after the sleep during which one has seen the man who died the previous day still alive – the corpse dead beyond recall, the bed prepared, the consecrated boxwood bough dipped in water, the candles lit.

Borluut had repudiated all memory. He felt himself victorious, free, calm like the bells – and age-old like the bells too, one would have said – when, examining them and listening to them, he found himself facing the Bell of Lust, covered in sins, which had originally aroused him and led him to thoughts of carnal pleasure, provoking his interest in Barbara, his love for her. The bell had tempted him, had contributed to the passion which had ended so badly. It was an immediate recall to the world, a reminder of humanity in the beyond to which he had escaped, been transfigured, was almost living a life eternal. Now the all-too-human bell had broken the spell of obliviousness. He felt the presence of Barbara once more. She belonged to his life as the bell to the tower. This bronze dress, hard and yet disturbing, was hers. All the sensuality, the intoxication of the flesh, spread over, wound round it in lubricious gestures, unsatisfied kisses. The metal of the bell contained endless women being possessed. In the same way Barbara embodied all women for him. She assumed herself the multiplicity of postures they adopted in these lascivious bas-reliefs, perpetually filling his desire with wonder. Faced with the Bell of Lust, Borluut realised that his belief that he had freed himself was vain. The world claimed him even at the top of the tower. Barbara was there, present and already forgiven. He felt that he still desired her. It was the fault of the obscene bell. From the very beginning it had been Barbara's accomplice. The first time he had seen the bell it was Barbara who had immediately come to mind. He had bent under the rim, looking inside, as if up a dress. He had started to imagine her flesh, the bare skin that could just be glimpsed.

Now the Bell of Lust once more took hold of him. It was Barbara herself in a bronze dress who had climbed the tower, slipping in beside him, tempting him, so quick to forget and not in the least repenting the recent scenes she had made, which had wounded him to the core of his being.

No matter! The images she wore on her dress brought back the memory of better evenings, evoking the ecstatic couple they had been, which was copied on the bronze . . .

Borluut sensed that he was once more in thrall to her. In vain he had believed he was *high above the world*. In vain he had considered himself liberated, finally free and alone. Barbara had followed him, spied on him and at that very moment was tempting him, vanquishing him once again. Barbara was in the tower, dressed in the bell. Borluut could not forget her, could not consign the world to oblivion.

Dejected and troubled, he made his way back down the dark stairs, the echo of his footsteps creating the illusion of other footsteps, close by and softer, as if the bell were accompanying him, as if Barbara had come to claim him and were taking him back to cheerless reality.

XII

The Monday gatherings at van Hulle's continued, but as an old habit, already mechanical. The years had chilled their initial enthusiasm. Gone the time of passionate declarations, seditious plans. They dreamt of a Flanders that was more or less autonomous, with a local count, with charters and privileges, as in the days of old. If pushed, they would have agreed that they were separatists. That was why they had the air of conspirators, as if every meeting were the prelude to a call to arms, brandishing words as if they were swords. Their first effort had been to impose the Flemish language everywhere in Flanders, at council meetings, in the courts, the schools and for all documents, deeds, state papers, public records, that is to make it the official language, replacing French, which had finally been banned, expelled from the town, as it had been during the often-quoted Matins of Bruges when all those who pronounced the difficult watchword *Schild en vriend* with a foreign accent had had their throats cut on their doorsteps.

It was van Hulle who had been the initiator of this restoration of their ancestral language to its former glory as a means of reawakening national consciousness. He had called conferences and incited a vast number of people to petition the authorities. He was truly the first apostle of the Movement, to which people like Borluut, Farazyn and Bartholomeus had rallied. Now the drive was slackening. None of their hopes had been realised, apart from the use of the Flemish language. And now that point had been conceded, they saw that it had not produced any important changes for Bruges. At most it was as if a dead body had been put in a different coffin.

They all felt they had been taken in by a beautiful but illusory dream. Often in the grey towns of the North you can see, through the screen of the windowpanes, a few people grouped round the sparse flame of a spirit stove with the teapot simmering on it. Thus they gathered, on the Monday evenings, around their project which, too, was now no more than a guttering flame.

Each had followed his own path. Van Hulle, grown old and disillusioned, had no more thought for the Flemish nation. Turned in on himself, he lived for his clock museum alone. Bartholomeus confined himself to his mystical cult of art, not unlike the Beguines among whom he worked, especially now that he was entirely taken up with the vast decorative painting which would cover one entire chamber of the Town Hall and which might make his name.

Only Borluut and Farazyn had remained faithful to their old ideal. But for Borluut that ideal was above all an expression of his sense of beauty. He had continued to adorn the town, saving the old stones, the rare façades, the rich relics. The restoration of the Gruuthuse Palace, which he hoped would be his chef d'oeuvre, was proceeding. It would be a treasure-house of stone, a unique jewel-case.

As for Farazyn, he still pursued his dream of a renaissance for Bruges, but by bringing it back to life, through action. One Monday evening he presented a new idea.

Before his arrival the conversation had flagged, dragging itself from one mouth to the next, falling on the way into great holes of silence where all that could be heard was the sound of Godelieve's lace bobbins. She was always there to refill their stoneware mugs with beer. Farazyn arrived, keyed up and full of his project:

'Yes, we're going to found an association. A fantastic project! It'll bring Bruges back to life, it'll be a gold mine! And we've found a name for it which says everything, a real clarion call: "The Seaport of Bruges".'

Then Farazyn elaborated his plan. Why hadn't they thought of it before? Bruges had been powerful when it was connected to the sea. The Zwijn silted up, the sea withdrew. It was the ruin, the death of the town. But what hadn't occurred to them was that even now the sea was no more than ten miles away. Modern engineers could perform miracles; renewing the link would be child's play for them. They would dig a ship canal and huge docks – even in the fifteenth century the sea had not reached Bruges, but only Damme, later only Sluis. There had always been a canal. If they were to rebuild it, the town would become a port again and therefore alive, busy, rich.

The others listened, looking indifferent, slightly disbelieving. As if waking from a dream, van Hulle objected, 'A seaport? All the towns have the same idea nowadays.'

'That's as may be,' said Farazyn, 'but at least Bruges is still close to the sea and once was a port.'

Borluut broke in, a slight impatience discernible in his tone. 'Do you think you can start up a port again, that you can start up anything again?' he asked. 'Archaism's absurd, in history as in art.'

Farazyn refused to let his optimism be shaken. 'The plans have already been lodged, a combination of financial backers has been promised. And the state will play its part. We will succeed.'

'I very much doubt it,' said Borluut. 'But in the meantime you will have ruined the town, destroyed what is left of the old districts, the precious façades, for your futile installations. Oh, if only Bruges could understand its vocation.'

Borluut went on to sketch out that vocation, as he conceived it. 'But does the town itself not understand it? The stagnant waters have given up; the towers cast long enough shadows; the inhabitants are sufficiently taciturn and stay-at-home.'

All they had to do was to keep on going in the same direction, restore the palaces and houses, let the bell-towers stand out from other buildings, embellish the churches, elaborate its mystical quality, enlarge the museums.

'That's the truth!' Bartholomeus broke in. He always emerged from his cool reserve in sudden bursts. Each time it was like a fountain in winter, thawing then quivering and suddenly soaring up in a long jet.

'Yes, Borluut's right,' he said. 'Here art is in the air. It rules over the old houses. We must augment it, revive the literary societies, bring together spectacles like those old popular processions, the *Ommegancks*. And pictures! Our Flemish

Primitives, for example. This is the only place where they ought to be viewed. It's only in Bruges that they can be understood. Imagine the town putting its gold and its energy into purchasing all the van Eycks and Memlings there are in the country. There's a use for your funds, Farazyn, if you get some. That will be far more beautiful than digging a canal and docks, shifting earth and stones. It would mean we would possess that divine *Adoration of the Lamb* with the angels clothed in clouds and, in the grass in the foreground, tiny flowers that form an unheard-of garden of precious stones. We'd also have that *Adam* and, above all, that *Eve*, whom the old master, in an extraordinary flash of genius, painted naked and pregnant, truly the mother of the human race. What a treasure it would be for Bruges, unequalled anywhere else in the world. That is what would make the town beautiful, resplendent, and would make people everywhere keen to come and see it. Look at the way even the little museum in the Hospital of St John and the shrine of St Ursula attract visitors.

Farazyn, annoyed at the cold reception of his project and the opposition it had aroused, said nothing more.

The others fell into an intimate silence in which they felt in agreement, dreaming of the same future for Bruges: pious souls would come now and then for a retreat in one of its convents; for those with artistic souls it would be a secular retreat, with the preaching of the bells and the exposition of the relics of a great past.

Following that evening at van Hulle's with Farazyn's announcement of the 'Seaport-of-Bruges' project, Borluut felt impelled to find out in detail how Bruges had been abandoned by the sea. A sudden betrayal! It was like being forsaken by one's great love. It had left the town forever sad, widowed, so to speak.

He searched the archives, looked at old maps, those of Marcus Gheeraerts and others, which showed the old communicating canal. But the earlier ones were missing, those which would have shown the North Sea close to the town, at Damme, which had been washed by the tides. Later they only reached Sluis; then the river silted up progressively, the sea withdrawing so that in its turn Sluis was repudiated, left in the middle of dry land. This change in the tides happened very quickly, in less than a century. Gradually all that part known as the Zwijn, which was originally an arm of the sea reaching into Flanders, filled in. The line could still be seen, a vast corridor of sand coming in from the coast, where the sea now stops.

One day Borluut went to see the dead river-mouth.

Everything was intact, preserving the shape of the past, as the mounds over the graves in country churchyards keep the shape of the body. Even the dunes open out on either side, no longer facing the sea but turning inland in parallel curves, like the remaining banks of a vanished watercourse. It was immensely wide, testimony to the fact that it had been an arm of the sea where the seventeen hundred ships of Philip Augustus performed their manoeuvres. It was here that the neat sailing ships, the schooners, the brigantines with painted poops came in on the tide carrying goods to the town: wool from England, furs from Hungary, wine from France and silks and perfumes from the Orient.

Long ago the place was famous all over the world. Borluut recalled that Dante himself had mentioned it in his *Inferno:*

> *Quali i Fiamminghi tra Cazzante e Bruggia,*
> *Temendo 'l flotto che inver lor s'avventa,*
> *Fanno lo schermo, perche 'l mar si fuggia.*

(Just as the Flemings, 'twixt Cadzand and Bruges,/ Fearing the tide that rushes towards them,/ Raised up a dyke to turn back the sea.)

It is in Canto XV where he describes the sands of the seventh circle surrounded by the stream of tears.

It occurred to Borluut that the canals of the towns here, abandoned by the sea, were also streams of tears, not only in Bruges, but in Damme and in Sluis, which he had passed through that morning on his way, a poor little dead town where he had seen one single vessel in the docks, giving it the illusion it was still a port. As for Dante's sands, he found them too in the dunes that had piled up. What an austere landscape! Borluut was alone, with nothing but the sky and water. No footsteps, apart from his own, marked the immense expanse, the white desert which this ancient outer harbour of Bruges now was.

It was an infinitely desolate spot, above all because of the dunes, the chain of lifeless hills of sand so fine it could have been filtered through the hourglass of the centuries. Some were clothed in a sparse grassy fleece, mangy green fur ceaselessly trembling as if afraid the time of shearing had come. But their melancholy appealed to Borluut. He had those eyes of the North which like to reflect things which are already motionless. And, above all, he saw an image of himself in them: a great torment that has subsided, a heart in turmoil that has resigned itself to severe, monotonous lines.

He sought counsel in this great calm, came to a deeper sense of the vanity of the world and of himself and his troubles as he contemplated the sandy hummocks aligned like enormous tombs, the tombs of towns killed by being forsaken by the sea. This sea, close beside him, stretched out limitlessly, a tragic sea, as variable in colour as in mood.

Borluut had often surmised its presence from fleeting glimpses caught at the top of the belfry while he was daydreaming after the carillon was finished. It could not be made out clearly because of the mist constantly woven into the air, the grey gauze that floats there and from which only the bell-towers divest themselves. However, as the sun sank, one could infer it from a shimmer, a gleam at the bottom of the sky . . .

Now Borluut was seeing it from close to. And to its very end, it seemed, from the way the line of the horizon merged into the infinite. It was bare. Not one ship. It ground out a dirge, in a glaucous tone, opaque, uniform. One sensed that all the colours were below, but faded. At the edge, the waves spilling onto the shore made a sound of washerwomen beating sheets of white linen, a whole supply of shrouds for future storms.

Borluut spent a long time walking across this solitary expanse, which was like the end of a continent. No traces of human beings. From time to time a gull screeched like a pulley-wheel.

He felt more cheerful, revived by the journey, released from himself and his poor life, uplifted by thoughts of the infinite. While he had spent his time lingering there, the tide had come in, sweeping across the beach, softening it, soaking the arid heart of the sand in a flood of tears breaking over it. The swell came from the open sea, dribbled a brief line of foam, seemed bound to continue its charge, generating itself from within – but it suddenly stopped at a precise limit, which was never crossed, a band along the beach fringed with a heap of shells, marked out with a border of glass trinkets. Beyond that the sand was compacted, it felt as if it was centuries old. No tide had ever reached it. That day's stopped too, just in time. No wave brought refreshment to the sepulchre of the ancient arm of the sea, dried up and dead beyond recall. The corridor of white sand remained empty and bare.

The town of Sluis was still there however, very close; the bell-tower could be seen, emerging from the trees, which the setting sun made seem more immense.

No matter. Henceforth the sea stopped and would go no further. The sea is changeable. It loves some towns, then leaves them, going to kiss others on the opposite side of the horizon. That is the way it is, we just have to put up with it, accept it. Are we going to run after the sea? Do we think we can tame it, bring it back, get it to mend its ways like a flighty mistress?

Here Borluut got a better sense of the obscure event that had been the ruin of Bruges. How absurd the 'Seaport-of-Bruges' project appeared to him now, seeing the Zwijn and what the past had been here, recreating the old drama of the sea. Was Farazyn the man, with his artificial waterway, to correct the monumental caprice of the element, its submarine will, its frenzied passion?

As for Borluut, his mind was made up: that day he had seen History, had lived History.

XIII

One Monday, after the customary soirée at van Hulle's, Farazyn accompanied Borluut as he made his way home. They dawdled, strolling aimlessly, carried along by the pleasure of chatting together, wandering along the canals. There was a slight mist in the air, casting a faint spell over the nocturnal town. From time to time the moon shone clear, creating a silvery chiaroscuro. And how enchanting suddenly to see the moon facing the moon in the water!

Together in the deserted shadows, Borluut and Farazyn, old friends, felt very close. They rekindled their shared past, distant memories, their initial patriotic fervour, which that evening at van Hulle's had shown to be slowly weakening. The soirée had been a melancholy one.

There had been little conversation. The words dragged, with a silence between each like the silence between bells striking. If the bells are sorrowful, it is less because of their mournful sound than because of the silence which follows, one of those long silences in which the sound dies away, sinks into eternity . . .

The great days of the Movement seemed past. Van Hulle, who had been the prime mover, in good times and bad, was undoubtedly growing old. He seemed uninterested in the world outside, leaning more towards private and secret pleasures. As for Bartholomeus, he had only joined them out of rancour, because the Flemish Movement, which had something of a conspiracy about it, served to express his own frustration at seeing his talent unemployed. Now that he had been commissioned to produce the decorative painting for the town, he was appeased, once more full of joy in his work and his mystic cult of art.

Even Farazyn, usually so loquacious, so impassioned, no longer spoke much, attending the evenings more out of habit.

'I just go to see Godelieve,' he told Borluut as they walked home.

Borluut said nothing.

'She's so delightful to look at.' And, with evident enjoyment, he went on to describe her, her ash-blond hair, her pensive smile, the pretty little movements of her hands playing with the bobbins as she made her lace; he evoked her whole being, his words creating a luminous presence in the night-time dark of Bruges where they were strolling.

Borluut listened, somewhat surprised, eventually amazed. He began to understand. Why had he not guessed during those Monday evenings? Surely there must have been glances, tones of voice, nuances in the way they said farewell and shook hands that ought to have led him to suspect what was now becoming apparent. He really was not very perceptive. His sensibility lacked antennae. He never saw things coming, only became aware the moment they were there right in front of him.

So the Gothic charm of Godelieve had worked; without words, certainly, just as the charm of a landscape works. That was the kind of impression she made, calm and profound. You looked at her in the same way as you looked at the horizon. To be honest, it was strange that her charm had worked on Farazyn, who was an outgoing, impassioned type, who liked to take centre stage, make a noise, dominate.

Is it true that love springs from the attraction of opposites? But, in the first place, did Farazyn really love Godelieve, or was what he felt merely a fleeting disturbance, an emotion that had plucked lightly at his heartstrings from having spent too much time observing her that evening, a momentary upsurge of feeling that would have no further consequences?

However, Farazyn had continued to enumerate her innumerable charms, concluding, 'She would make a delightful wife.'

'I don't think she'll ever get married,' said Borluut.

'Why?'

'In the first place, because it would make her father too sad.'

'I know,' Farazyn replied. 'He adores her, cossets her like a little child almost. Poor old fellow.'

'Yes, no one can approach her. She never goes out without him accompanying her. At home he's always at her side. They're like each other's shadows.'

'No matter,' said Farazyn. 'She must dream of a different life.'

Then he dropped his mask and confided in Borluut. He liked Godelieve immensely and was thinking of marrying her. For a long time now he had been trying to make his sentiments known to her, but what was a glance of avowal, an expressive look, a squeeze of the hand in a handshake? Feeble signs! Especially since Godelieve always had a vacant look, her eyes elsewhere, eyes that constantly had to be *brought back* to the conversation.

In order to be more explicit, he had tried to see her alone for a moment, when he came for the Monday soirées, either by arriving early or by being the last to leave. But van Hulle, jealous guardian of his treasure, never left her.

Farazyn suggested that Borluut should collude with him. It would be nice for them to be linked by family ties, and useful as well from the point of view of their influence on the direction of the Movement. For example Borluut could invite Godelieve – alone – for lunch one Sunday. Farazyn would be invited as well. And after the meal they would be left alone for a while, as if by chance.

The meal was arranged in accordance with the friends' plot. The old antiquary had grumbled, but since he was none too steady on his legs and concerned about his health during those harsh and snowy winter months, for once he had to give up the idea of accompanying Godelieve. The meal was by no means a dull affair. The table sparkled with the glitter of silver and crystal. Each one of them seemed to have overcome their own heartache. They were all in festive mood. Farazyn spoke a lot, elegantly, forcefully, profusely, with an ebb and flow of ideas which he cunningly channelled into gentle waves that washed round Godelieve. He spoke of life, of men's struggles, and of love, which provided respite for them, a staging post on their journey through life, an inn full of smiles and tender care. Barbara joined in with lively, if slightly sceptical, comments on happiness, on the importance of passion. Farazyn stuck to his guns and argued, in fiery, flowery speech, the rather facile and showy eloquence which he brought to everything he said, empty phrases, iridescent bubbles with which he juggled tirelessly, inexhaustibly.

Godelieve remained inscrutable.

Once the coffee had been served, Barbara made some excuse to leave the room. After a few minutes Joris joined her.

When, one hour later, they returned, twilight was already filling the spacious dining room. The short days of these northern winters!

Godelieve and Farazyn were still sitting in the same places. Neither of them had moved. Barbara realised immediately there could not possibly have been any closeness between them. Their words had not come together for one moment. They had made conversation from either side of the table, as if from two sides of a river that could not be crossed. Evening came, hastened by the heavy curtains draping the windows. Darkness descended on the room, descended on them. The end of the day and the end of love!

They did not bother to light the lamps, as if it were better to make the half-light appear the cause of the half-silence of a conversation that followed a disaster and could not pick up again.

Soon Farazyn rose and said farewell, slightly embarrassed, unseated from the prancing steed of his fine self-assurance.

As soon as he had left, Barbara darted over to Godelieve, snapping, 'You refused him?'

'What?'

'Don't pretend you don't know what I'm talking about. You refused him. I thought you would!'

Godelieve seemed unmoved. She replied in her gentle voice, 'I have no wish to get married.'

Then she added, with the slightest touch of reproach, at most a shadow, the reflection of a cloud, in her luminous voice, 'Moreover, I think you might have warned me, asked me beforehand.'

At once Barbara openly expressed her annoyance.

Godelieve hesitated to reply. It was only after a pause that she declared, 'I prefer to stay with *our* father.'

The italics were in her voice. Barbara, quick to take offence, saw it as irony directed at her. Immediately she vented her anger. 'You're being absurd! Our father! No doubt you're insinuating you're the only one who loves him. Oh yes, you and your mawkish ways.'

The discussion was becoming more and more acrimonious. Eventually Godelieve said nothing more. Joris tried to intervene, to put in some calming words. Barbara turned on him. 'Are you going to lay the blame on me now? You're the one who invited them.'

Barbara was restless, standing up, sitting down, pacing round the room. It was a monologue in which she gave vent to complaints, grievances, her regret at the failure of such an excellent plan, and cast angry reproaches at Joris, at Godelieve, who sat there in silence, as if they had come round to her point of view.

She turned to Joris. 'Come on, say something. Persuade her. You tell her she's being unreasonable too.'

Not long after that Barbara, furious, went out, slamming the door, leaving the room in a swirl of skirts like the wake of a tempest.

Twilight had deepened. Joris and Godelieve were bruised and in receptive mood. They sat there facing one another, not saying anything, scarcely able to see each other. For each the other was a comforting apparition, a silent shadow which seemed no more than a memory of itself, that which persists in mirrors or in the mind. After Barbara's vehement outburst they both savoured the sweetness of the silence, a silence which seemed convalescent, begging to be spared violence. They sensed that nothing needed to be said. In silence, minds understand each other.

Joris had detected an irrevocable decision, mysterious reasons which it was better to leave untouched and against which words were powerless. Since Barbara wished it, he ventured to advise Godelieve, to plead the case of his friend who had been rejected, but very discreetly, for no more than a moment.

'It might perhaps be best if you did marry –'

But Godelieve stopped him with an imploring gesture, a look of distress. 'Oh, don't say that. You . . . you of all people!'

It was a cry that revealed everything, like a flash of lightning exposing the bottom of a valley. Joris saw the depths of her soul. He became aware of something he had merely suspected, had almost forgotten since the time when van Hulle had thoughtlessly revealed Godelieve's feelings.

He had assumed it was one of those vague passions such as all young girls have, a stirring of the heart that settles on an object at random, a spreading of the wings on the edge of the nest.

Now he sensed that what she had felt for him might perhaps have been true love. Was that love the reason why she remained disillusioned, refusing any further attempt at happiness? Was she one of those women who, after a single trial, cast the key to their heart into eternity?

Joris continued to look at her without saying anything, without seeing her any more, lost in reverie, conjuring up the melancholy charm of things that have not come to fruition, projects that have been abandoned, journeys that were never undertaken, everything that could be and will never have been.

XIV

Borluut's home life was becoming drearier and drearier. The mysterious state of Barbara's nerves was getting worse. Now her fits of anger were more frequent and lasted longer. Again and again the slightest thing – some domestic annoyance, being contradicted, a breakage, a minor misunderstanding – would send her instantly into a rage, a storm that swept through the house, leaving behind it nothing but dead leaves. But now, to make matters worse, these crises persisted, leaving her drained, prey to sombre thoughts, ashen faced, with the tears running down like rain on a tomb. Joris was moved and, even though still smarting, cut to the heart by the scene she had made, offered soft words, the balm of friendship and reconciliation. Tentatively he placed a soothing hand on hers, sketched a caress on her cheek, trying to exert a calming influence. Barbara pushed him away harshly and her lips, shut as tight as a clasp, suddenly opened in an explosion, another rockfall of violent words. Joris did not know what to do, how to reply, to mitigate these scenes which left him bruised to the very soul. Trying to avoid them was pointless, they occurred of their own accord. It was as if Barbara's moods had their seasons, the equinox returning regularly. The plan he made in advance to remain silent, to give way immediately, was vain as well. Despite it, he was still at a loss every time, incapable of deciphering the scrawl of nerves.

Initially he had simply put it down to her character, assuming she was by nature irascible and capricious. Now he was forced to the conclusion that there was something beyond her control in her fits of temper. 'Obviously she's ill,' he told himself.

And he thought of all the strange neuroses which, from time immemorial, have debased humanity, a tangled skein strangling the will, the soul entirely. A scourge that had worsened during this century as a consequence of the decline of the races and the accumulation of heredity. In Barbara's case he recalled the premature death of her mother, also the victim of an obscure malady.

'No matter,' said Borluut, 'whether she's ill or simply ill-natured, I suffer for it all the same. And I suffer from *being in doubt*. Where does illness stop and ill-nature start? Up to what point is it conscious or unconscious? Even if the anger wells up of its own accord, a person still chooses the words. Thus hatred hesitates, alternating with pity. Be that as it may,' Borluut concluded, 'she has still drained the sap from my life.'

In such moments he felt sorry for himself, bewailing the dead end in which his destiny was locked, not even sweetened by sorrow.

Other families are saddened by illness, but there are illnesses in which the suffering only serves to increase love. A woman grows palely delicate, more spirit than flesh. It has a sweet sorrow, like the evening before a departure. The curtains round the bed quiver like a veil . . .

A state of ill-health such as Barbara's – assuming she was not simply ill-natured – was tense, hostile, discouraging tender care, rejecting soothing potions, tainting the flowers that were brought to keep the patient company. Such illnesses are exasperating, with the result that people soon distance themselves.

After being torn this way and that, between painful alternatives, between violence and renewed tenderness, Joris felt that his love was over. He had finally retrieved his heart, it was no longer at the mercy of these tides, of the ebb and flow which toyed with his happiness. Now he felt he had won back his freedom, was master of himself once more, unaffected by the daily ups and downs, alone in the farthest recesses of his soul where every one of us can reach and possess his own self. One sorrow remained: not to have at least the compensation of children and that his home was as silent as his heart. That, too, was doubtless the consequence of Barbara's condition. Yet in the past he had so often dreamt of having a numerous family. He remembered how, during their engagement, he had taken Barbara to the Museum to see Memling's great triptych with

St Barbara, her patron saint, and been moved at the sight of the donors surrounded by their five sons and eleven daughters, a patriarchal family, their faces juxtaposed and resembling each other. He had imagined himself having a family like that painted by Memling of Willem Moreel, the burgomaster of Bruges.

Now the dream had ended in a wife without love and a house without children.

What is more, Borluut had very little social life. He was not of a very sociable disposition, finding banal conversations and ordinary company tedious. His old house on the Dijver, with its blackened façade, its high windows in their wooden frames with small panes of greenish glass, the colour of the canal facing it, was somnolent, closed, the blinds drawn, like a house whose owners were away. The bell hardly ever rang, at most a delivery or a client. Barbara had no friends at all. The bell would make a short, sharp sound, as if to emphasise the vast and immutable tranquility, before the corridor immediately became a path of silence once more.

Borluut did not even go to the Monday evening soirées at van Hulle's any longer. They were his last diversion and he missed them. They had stopped of their own accord, so to speak, each of the guests attending less frequently, then giving up. Bartholomeus had adopted a cloistered existence in order to concentrate on the painting for the Town Hall he had started, becoming more and more like the Beguines among whom he worked. As for Farazyn, he found it difficult, after his venture of the heart with Godelieve, to spend a whole evening each week in her presence. He was, moreover, annoyed at her rejection of him and even broke with Borluut, claiming he and his wife had, if anything, dissuaded the young girl. The whole affair had been distorted by indiscretions, gossip and spiteful comments.

Borluut felt he was alone.

Separated from everyone as he was, he rediscovered his love of the town, indomitable and more fervent than ever. At bottom he had never lived other than for that dream and in that dream. To adorn the town, to make it the most beautiful of towns. Even when he climbed the bell-tower, exhausting himself at the heavy mechanism of the carillon, it was to embellish the town, to crown it with the wreath of iron flowers. All his restorations and reconstructions were directed towards the same end, to give each street its surprise, its escutcheon of stone, its façade ornamented like a chasuble, its carvings sinuous as a vine. He was the one who had saved all these treasures of the past from death, had exhumed them from the plaster, the mortar, the whitewash, the bricks – from the vile winding sheet of ignorance. It was as if he had brought them to life, had created them a second time.

A great effort! A visionary genius! The people of the region started to become aware of it. By a painful irony of life, his professional situation brightened the more his home life clouded over. Work and commissions poured in. He found and renewed hundreds of fifteenth- and sixteenth-century houses. What is more, he had just completed his reconstruction of the Gruuthuse Palace, which he considered his masterpiece. When the old town house was handed over to him it was in a wretched state. A noble edifice fallen into sad decay. The façade still bore the arms of Jan van der Aa, lord of that place, who had adopted them in 1340. The king of England had stayed there at the time of the Wars of the Roses. Now the ancient palace had reached its nadir. It was used as a pawn shop. The cast-off garments of the poor within these walls which themselves looked like the cast-off garments of the centuries. Poverty within poverty, like tears in the rain. Borluut had looked at the palace as one might look at a beggar. How could one make the beggar suddenly abandon his rags and appear dressed in sumptuous fabrics and rare jewels, in all the splendour of a prince returning to his town? How could it be cleansed of the grime of ages?

Borluut performed the miracle. He galvanised the ruins.

He gave blind windows back their sight, cured the crippled gables, made the hunched turrets stand up straight. He revived the bas-reliefs eaten away by rain and time, fleeing faces, recollections lost in the depths of memory which suddenly emerge and come into focus. Everywhere there was renewal: the open-work balustrade stretched out unbroken, the stone garlands blossomed, the ogival arches drew their new bows.

Borluut's restoration was complete. What was going to become of the former palace now it had been rebuilt? But do things not call out to each other? There are mysterious analogies, there is a rhythm driving the universe. Destinies come together. When the house is built, the occupant it deserves comes, the one that was meant to come. Thus when the Gruuthuse Palace became a beggar, sitting on the side of a canal in Bruges, weary from its long journey through history, it only housed the poor, those who resembled it. They had turned it into a pawnshop.

However, as soon as the Palace, as if touched by a magic wand, once more became itself, its destiny changed. At that time an old dowager died and bequeathed to the town a marvellous collection of Bruges lace, to be preserved and exhibited there. Now that the Palace was a piece of lace in stone, it simply had to become a museum of lace. Mysterious attraction! Everything fits. What happens to us is what we deserve. Things turn out according to what we have made of our soul.

These frail marvels, embroidered with needles, embroidered on bobbins, were set out in the rooms. There are some which must have taken a whole life, for example the hunt, in which we can see the huntsman, his dog and the partridges; or this passion, signed in 1529 by the sister of the bishop of Bruges who included in it Saint Veronica's veil, St Peter's cock, the sun and the moon. And there are unique pieces: the altar cloth from the first communion of Charles the Fifth, given by him to the church at Oudenaarde and transferred here, with his coat of arms in one corner, the crown of the Holy Roman Empire placed on the Paschal Lamb, which seems overwhelmed by it, crushed beneath the burden, inexorable even for One who is divine.

Everywhere this exquisite lace is spread out before us, in wide strips or symmetrical rectangles. Infinite flights of fancy: flowers, palms, a tangle of lines as mysterious as the lines of one's hand. Is it not like a stained-glass window in linen? Is it not like a geography of threads: brooklets, pools, an accumulation of frozen water, a calm flow, in one place dried up, ending in a void, in another spreading out in meanders, in little waves coming together and parting.

These intermediary strips linking the rosettes, the scattered motifs, are characteristic of Bruges lace. Other styles are like filigree. Bruges lace is like a more solid piece of silverware, though still very delicate. A white garden! Daisies and ferns of frost on a windowpane that will vanish if you breathe on them.

There were some pieces in the valuable collection going back to 1200. Was it not logical that they should end up there? Could such a delightful idea as collecting lace arise anywhere other than in Bruges, Bruges of the Beguines, those perpetual lacemakers, Bruges with its monuments of stone guipure, where it was realised with a name as sweet as if it came from the lips of angels and which sums up the whole town: 'Museum of Lace'.

When the restored Palace was opened it was greeted with wonderment which increased Borluut's reputation.

He was rewarded with public recognition, banquets were given in his honour, serenades.

At the same time another honour was accorded him which touched him more deeply. The ancient guild of the Archers of Saint Sebastian unanimously elected him its head. It was the oldest society in the town; since 1425 it had received an annual payment of a hundred Paris *livres* from the council. It had, moreover, taken part in the crusades. That was why, during the processions and pageants in which it takes part even today, its ancient banner is surrounded by a retinue of little negroes, Turks and men on horseback wearing turbans. The company still occupied the same premises, the old palace with the turret, as graceful as a slender maiden, at the end of Carmersstraat, where it settled during the sixteenth century. Everything was preserved there intact: the book of funerary bequests which each new member signed, allocating sums for his funeral mass and other minor expenses after his death; the jewels given by the Duke of Gloucester and the sovereigns who belonged to it, that is presentation cups, a bird and a sceptre in chased silver, the insignia of the King of the Shoot and of the Guildmaster. In the hall of honour were the portraits of all those who had been one or the other, holding in their hands painted representations of the centuries-old pieces of silver which were still displayed in their cases. These portraits immortalise the greatest names in the history of Flanders, since the Guildmaster was chosen from among those outstanding either by birth or services. Jan Breydel, the butcher of Bruges who led the uprising against Philip IV, was Master of the Guild of Archers of Saint Sebastian, as was Jan Adornes, a crusader and donor of the church in Jerusalem, which contains his image in stone over the tomb where he lies. Because of the great memories associated with it, this is one of the most coveted honorary positions in the town. It was offered spontaneously to Borluut. His name alone qualified him, since he belonged to the ancient nobility of Flanders (one of his ancestors was the hero of the Battle of Gavere), but it was above all his glorious achievement in the resurrection of the Gruuthuse that brought him the votes. Once elected, he was invested according to the rites; as was *de rigueur*, the inaugural banquet included the traditional dish of cockscombs, an allusion to archery and to the feathered targets that are shot off the pole.

Borluut was happy. In this way he relived the past, was for a moment part of the age of glory. He had rebuilt the setting, now he had come upon its spirit. The ancient soul of Flanders lived on in the guild, in the faded folds of its banner, on the lips of the old portraits, which would give him their silent support, thus becoming the champions of the Movement. Borluut experienced the joy of a dream come true. He had been right to love the town, to recreate its past, to want it to live in beauty, to make it into a work of art, *his* work of art. His love of the town, at least, had not deceived him, in his moment of triumph he felt it was reciprocated.

What, then, were his trifling personal troubles, his gloomy house, his irascible wife, the occasional cries and quarrels, the daily ashes of his hearth? *High above the world!* He climbed up into his dream as he climbed the tower. His dream too was a tower from the top of which he could look down on the town, loving it more and more as he watched it in its sleep. It was so beautiful.

XV

One winter's day Borluut was granted his absolute ideal, a peak of harmony in which the town finally became a work of art, with the colours of an old painting in a museum. Snow and gold! The flakes had accumulated during the night. Now, as he climbed the bell-tower, the sun emerged, adding its sheen to the whiteness. The town seemed transfigured, and so pure! The very swans on the canal banks were humbled. An unearthly whiteness, diaphanous, such as only lilies have.

Everything was white. Borluut had always been susceptible to the charm – the intoxication, the sensual pleasure, so to speak – of whiteness. Even as a child his fingers had trembled at the touch of linen. The fresh altar cloths on Sunday, the sheets drying in the bleaching fields around the town, the priests' surplices during the Procession of the Holy Blood sent a shiver to his eyes, like the caress of something with a hint of the divine.

That morning Bruges had laid itself open to him in a unanimity of whiteness. The old roofs, usually gardens of red, had become sloping white flowerbeds. The frost had put screens of lace over the windows. The bell-towers were officiating in ermine copes.

Mass for a dead virgin. *Deuil blanc*, wreaths made of hoarfrost pearls and the soft pall of snow! The town seemed to have shrunk, you would have thought it was bigger. The cause was its robe of white muslin. Bruges had died dressed like that. Can there be anything more sad than a girl dying on the day of her first communion, in her new dress. A little bride of death . . . That was Bruges.

Borluut surveyed it, stiff and immaculate. When the time came to awaken the carillon, he trembled, hardly daring to touch the keys. What hymn was chaste enough, what Beguine anthem fluid enough to modulate such a sweet death? Tentatively he hazarded muted phrases, soft arpeggios, themes merely sketched out, chords falling like autumn leaves, spotless feathers drifting down, shovelfuls of snow, as it were, poured onto a coffin that had already been lowered into the snow.

Everything was in harmony. It was as if the carillon were coming from beyond the world, while the town already seemed to have entered eternity.

XVI

Barbara was superstitious. With her Spanish complexion, that flesh with the bleeding gash of her too-red lips, her face reflected her soul. She burnt inwardly with a faith, a dark, violent religion, also Spanish, full of agonies, of wounds, of candles, of the fear of death. Her existence was tormented by a hundred superstitious fears, like the fibres of a hair-shirt. She spent every Friday and the thirteenth day of every month in suspense, expecting some calamity. A broken mirror presaged a death. And it was true that several times her premonitions and dreams had been confirmed. Perhaps she was fore-warned of what was to come because of her strange neurosis, her nerves in communication with the invisible, tying their threads to coming bereavements, to bells about to ring out, to hearts which shared an ascendant sign and even to the heart of God. Mental telepathy going from soul to soul, as astral telepathy goes from star to star.

Recently she had gone for a walk with her father who, despite his sedentary existence, had suddenly, on a whim, decided he would like to go out with her, in a fit of tender-ness, overcome with affection, as if at the last minute he had felt remorse, regretting the long coolness between his daugh-ter and himself. They had spent a long time strolling around aimlessly, taking it slowly, the rhythm of their gait governed, as it were, by the cadence of the bells which that afternoon were ringing without respite from the top of the scattered bell-towers. Parish bells tolling for the funeral masses of the morrow. On the door of Saint Saviour's, and also on the ancient walls of the Church of Our Lady, Barbara saw more of the large funeral notices than she had ever seen, the customary public announcements of the service, like posters for a play. The name of the deceased leaps out from them, with star billing. They had also encountered a coffin carried by a join-er's labourers which was being taken, uncovered and empty, to some bereaved household. Truly, death was in the air, was all round them.

A more conclusive portent was needed. All of a sudden, as they came round the back of the Hospital of Saint John, they saw a gathering on the little bridge. Men were shouting, women throwing up their arms, pale with horror. They were told that a body, flaccid and distended, had just been seen floating in the leaden waters of the canal. At that point they deepen, renouncing all reflection, appearing to go down forever. Had the drowned man returned from that abyss of silence? Had he seen the bottom of the canal?

Death here seems aggravated. It is an end worse than death. Does a person have to have reached the infinite of despair to throw himself into those waters?

Barbara dragged her father away so that they would not have to witness the horrible spectacle of the drowned man being pulled out of the canal. They hurried off, silent now and haunted by funereal images. There was no doubt that the old antiquary was thinking of death, of *his* death. That was what Barbara thought, but she did not have the strength to distract him, to find words to counter what was already inevitable.

One night not long afterwards she awoke with a start. The front-door bell had rung in an accumulation of feverish strokes. Immediately Barbara thought, 'It is bad news ringing.' And indeed, someone had been sent to tell hem that van Hulle was in a critical state. In bed and almost asleep, he had had an attack, announced by a great cry that went right through the house. Now he was lying there, inert.

What it was they did not know. The doctors had not yet arrived.

Words gabbled in haste by a servant; the household roused, great confusion, anxiety, sobbing; then the race across the sleeping town, on a warm summer's night which seemed completely incompatible with the possibility of death.

When Barbara arrived with Joris, van Hulle did not recognise them. His eyes were shut; his head was flung back among the pillows, crushing them as if it were weighed down by all the blood that had rushed to his brain. His skin was marked with little purple lines, those veins of blood that October brings to the vine leaves. Rasping breath, the noise scraping away at the silence. Godelieve was standing beside the bed, bent over the patient, paler than the sheets, appearing to offer him her own ample breath and ready to give him her whole life. Doctors arrived; in the panic several had been called. They observed, palpated, suggested vague palliatives, declared that it was too early to form an opinion, that they would return in the morning, then withdrew, gravely indifferent.

A long night, an interminable night, a gloomy vigil, which became even gloomier when day broke – the lamp in distress as it struggled against the clear light of dawn.

It was evident what had happened. Van Hulle had suffered a stroke, which, moreover, had been presaged by certain warning signs – flushes, drowsiness.

When the doctors returned, his condition was declared serious, his chances of recovery minimal.

Godelieve was still at his bedside, administering the remedies, fighting, hoping against hope. She found strength in her love for her father, that tender love which he had returned with such attentions and caresses, a unique affection, the sweetness of which was theirs alone, the delight of exchanges every minute of the day. Even now she was appealing to him, with his name, her name, all the little terms of endearment with no real meaning that they used for each other, the names of animals or flowers, monosyllables, adjectives, abbreviations, baby talk, the conventional signs, the private vocabulary of those who love each other, as if to show that they are *a different person* for each other than for the rest of the world.

At the same time she was kissing him, his face, his hands, covering him with kisses, imagining she could flush out the illness and that it would disappear when she had placed her lips everywhere.

Barbara, on the other hand, was pacing round and round the room, filled with anguish, on edge, breaking out into fits of sobbing, at other times flinging herself into a chair, completely drained, her gaze apparently fixed on the distance, beyond the world.

As for Joris, he was kept busy all the time. During the night he had had to go to call the doctors, then rouse a chemist, get him to mix the potions. In the morning he had to go and see the priest, to ask him to bring van Hulle the extreme unction and the viaticum.

It was a sorrowful moment for the old house when the priest entered in alb and stole, bearing the host in the pyx, preceded by an altar boy who was ringing a small bell. The servants had come into their master's bedroom as well. Old Pharaïlde, who had been in service with him for more than twenty years, was crying, large tears rolling down, scattering pearls of water among the beads of her rosary. Everyone knelt. Godelieve had placed a small altar on a chest of drawers, a white station with, as an altar cloth, the still unfinished lace veil she had been making for the statue of the Madonna in their street, never imagining, as she intertwined the threads each day, that she was weaving her father's death-veil. The ciborium was placed on it. The prayers began, private murmurings, flights that scarcely took wing, Latin phrases skimming the surface of the the silence. When the priest anointed his forehead and temples with the holy chrism, vague spasms crossed the face of the dying man. A last trace of sensitivity? Barbara was very close, her nerves stretched to breaking point, and every possible alternative was reflected in her face, the face of a temperament as responsive as a mirror and which lived on reflections.

But now the priest had taken the ciborium from the chest of drawers. He went over to the bed, holding the host in his fingers. They all bowed. The altar boy's little bell rang out once more with its high-pitched yet sweet sound. A delicate peal, an acoustic aspergillum sprinkling the prayer-filled room with little drops of sound.

Van Hulle's mouth had been held open to allow the host to be inserted. It seemed to those who were nearest that it emitted a faint murmur before closing. Barbara seemed frightened, then suddenly hopeful. She claimed that her father had tried to speak, that she had distinctly heard what he said, even though it was faint and half muffled. He had said, 'They have chimed.'

Unconscious babblings, confused images of delirium! Perhaps, too, from the depths where he was stuck he had sensed, through successive waves in the water, what was happening on the surface of life. That would explain the words vouched for by Barbara. Of the ceremony of extreme unction he had doubtless only registered the sound of the altar boy's little bell; some of his faculty of hearing must have survived and transmitted the sensation to the brain, thanks to one last clear nerve. 'They have chimed.' He may have heard the tinkling, an instinctive vibration of the eardrum, the ultimate echo of life. On the edge of death, he heard the bell ring and, given his obsession, taken it for the chime of a clock.

But then why the plural? Presumably Barbara, her nerves on edge and her gaze fixed on death, had imagined words which had come from within her.

The whole day his death rattle sounded through the quiet house. And because of the great religious silence, the church silence that illness creates around itself, the confused grating of the tick-tock from the museum of clocks could be heard. The pendulums swung to and fro; the wheels seemed to be grinding out time; it was a continuous noise, slightly hoarse, articulating the flow. Godelieve felt moved when she heard them. Her father had loved them so much. Along with her they had been his most constant, his dearest friends. What was going to become of them without him? Barbara, on the other hand, found them irritating; the noise racked her nerves. She asked Joris to silence them, to stop the large pendulums, which were pulling her heart to and fro, the wheels that were constantly tearing at something inside her.

The house was completely hushed. It was as if it had died already, before its master.

Towards evening his condition worsened. His rasping breaths became deeper, more spaced out. The little purple veins broadened, the whole of his face was flushed; the sweat continuously welling up in huge drops formed a kind of crown of tears round his forehead. His body kept being shaken with violent shudders. The old man, still robust, was fighting against death. He had stretched out his legs, bracing them against the foot of the bed, the better to resist.

All at once the battle seemed over.

There was a respite, an improvement. The little veins faded, serenity flooded his face, the beginnings of a smile, a sort of otherworldly light, as if his brow had been touched by the light of some unknown morning. In amazement, those around saw the sick man stir, come back to life, so to speak.

An expression of bliss, of immense joy on his face, they heard him repeat, distinctly this time, 'They have chimed . . . They have chimed!'

Then, raising himself up a little, he leant on his outstretched arms, like a swan leaning on its wings as it tries to rise from the water when it is dying; and the old man expired – as if taking flight – in a blaze of white.

One moment later Barbara fell to the ground, rigid and ashen-faced. Joris had to carry her to a bed where she lay prostrate for a long time. When he returned to van Hulle's room he looked on his old friend, that noble heart, the first apostle of the Flemish Movement. He lay there, looking like one of the elect . . . Already so little of the human about him. He was his own marble effigy; a bust copying what he had been, but with the transfiguration of art, the beauty of a purer material. Godelieve had quickly laid out the body, doing as little as possible so as not to disturb him, not to harm him. She was on her knees praying, bathed in silent tears, at the foot of the bed.

When she saw Joris, she said, 'Barbara was right. You heard his last words? He repeated them: "They have chimed." '

'Yes. He'll have been thinking of his clocks. It was his life-long dream. He must have thought that at last they had all struck together.'

Godelieve went back to her prayer and her tears, suddenly seized with remorse at having spoken in the presence of her dead father, even if it was to talk about him.

At six o'clock on that summer's afternoon the heat in the

room was oppressive, a room rendered fusty by the smell of death and of potions. It needed fresh air. Joris opened the window giving onto the garden and those of the neighbouring houses: open spaces with grey courtyards, green lawns and trees. Borluut looked without seeing, melancholy from the contemplation of death, which had been an example to him, a lesson promulgated from the threshold of infinity, so to speak.

'They have chimed!' Borluut had understood straight away. Dying, the old man had attained his dream. His hopes, his wishes had not been in vain. It was by desiring things that one came to deserve them. Human striving was not vain. It was the striving alone that counted, since it came true when it reached its conclusion. It was sufficient unto itself, it was its own consummation.

The old antiquary had so fervently desired that his clocks would, one day, sound in unison. And he did hear them strike, all together, the same hour, the hour of his death. In death everyone's dream is fulfilled. In the world beyond we achieve the thing we coveted during life. Thus we are finally ourselves, made whole.

Borluut plunged into an abyss of reverie, thinking of his own case. Up to now he, too, had been living in a dream, devoted to the beauty of Bruges, with that one love and that one ideal, which had already consoled him for the daily disappointments of an unhappy marriage. He must hold on to his dream with an immense and exclusive desire. For the dream, he thought, was not just a dream but *anticipated reality*, since it would be fulfilled at the moment of death.

Meanwhile the man who had joined the elect was resting in peace, no noise coming in through the open window. All that could be heard in the silent room were the few flies flitting to and fro, black snowflakes, music of two wings. And it was solemn, the hum of these little flies that had been sent, it seemed, with the sole purpose of rendering the silence perceptible, the silence of which we are only aware, which we can only measure, against the sound and which appears vaster the fainter the sound. Thus the silence seemed more silent, the dead man more dead. The ephemeral insects made eternity comprehensible.

For a long time Borluut listened unconsciously to the buzzing of the flies, one of which, now and then, ventured onto the bed, even onto the face of the dead man, no longer afraid of him.

PART TWO

LOVE

I

After van Hulle's death, Godelieve had gone to live with her sister, in Joris's house. She had been afraid of staying by herself because of her dead father, because of her memories of her dead father.

'What are you afraid of?' she was asked.

'Of everything and nothing. You always think the dead aren't entirely dead and that they're going to come back.'

Godelieve was startled by her own shadow, the sound of her own footsteps, the least unfamiliar noise. Her reflection rising up in a mirror would come towards her like a ghost. It was above all in the evenings that she was afraid, becoming a child again, looking under her bed, shaking the silent folds of the curtains. She felt she was going to come across a corpse at any moment.

The terrors that follow a death! And worries about the dead man himself, concerns that his eyes had not been properly closed. And the faint implacable odour which persists in the rooms, musty and obstinate: the sweat of the death-throes or burnt wax.

Godelieve had had to leave the old house in Zwarte-Leertouwersstraat. She thought it would be just for a short while, long enough for her memories, the images and the funereal stench to dissipate. Now months had passed and the temporary arrangement seemed to have become permanent.

These scenes of death had made a vivid impression on Joris as well. That always happens when we are present and the person concerned is someone close. We always relate them to ourselves. We see ourselves lying there, when our time comes, pale with the ultimate pallor. Suddenly, in the middle of our daily routine, our ambitions, our sorrows, our affairs, we are confronted with a vision of the only reality. What we are is brought face to face with what we shall be. To tell the truth, Joris often thought of death. Sometimes, when he was looking into a mirror, he would almost close his eyes and see himself, because of the distance and the paleness the mirror gives, with the simplified face drained of blood he would have when he was dead.

He had, however, been even more deeply moved by van Hulle's death. For him it had been a kind of example, a solemn lesson from the edge of the tomb. During the weeks that followed he recalled the old antiquary's final visions, which must have sweetened his death throes, and the ecstatic smile on his face. For a long time he continued to hear his cry at the moment of death: 'They have chimed!' He had realised his dream through having desired it. We must make ourselves worthy of fulfilment . . .

Joris remained pensive, taking stock of himself, of his life.

He, too, had been living in a dream. If we earn the right to our dream by renouncing the world, then he could earn it when his time came. For he had certainly renounced the world as far as he himself was concerned. He had devoted himself to the town, expressing himself entirely in it and through it. Doubtless he, like van Hulle, would be granted a vision of his ideal at the moment of death.

But that moment is brief. And in his case the realisation of the dream would be so anonymous! Others, the artists, the creators, must see themselves in that instant as immortal, crowned with a laurel wreath which will cool the burning sweat on their brow. Because of the impersonal nature of his work he, a little like van Hulle, would only be able to exclaim as he died, 'The town is beautiful . . . The town is beautiful!' without enjoying a sense of personal pride, without conquering death through the knowledge that his name was already on its way to the centuries to come. It was for that hollow conclusion that he had renounced the world.

For a long time Joris was disturbed, perplexed, uncertain of his destiny and of himself. Up to this point he had followed a broad, monotonous road, without stopping, without looking around. He had lived his life, drawn on by a unique goal, a rare ideal, but all at once he had started to have doubts about it.

The death of van Hulle was a point at which he paused to examine himself. Had he perhaps taken the wrong direction? Was there not a better means of achieving happiness, and of achieving it immediately? Was it not a delusion to renounce the world just in order to see, for a moment, one's dream realised? Thus the lesson of death turned against itself.

Joris trembled at the idea that he might have been wrong. Fearfully he wondered, 'So many years already wasted as far as happiness is concerned!'

It was the tower that was to blame.

He had wanted to climb *high above the world*. To ascend into his dream. Now, at the death of van Hulle, he had come to see the certainty, but also the futility, of the realisation of a long-held dream. Perhaps the world offered more. There were pleasures that were more tangible which he had never considered, but in which other men found their joy. Like him, van Hulle had ignored and rejected them for the pursuit of a goal *which was only within him*. The Flemish Movement, of which he had been the first apostle, already seemed a beautiful illusion. It was collapsing. Joris foresaw that he, in his turn, would devote his energies to it in vain. And as for his devotion to Bruges, it was as futile as the devotion to a tomb.

To live! He had to live in the world. Life is such a fleeting thing. It was the bell-tower that had discouraged him and given him a taste for death. Now, when he entered it, with each step he climbed he felt he was leaving behind a new possibility of joy. Henceforward there was doubt in his mind as he climbed the tower. It seemed to him that he was wrong to abandon the world where there was something calling to him, holding him back with a voice close to his ear and mysterious promises. On the narrow stairway, with its darkness and sepulchral damp, he felt, just for a moment, as if he had ceased to be, had anticipated his death. During those days he did not linger at the top of the tower any more after the time appointed for the carillon. When he came back down he had the impression he had gone there to die a little.

II

In becoming part of Joris's household Godelieve brought, if not an improvement, at least a respite. Barbara, slightly distracted and influenced by her sister's presence, restrained herself more, curbed her fits of anger, her frequent contrary moods, her constant irritation with her husband. Gentleness can be contagious. Godelieve's arrival there was like a pocket of silence appearing in the forest, like the wine-cup the King of Thule cast into the sea. She seemed so agreeable, with the graceful arch of her countenance, her forehead as smooth and pure as a temple wall, her beautiful honey-coloured hair; and a voice of the same colour as her hair, never darkened by impatience, her never changing, placid temperament, accepting everything with docility, the docility of the canals in which the skies and houses, reflected, come to a standstill. Godelieve, too, was a mirror of calm.

Behind its curtain of ever restless trees, the old house on the Dijver enjoyed a little peace and calm, a relaxation of tension, such as a truce brings, the empty quiet of a Sunday morning. Godelieve wove her spell. She went from one to the other, it seemed, pouring balm on their wounded hearts, healing, reconciling them, like a Sister of Charity between two patients.

Did she suspect the silent drama being played out and seek to resolve it, to bring it to the peace of forgiveness? Or was she perhaps simply being herself, radiating pure goodness?

Whatever the case, a new dawn broke in Joris's household. He above all rejoiced in the unexpected quiet. Everything seemed changed. He felt he must be in another place. It was as if he had returned from a tedious journey and was coming home in the spring. A sense of toleration was released within him, a love of the world and of men. He went out more often, and no longer, as previously, to the mournful canals, to the ecclesiastical districts. He no longer avoided other people, was more sociable, interested in the chance encounters of the street. He seemed to be a different person. Did he have new eyes? Formerly they had been full of withered things. In his eyes the whole world had been withered. And it had been because of Barbara, harsh, irascible Barbara who had disappointed him, maltreated him, made him disillusioned with everything. Woman is the window through which we see the world.

And now a different woman had come. Oh, the perturbation of a man who is still young when a woman becomes part of his household!

Borluut felt as if the house were brighter, the air warmer. Godelieve's large eyes were like two new windows, wide open. Inside, where it had so long been gloomy, it was less sad. Voices could be heard, resonant like voices among ruins. There was conversation at table, the meals were not cut short any more. Joris described his projects, his ambitions; Godelieve expressed interest, drew Barbara into the conversation. Sometimes she talked of her father, prompted by some detail, one of his favourite dishes, a victory for the Movement, a shared memory which brought all three together. And the love they had shared for the old antiquary, their laments at his passing, made them feel closer. It was as if they were holding hands around his grave.

As the months passed, Borluut was more and more amazed at Godelieve's gentleness. Nothing disturbed it for one single minute, not even Barbara's fits of impatience, which were sometimes directed at her. An equable temperament, seraphic mildness. Her voice came and went, folding and unfolding like a large white wing, always level, with the same spotless words, the same arpeggio of feathers. It had a calming effect, the simplicity of a sky breeze, something peaceful, soothing. Now Borluut could comprehend old van Hulle's affection for Godelieve, his jealous, cloistered existence with her; it had been like living with an angel – a foretaste of paradise.

Now that Borluut was living with the two sisters, he compared them: Barbara, Catholic and violent; Godelieve, mystical and gentle. One was the Spanish graft on the race; she was truly Spanish in the pleasure she took in causing suffering, her body like an executioner's fire, her lips like an open wound; a taste for torture, inquisition and blood. The other was the original, fundamental type, the fair-haired Flemish Eve of van Eyck and Memling. And yet, despite all that, they were not too different; the centuries and heredity had diluted the foreign blood. When one recalled their father's face, one could see that they shared the same features. They both had his slightly aquiline nose, his high forehead, smooth and calm, and those eyes, the colour of the canals, of people who live in the north, in the countries bound by water. Each one of them resembled him in her own way and thus each resembled the other.

At most there was a different lighting. It was the same flower, but in the shade or in the sunlight, born during the day or born during the night.

That had made the difference and Borluut's fate had been determined.

Seeing how they resembled each other, now that he was living with both of them, only increased Joris's vexation and grief. What ill-luck to have chosen, between two almost twin sisters, Barbara, who was irritable, cruel and neurotic, who blighted all his joy. But do we not always love that which will make us suffer? It is the secret of Fate, which does not want us to be happy because unhappiness is the rule, because capturing joy for oneself would discourage other men from living. Our will does see the trap and tries to save us, to get us to make a different choice. But Fate is stronger and we rush headlong into unhappiness.

Now that, with Godelieve living in his house, he had become aware of her angelic sweetness, Joris was all the more able to appreciate his irreparable ill-luck. To think that he could have been living surrounded by that goodness, that tranquility, that calm affection, that soft voice, that ever-acquiescent soul. He had come so close to happiness. The most depressing part was that he had sensed it, had hesitated for a good while over his choice. Now Joris recalled how he had long been undecided, uncertain about his passion.

Whenever he had gone to visit van Hulle, some instinct had told him the house contained his future, but nothing more precise. He sought an answer, but his love, lacking clear vision, wavered between the two faces. And in this it was above all the bell-tower that was to blame. He remembered how he kept being drawn to the Bell of Lust which, for some unknown reason, provoked within him a desire for Barbara, a vision of her body, slim and supple like that of the women swooning in ecstasy in the bronze reliefs. At the top of the tower, he wanted Barbara. When he came back down into the world, he loved Godelieve. And she had loved him. Why had she not spoken instead of Barbara, who had boldly made up his mind for him, committing him with one brief, irrevocable kiss? There was not the slightest doubt, it was all down to Fate. Joris realised how little the choice had been his. But who can choose in love? Circumstances envelop us, act of their own accord, tie threads we only become aware of once our hearts are bound.

What is it that decides the happiness or unhappiness of a whole life? Now Joris realised how decisive the choice between two alternatives had been for him. In choosing Barbara, he had embraced all the unhappiness; in choosing Godelieve he would have embraced all the happiness.

And that had been decided in a moment, by a single word, a minute detail. If Godelieve had made a sign, uttered a word, given him a glimpse of the shadow of the love within her, everything would have turned out differently. Three lives would have been changed. And his life would have flowed along happily, like a stream over a bed of flowers. But Godelieve had not spoken and he had not suspected anything. It was van Hulle who had revealed it, at first fearing, when Joris asked for his daughter's hand in marriage, that it was Godelieve he wanted, becoming alarmed, panicking at the thought of losing her.

Now Joris thought about Godelieve's love. 'How much did she love me?' he wondered.

It had certainly not been one of those fleeting passions, a light haze, a dawn mist in a young girl's heart which soon dissipates. With her the emotion must have persisted. Joris recalled another scene, a later one when, at Farazyn's request and to humour Barbara, he advised her to marry his friend. Immediately she appeared anxious, with a distraught expression, an imploring gesture: 'Oh, don't say that. You . . . you of all people!' That was all she had said and he had remained silent, guessing at a great secret that was dead and buried and that he did not want to know.

And now he was seized with a desire to throw light on this mystery. Perhaps it was because of this one unfulfilled love that she had renounced love altogether. There are hearts that are not made for new beginnings. Having failed to marry him, she would have abandoned the whole idea of marriage. And that without rancour or bitterness, either towards any person or towards life, all gentleness and resignation, having folded her chaste love away within herself, like the trousseau of a maiden who had died on the morning of her marriage.

Joris was saddened at the thought of all that time in the past when he had been so close to happiness without realising it, without grasping it. He bemoaned himself, Godelieve, the wretchedness of life. Moved, troubled in some way, he still wondered, as if speaking in a low voice, 'And now, has she completely got over it?'

She seemed so placid, her eyes elsewhere, appearing to float rather than to walk. Nothing disturbed the steadiness of her voice, her even phrases which gave the impression of the texts on the banderoles in paintings by the Primitives. You looked for a narrow scroll coming out of her mouth. Her words undulated silently.

Nevertheless Joris noticed how she was concerned to soothe Barbara, to take everything on herself, to avoid conflict, to conciliate at the least alarm. It required unobtrusive and loving attention. Barbara, irascible, prickly, quick to take offence, was not very responsive. Godelieve would increase her sisterly efforts. Sometimes, thanks to her, the atmosphere relaxed, conversation was open, more amicable. She stood between them like a canal between two stone embankments. The embankments are face to face, nevertheless apart and will

126

never unite, but the waters mix their reflections, merge them, appear to join them together.

Thanks to her, life improved for Borluut. He spent several months of calm. However, one day Barbara had another violent fit of anger and, this time, refused to be intimidated by Godelieve. As always it had been set off by a trifle: Joris had lost a key. As they looked for it, Barbara became irritated, started to dwell on his carelessness, brought up old grievances, imaginary wrongs, immediately expressing herself in the harshest terms. And now Joris, less resigned on that particular day, or perhaps encouraged by the presence of Godelieve, hit back, reproaching Barbara for her lack of consideration, her perpetual bad temper. The debacle was instantaneous. Barbara turned livid and started to scream, emitting a whole avalanche of hurtful words which erupted like stones, raining down on Joris, cutting him to the quick. Although wild with rage, Barbara did not hit out at random. She found sensitive spots, chose the most wounding insults and allusions. Joris felt he was tied at the stake with the flames of her Spanish anger licking round him in a blaze no one could have stopped. But that did not prevent the other tortures of inquisition being deployed: an old reproach poured into his ear like molten lead; then a sudden look of hatred pierced his eyes with a red-hot needle. It went on for a long time. Barbara paced up and down the room, truly ablaze.

Then her furious anger abated, subsided, having consumed itself for want of fuel since Joris had quickly fallen silent, realising he should do nothing to aggravate the situation, which would immediately end in disaster, approaching tragedy, death.

Godelieve looked on, silent, stupefied, feeling powerless in the face of an outburst more extreme than she ever could have imagined. Barbara on the other hand, having exhausted her anger and her nerves, left, slamming the door as usual, filling the stairs and corridors with her final cries, with the sound of her staccato footsteps growing fainter in the silence.

Joris, overcome and embarrassed, had gone over to the window that looked out on the garden, leaning his forehead against the glass to cool his fever with its chill moisture, to alleviate his sorrow.

Godelieve watched him. When, a moment later, he turned round, she saw that his eyes were filled with tears. How distressing to see a man cry! Moved to compassion, more than a sister, pity bringing out the mother in her, she went up to him and silently took his hands, not finding any words, not daring to touch the deep, intimate wound for which the balm of a look was sufficient.

To explain, excuse the cruelty of the scene, Joris said, 'She's unwell.'

'Yes,' said Godelieve, 'but you are unhappy?'

'Very unhappy . . .'

Joris wept. Unable to hold back any longer, he burst out sobbing, as if his heart itself were leaving, were rising up as if to die in his mouth. The moans of an animal or a child that cannot take any more, a cry no longer human, howling loud and long.

Godelieve felt old memories come alive again, everything she thought had been dead and buried in her heart. Forgotten dust fluttered and, thinking of what might have been, she whispered, 'If only it had been God's will.'

And seeing Joris weep brought her to tears as well.

Mute consolation. It is in silence that souls finally come together, listen and speak to each other. They tell each other things their lips never can. For them it is as if they were in eternity already. And the promises they make each other in such moments will never cease.

Godelieve and Joris felt their souls touch. They were united by a communion stronger than love. Henceforth there was a secret between them, an exchange more sacred than that of kisses: the exchange of mingled tears.

III

'If only it had been God's will.'

From that point onwards Godelieve's words affected Joris, obsessed him, coloured the air around him, filled his sleep with images. The lament of unallayed regret! The murmur of a spring one thought had dried up! A cry of avowal suddenly bursting forth, ringing out in his unhappiness like a voice in a graveyard. At a stroke the young girl had given away the secret of her life. Her love, which he had thought superficial and ephemeral, persisted, reappearing here and there like the water of the canals in the town.

Joris recalled the successive proofs: van Hulle's revelation; Godelieve's later half confession, when he had encouraged her to marry Farazyn; now, finally, the decisive words which had slipped out, almost instinctively, with the sincerity of a gesture.

'If only it had been God's will.'

So she had not got over it, never would get over it. There are women whose love only ends with death. Now Joris understood the gentleness she spread, her willing presence about the house, her concern to mitigate any discord, the calm her look brought, the sweetness her voice gave. In the troubled house, she was a haven of silence. She was trying to bring happiness to his home. Perhaps that was the reason why she had come to live with them, out of the affection she still bore him, in order to offer him her protection and comfort, like a sister at least, a Sister of Charity who would dress his hurts whenever he was wounded and bleeding. And to think that she could have been his wife! He kept on going over the chance he had missed, the blissful life he would have led. He repeated to himself Godelieve's nostalgic sigh: 'If only it had been God's will.'

From now on, when he climbed the tower he no longer had the impression he was moving towards death. He was accompanied by the words of brightness. They went before him, climbing the dark steps one by one. They left him behind, running to the top in one breath, then coming back down to meet him, swelled by the wind, panting from the run. No longer was Joris alone. He climbed with the loving words, which were the voice of Godelieve. And he replied to her voice. He spoke out loud, told of his hopes, expunged the hateful past, spent hours conversing with her. Now the belfry no longer frightened him; he no longer blamed the tower for taking him away from the world.

On the contrary, he took his world up there with him. The voice of Godelieve was Godelieve herself. She had followed him to the glass chamber. She was there beside him, invisible but present and murmuring. They said the kind of things to each other that we only say at the tops of towers or of mountains, things that belong on the threshold of infinity and that God can hear.

It was for her that Joris played the carillon. He used the bells to illustrate their story. It was like an encounter between misfortune and joy: at first a lamentation among the basses, a surge of deep sounds, black water pouring from inexhaustible urns, a flood of sound telling of disaster and endless despair; then the pure white ascent of a fragile little bell, soaring persistently, growing, the silvery fluttering of a dove come to announce salvation and the rainbow in the sky. Everything within the carillonneur took flight from the tower.

He himself was not always aware of what he was playing, of the way the bells rang out his very soul. This time, however, he was and he admitted to himself that Godelieve was the dove of the Flood, the little bell lighting up the disaster. Because of the words, which no longer left him and had climbed the tower with him, he gradually succumbed to the spell. He was no longer in a hurry to come back down since he had taken his world up with him. Godelieve was his world and her voice was up there with him. Now they were together. Joris lingered for hours, answering the voice, anticipating a better future. What it would be he did not know.

At first he was entirely taken up with the inner turmoil caused by the fact that tender words had come into his life. But gradually his dream took shape. In the carillon the little bell sang louder, came closer, pecking at his heart. At the same time the outpouring of deep sounds, the black water of the large bells, dwindled and soon dried up completely. All that was left was an immense joy with the fluttering wings of the dove, the little bell that was the words of Godelieve become her own soul. Yes, the soul of Godelieve enveloped him, came to put itself round him.

Joris felt himself entirely bathed in a new light, the brightness, like a new dawn, of love starting again. The return of life to the world after the flood that had seemed final. The sweetness of a *second* love.

And this one so chaste, principally of the mind! Joris thought of Godelieve as he would have thought of a sister who had disappeared as a child, was believed dead, and was now found again, an additional, unhoped-for affection.

When he imagined her watching over him, consoling him, it was not so much as a real woman, more as a guardian angel. This kind of second love, a love of our middle years, is so different from the first, especially for those who have suffered. It is like a refuge, the balm of trust, of one soul speaking to another. At first the flesh had little part in it. Joris avoided even the merest hint of a thought about Godelieve that was not full of respect. She was so chaste, enclosed in her decorous gowns, mystical, pious even, with a deep, personal faith. How different from his former passion for Barbara! Here, in the belfry, he was in a good position to compare, for it was here, because of the Bell of Lust, that he had conceived his violent desire. His senses on fire, his face feverish, he had pictured that love as one might picture a crime. He had sought her body, imagined her orgasm, in the obscene bell. Now that his whole being was flooded with an immense affection for Godelieve, he was afraid of the Bell of Lust. He no longer ventured onto the upper platform where it hung, beside the bell that rings the hours. He avoided it, he detested it like a bowl full of sins, like a fiendish image that would have defiled and degraded his pure vision. Godelieve, being for him only a soul, was embodied in the little bell whose pure song at that time was soaring, dominating every piece on the carillon, music of dispersing clouds, of a brightening sky which, once more, represented his life.

IV

Since Godelieve's half avowal, her elegiac sigh, Borluut felt suffused with an indescribable sweetness. In the great disaster that was his life, someone had taken pity on him, someone loved him a little.

Henceforward what did Barbara's harshness matter, the miseries, the scenes, the unpredictable days, the loveless nights? Godelieve was present, attentive, loving, already a lover, perhaps . . . Yes, she had revealed herself in those words which from now on lived within him, growing, like letters carved on a tree. Godelieve had loved him, still loved him. The thought sent Borluut into a quiver of agitation and expectancy. Of regret, as well. They had both let happiness slip away without stopping it. How could they have been so blind? What mirage had dazzled them? Suddenly they could see clearly, could see each other, as if in bright daylight. But it was too late. Happiness is for two to be as one. It was a dream that was now impossible.

Nevertheless Joris was elated, glowing with the revival which had set his heart alight. Since Godelieve had spoken those words, he felt something unforeseen and delightful within him, something that was not music, yet sang, a brightness that did not come from the sun, yet shone. The miracle of the springtime of love! Yes, love had sprung up inside him once more, for he suddenly felt he had a new heart and new eyes. Life which, but yesterday, had been old, faded, worn down by strain, by the centuries, now seemed new-born, as if it too were emerging from a flood with fresh faces and green shoots.

New love gives birth to a new universe.

Borluut's wonderment was combined with a feeling of convalescence. Imagine an invalid who has long been prey to fits and torments, debilitated by the half-light, the sickly smells, the insipid diet, the feverish fluttering of the nightlight, his mind fixed on dying; then the sudden reversal, recovery, the sick-nurse immediately becoming his lover.

Thus Joris went straight from death to love. For he was in love.

What at first had been merely a tremor, a frisson at the presence of a young woman in his house, soon became an obsession, love, the intoxication of a shared passion.

The fact that he was living with her under the same roof fostered his imagination. They were living together, day and night, in the same house, like a couple that had overcome desire. It is true that they were frustrated by the presence of Barbara, but their souls spoke to each other in that spiritual union the sole aim of which was mutual consolation and mutual regret. Their eyes would meet, would touch. Oh, the caress of eye on eye, resembling that of lip on lip and already with a thrill of sensual pleasure!

Something carnal was born between them.

Through living together under the same roof they continually unveiled a little of their intimate person to each other. Godelieve, so utterly chaste, did not think of the danger of appearing in a simple morning gown. Her figure showed through such rudimentary attire. Joris could see her better behind the few folds, the more yielding material. There were fewer veils between them. Sometimes too, her hair, only perfunctorily dressed in the morning, suggested hair dishevelled during lovemaking. Thus, little by little, Godelieve came to seem for Joris a woman he had possessed and who no longer had any secrets from him. It was the result of their life together in which they revealed a little more of their selves every day.

Joris went over the rapid development: at first, when he had learnt that Godelieve still loved him, he had felt an infinitely grateful affection for her gentleness, for the care with which she surrounded him; then came the bitter regret for the happiness they had missed, the growing desire to correct the double error. Since the very beginning their will had been to love one another, Fate alone had prevented them. Why should they now not accomplish their will and love one another?

They should have been man and wife and had not been. They could still become that.

And was it not as if Fate had repented, chance bringing the two of them together under the same roof, appearing to let them follow their own destiny?

They yielded: furtive glances, hands lingering when they met on the same object, all the stratagems of seeking, avoiding, finding each other. Brushing against each other, touching lightly, as if by chance, each fearful of the other, of themselves, and above all of the Witness, the tragic figure of Barbara, who had not yet noticed any signs. Moments of infinity, fleeting thrills, joys that were over in a flash, dewdrops which contained a taste of heaven. For a long time they savoured their hidden love. It even seemed to taste better for being hidden, more intense for being intermittent. Words tossed in the air, caught on the wing, half kisses, hands squeezed in passing – all the beginnings, all that is best in the Eternal Adventure. And with no consummation possible, nor yet desired. It was delightful to hope for everything and attain nothing, to spend their time on the constant lookout for a propitious moment, to harvest the corn ear by ear.

Their happiness was precious to them, as if it had been saved up, put away for a rainy day, and already amounted to a considerable sum.

Joris felt fulfilled. He was without further desire, without further ambition. His work was neglected. He did not finish the projects which were in train. In his study the files, the compasses lay scattered around and his plans, his drawings remained uncompleted on the paper, like buildings halfway up in the air. He had stopped working, stopped accepting commissions. He was no longer interested in his restorations. He was bored by all those old buildings, those ageing façades to be rejuvenated. They were surly old dames, their cracks like the wrinkles of old age, their ancient leaden windows like sad eyes that had looked on the dying. He no longer wanted to live with the past. Associating with old things makes your heart old. He wanted to be young, to enjoy the present. And his only occupation was with Godelieve's face.

Alone with her face, he strolled round the town, climbed the bell-tower, mingled with the passers-by, idle and contented. He was no longer bitter, no longer sought solitude; he would have liked to have friends, to take part in public festivities.

Sometimes he went to the Society of Saint Sebastian. It was his duty as Guildmaster and he had long neglected it. He watched the archers, admiring their skill as they drew their longbows, aiming at the targets or the feathered birds on the tall pole, so tiny in the distance that it needed a sure arrow to dislodge them. He liked being in the ancient and picturesque premises with the slender turret, its masonry tinged with warm, pink skin tones, amid the bustle of games, where people spoke their minds and took long draughts of the free-flowing, foaming Flemish beer. It was a corner that preserved the life of the people, intact, flavoursome, a coloured picture of the past, saved by chance. He mixed with men again, in a familiar and friendly manner which made him popular. He soon had a devoted following who admired him, loved him.

Lacking occupation, Joris started going to see Bartholomeus again, whom he had neglected for a while. Incapable of working himself, obsessed by Godelieve and his love for her, he spent whole afternoons in the painter's studio, talking about art, smoking, daydreaming. He had not seen his friend for a long time. Bartholomeus had shut himself away, cloistered himself completely, the better to devote himself to his work, to have solitude and silence to carry out the series of large-scale paintings which he wanted to make his masterpiece, the realisation of his great dream of glory.

'Well, then' Joris asked, 'how far have you got?'

'I'm making progress. I'm still doing studies and I need some research for certain parts, but the overall design is complete.'

'Show me.'

Borluut made as if to stand up to go over to where some canvasses were stacked, but turned to the walls, mysterious, the wooden stretcher a sign of the cross. Bartholomeus immediately shot up, protecting them with a nervous gesture. He did not like to be caught in the middle of his labours, to show his canvases before they were finished.

'Don't! They're just roughed out, not much more than sketches. But I know what I'm going to do. Listen. Since it's a decoration for the Town Hall, that is a building that belongs to us all, it will be a dream evoking the town itself, what makes its soul. It will be enough to take a few distinctive features, a few symbols. Bruges is the great Grey Town. That is what I must paint. Now, grey is made up of black and white, as is the grey of Bruges. What needs to be done is to choose the blacks and the whites that go to make it up. On the one hand – for the whites – there are the swans and the Beguines. The swans will form one panel, setting off along a canal with one of them in a flurry, pressing its wings down onto the water, trying to rise from it, just as a dying man tries to rise from his bed; for it is indeed dying, and singing, to symbolise the town which is becoming a work of art because it is in its death throes. Then, forming a second panel and still for the whites, the Beguines, who are also swans; they displace a little silence as they walk, just as the swans displace a little water as they swim; and I will paint them just the way they pass, down below, framed by my window as they cross the close after mass or vespers. For the blacks, on the other hand, there are the bells and the cloaks, which will form another pair of panels. The bells, the colour of night, will be seen making their way through the air, meeting, going from this tower to that to see each other, little old women stumbling along in their worn dresses of bronze. Then the cloaks, which are not so much the garment worn by the women of the people as other bells, large bells of cloth swinging in the streets, bells down below whose rhythm is parallel to that of the bells up above. There you have it. In short: the white of the swans and the Beguines, the black of the bells and the cloaks; black and white mixed, that is the grey of the Grey Town.'

Bartholomeus had spoken passionately, his look elsewhere, a gleam burning in his eyes like the reflection of an invisible sun with which he was communicating. His handsome monkish head with its pale complexion and fine black beard recalled the painters of the Italian monasteries who recounted their dreams on the white of the walls. Bartholomeus had sketched out his own dream as if he, too, were in a cloister, living a chaste, solitary life in this nuns' enclosure, surrounded by the sound of hymns, the freshly whitewashed houses, a paradisal light in which even the shadows of the clouds took on a silvery luminescence. His appeared to be a complex temperament. That was because he was close to the infinite. He naturally found mystical analogies, the eternal connections between things.

Borluut listened to him talk of the themes of his painting with interest, with admiration. Then, at the thought of their profound and mysterious beauty, but also of their inaccessibility to those who had commissioned them, he could not help commenting:

'That's superb! But what are they going to say?'

'Ah! They'll be astonished, that's for sure. They've already given me some advice. What they would like are episodes from Flanders's past, historical painting, of course. The usual things: the Matins of Bruges and Breydel and Koninck and the commune's fight for autonomy. It's all become a carnival, a play with the heroes in costume, the props, the hand-me-downs of the centuries, which provide a living for our bad painters, our bad musicians, all the charlatans who produce large-scale canvases and cantatas. Deeds should be left where they belong. All that could be made in that way would be a vulgar daub with the scene at the Battle of the Golden Spurs, sublime in itself, where the guilds and corporations take a handful of earth, eating the earth for which they are going to die.

This led Joris and Bartholomeus to talk of the Flemish Movement, for which they had shown such enthusiasm in the past, when van Hulle had still been alive. They confessed that the impetus had gone, their efforts had come to nothing.

The painter had turned his mind away from the town and other people to devote it entirely to his work which, henceforward, was the only thing that mattered to him. He spoke of his art as a man might speak of his beloved.

He described the obsession with an idea, which would suddenly appear, like a chance encounter, like a passion taking over your life; and the intimacy of living with the idea, the silent conversations in which it unveils itself or refuses to give itself to you. At times forthcoming, at others cold, as if sulking. Are you going to prevail over it? Now it appears naked on the canvas. The caresses of the soft brush, slow or feverish! No respite any more. You dream of it at night, see it ever more beautiful, adored down the centuries.

As he spoke, Joris listened, compared. Was that not the way he loved Godelieve, the way he was haunted by her, held conversations with her in his head, was visited by her even in his sleep? Did the love of art truly give one the same ecstasies as the love of a woman? Joris had assessed the painter's happiness: it was more serene, more certain, even more noble, perhaps. He felt some concern, the beginnings of regret. He too, in years gone by, had loved his art, had striven for a great and lasting work, had dreamt of the restoration and resurrection of Bruges. Now he was about to sacrifice his love of the town to his love for Godelieve.

For the first time he was visited by doubt, stood back from his passion, felt some hesitation at the prospect of the affair.

His feeling of unease remained as he made his way home, not daring to look at the old façades, the stagnant water, the enclosed convents, everything which counselled the renunciation of the world, the cult of death. In a low voice he repeated to himself. 'Live! I must live in the world.' And, as he approached his home, Godelieve's face appeared once more, shining on him in triumph, rising within him like the moon in the canals.

V

Barbara's nervous disorder was getting worse. She had lost weight, her complexion was pale. At the least annoyance – a breakage, a servant leaving, a remark that was made – she would immediately get worked up, lose her temper. The storm-clouds never cleared from the house, Joris and Godelieve lived in constant expectation of the next thunderclap. They had to keep a constant watch on themselves and exercise limitless patience, yielding to her humours like the harvest before the wind. It was easy for Godelieve; already as a child she had become accustomed to them, bending before her sister's ungovernable outbursts. Her innate gentleness remained calm, serene, unruffled, always the same, as smooth as a frozen pool that neither the breeze nor the violent north wind can disturb with the least ripple. Joris found it less easy to resign himself to all these whims, these shifts in the wind, these contradictory impulses, never being sure what was coming next. Moreover nervous irritation is contagious. At times he himself was at the end of his tether and rebelled, reasserted himself in his male pride. But he did not keep it up for long. Barbara, used to meeting no resistance from anyone, quickly flew into a wild fury, hurled abuse at him, became aggressive, went towards him. One day, beside herself with rage, she flung a horrible threat at him, in a hoarse voice it was painful to hear: 'I'll kill you.'

Joris felt sorry for her, felt infinite pity deep within for this poor creature, who doubtless could not help herself, while he himself was so far away, having taken refuge inside himself, in that dark recess, that farthest chamber of the soul which no one can enter. It was there that he met Godelieve, smiling silently at his love. What did anything else matter? These eruptions left Barbara drained, a crumpled rag of flesh and nerves, a sail slumped at the bottom of the mast. She lay down for a long time, pale and unmoving, moaning too because of the tingling pain in every limb: threads stretched along her legs, knotted at her knees, the skein continuing up into her throat, blocking it so that she was suffocating.

She complained to Godelieve, 'I'm aching, aching.'

And her voice became high and thin, cracked, a little voice breaking, the voice of a sick child crying for help. She curled herself up, would have probably liked to cuddle up, to warm herself against someone.

'And I'm so cold as well.'

Then Godelieve, moved to pity, would cosset her, wrap her in shawls and run her hands over her – the contact pacified her, soothed her, as if they possessed an invisible, calming force. At that point Barbara would become aware of her fits and seem embarrassed: 'I don't know what I'm saying.'

Immediately Godelieve went to tell Joris, to heal his wounds, to bring him back and attempt a reconciliation which at least would bring peace, if not forgiveness. But he refused in a sad voice: 'She has caused me too much suffering. Aware of it or not, she has bruised my heart too much.'

Godelieve tried to work on her sister, ventured a gentle reproach: 'You're hurting yourself and your hurting others.'

But Barbara, only temporarily pacified, bristled, her anger and her complaints returned, this time directed at Godelieve. She reproached her sister, imagining grievances, wrongs, finding a hurtful intention or inflection in everything she said.

'I want to die!'

And all at once she opened the window, as if she were going to throw herself out. Instead, she swept out of the house, scarcely pausing to put a hat on her head, a coat round her shoulders, and started to stride along the strrets with hasty steps, towards the canals and the ponds on the outskirts of the town, looking as if she intended to throw herself into the water and was choosing her spot. Joris was told and hurried along after her, pale himself, as if he were about to faint, his heart beating like a clock in his chest, anxious, his fear of a scandal intermingled with the first stirrings of sorrow for poor Barbara, whom he believed he no longer loved but whom he could not bear to imagine dead, covered in blood from a fall or with Ophelia's water plants.

In spite of everything, he remembered the beginning, saw her once more in her white bridal veil, thought of her lips that had been so red.

Barbara had bouts of nervous exhaustion, of melancholy, which made it easier to feel sorry for her. Things were less strained, it was a period of depression after one of over-excitation. She seemed to emerge from the ruins. It was as if she had been walking in the rain for a long time; there was something faded about her. Looking at her made one think of a shipwreck and that she must have seen death.

She seemed to regret having escaped it, to still be sitting in his house.

'I'm in your way,' she sometimes said to Joris. 'We're unhappy. It would be better if I were to die.'

Joris gave a start. But she couldn't have guessed his love for Godelieve, which he kept secret, shut up deep inside himself. But does instinct not sometimes see things that are invisible to the naked eye? Joris dismissed the suggestion which frightened him and which had touched on something he did not want to think about.

Far from letting her die, since Barbara seemed to be ill they had to relieve her suffering, find a cure. He summoned a doctor, informing him in advance about the case. The diagnosis was clear: anaemia and nervous exhaustion, the old blood in decline, the scourge of the age which had even reached those out-of-the-way towns. In Barbara it was hereditary. The remedy? Her condition would improve later, with age. In the meantime taking the waters would alleviate it, the mountain air would tone up the nervous system, have a calming effect. It so happened that Barbara was in contact with some cousins who lived in a spa, a little village in Germany where she had visited them in the past. She had no objection to going there again. But she insisted on going alone, with no one to accompany her, thus breaking with her present life for a while, cutting the bonds which attached her to her family, losing all memory of the home where she had spent such black days, setting off on the journey as if she were going to a different life. Was her irritation with those around her, those rather than others, perhaps not one of the symptoms of her illness? She did not want them with her and left by herself a few days later. In vain Joris had offered to accompany her, as had Godelieve, even more insistently, racking her brains for reasons, constantly changing tack, thinking up specious arguments, promising she wouldn't take up any room at all, wouldn't be a nuisance, would be there to pamper her.

The fact was that Godelieve was afraid, terrified, at the thought of staying alone with Joris. Barbara's departure would open the door to danger. As long as she was there in the house, Godelieve felt protected, sweetly secure. True, since she had always loved Joris she had not managed entirely to stop herself loving him, nor letting him see it. She was not too ashamed of all the little pleasures they found, almost by chance, as soon as they were alone together: a swift embrace, lingering hands, a brush of the lips, all the endearments of a love which is scarcely carnal, in which it is the souls that mate.

Godelieve consented to these harmless kisses, which did not seem very different from a sister-in-law's kisses. She could have openly acknowledged them, though not the inner turmoil they caused her, the divine reverberations that went through her whole being, as if a host imprinted with Joris's face were coming down into her.

And was it not a good work, a work of domestic charity and of human compassion, to grant Joris the comfort of a little tenderness, a cooling draught from her young lips in the arid heat of his home. No, she had no cause to blush at her love, she was not ashamed to talk to God about it.

But she had a vague feeling that everything had changed now that Barbara had left. It meant the end of her security, the innocent intimacy, their pardonable liberties, their pure, unstained love, which could have lasted to the end of their days. They were going to be alone together and therefore free and open to the worst temptation.

Having dinner that evening, the two of them together, they both felt very awkward. Godelieve had blushed as she sat down. She realised that from now on she would always blush in Joris's presence. He was smiling, exultant, amazed, all of a tremble. Could it be that chance had decided, for a moment at least, to restore their destiny? They were together in this house that was theirs, alone together, in the lamplight, like a happily married couple. It could have been – it *was* for the moment. An intimate, almost conjugal evening together. Joris opened his heart, poured out his feelings. Godelieve listened, acquiescent. She had taken up her lace, manipulating the bobbins, often not concentrating on it but reassured by the interplay of the threads with which she kept her hands occupied, for a long time, out of fear that Joris might take hold of them . . .

VI

Love burst out in them like spring. One sunny day is enough to turn all the peach trees pink, to cover the old walls with leaves. And thus their prejudices, their fears and their scruples vanished in an instant under an explosion of flowers, that rising tide of fragrance signifying renewal. They knew resistance was vain. The season was ripe, the inevitable had arrived. It was the normal course of Nature, their will triumphant after all the trials, the waiting. They became a couple who, long engaged but separated by time and tide, belong together and are reunited. And it was not mere chance they had to thank, something more mysterious had arranged everything: Barbara's worsening nervous exhaustion, the discord in the home, her solitary departure leaving them together, prey to themselves. In reality their destiny had resumed its course, was once more flowing downstream after having disappeared for a while among rocks and gone underground. All the time during which they had been unable to see their reflections in it they had felt as if they were lost. Now each could see the other's face as their lives flowed on.

Now all the rest seemed to have been so short, so insubstantial, so unreal; already it was past. Not two days had passed since Barbara had left, since they had started to live together in the intimacy of the house, and they had the impression they had always lived like that. Living like a perfect couple. Shared harmony, never marred by the slightest difference. Joris was constantly filled with wonder at Godelieve's gentleness, her angelic temperament, always true to itself, as if her soul were under glass and nothing, not the tug of a nerve, not a word, not a wind, not a grain of dust from the world could reach it and affect it.

Oh, the calm assurance such a presence brought to his home, the steady, constant light such a love cast!

Joris made comparisons, still recalling now and then the

wild flame that was Barbara which always either burnt him or sent him into semi-darkness. How he had suffered for his mistake, for having listened to the bad advice of the bell, for his lack of clear sight when he came back down from the bell-tower!

He was now in a position to judge what a delightful life would have been his had he chosen Godelieve. And that could have been, would have been, had not Barbara intervened and at a stroke, with one irrevocable kiss, desecrated and ruined their future.

But now his mistake was being put right; circumstances were conspiring with him. God Himself seemed to be tempting them.

The time had come to restore their destiny.

During the day they enjoyed the enchanting illusion that nothing of what had been had happened. Not once when they were together at table did they sense an empty place, at no moment did Barbara's absence come between them.

Only during the evening, as the time to go to bed approached, did Joris fall prey to a fever of agitation. He fell silent while in his mind's eye he imagined Godelieve in her bedroom, already in the intimate whiteness of her underwear. He pictured her, using the way she had looked on certain days in the past, her hair not properly dressed and in her morning gown, not suspecting the arousal it caused, nor its surreptitious aid to future images. Joris visualised her pink on the pillow with, all around, the blond stream of her hair, playing in meanders round her head. He would have so liked to see her asleep.

The evening drew on. Neither dared give the signal to part. They were unaccustomed to being parted. They had spent the day together, just the two of them, a couple enraptured, perfect lovers who are alike, think the same thing without having to say it, vibrating in such unison that they remain silent together to let their souls communicate. And it had long been so, always, since those far-off days when their souls had been betrothed.

One evening Joris was more affectionate, more tender. He

followed Godelieve down the corridor and up the stairs as she made her way to her room. He delayed his goodnight and took her hands, pressing his face against hers. He recalled their past: Godelieve had fallen in love with him straight away, and he, basically, had never loved anyone but her. It was Fate that was to blame. But Fate had relented, had brought them back together. Should they fight against themselves now?

Godelieve, pure as she was, was not an innocent. She guessed, understood Joris's tender entreaty, still quivering from his words, his caresses, his emotion, the fire in his expression, youthful once more. At the same time the great mystery, of which she was ignorant, filled her with alarm. Her voice changed as she asked, 'What is missing from our happiness?'

Joris stammered a reply.

Godelieve murmured, 'It would have been so good to continue as we are.'

Joris said, 'Who will know?'

'God will,' Godelieve replied sharply.

As she spoke, she pulled away in consternation, suddenly recovering her old self. God! The word had rung out in her confusion, in her first steps towards defeat, like one single bell, all the more tragic for being one single peal. Her expression became solemn, was transfigured, lighting up the gloom. Certainty flooded her eyes like dawn breaking. She looked Joris straight in the face, serenely. She took his hands, with nothing sensual in the gesture now, as if they were just flowers she was taking. And she said, in a voice which sounded as if she were praying out loud:

'Yes, we must belong to each other. But not like this. First we will go to the church. I feel that my love is so blameless that I want to take it to God, to have it blessed by God. God will marry us, if you're willing. Tomorrow evening, in the parish church? After that I will no longer be myself . . . I will be yours . . . I will be *your wife*.

The following day, towards six o'clock, Godelieve made her way to St Saviour's Cathedral. Joris had expressed a preference for that church, thinking it more beautiful and wanting their love to be surrounded by beauty. She entered by a side door and went to wait for him, as agreed, in one of the chapels in the apse. She was afraid, though without knowing why. Who could have guessed? Who would have suspected if they saw them together? Was she not his sister-in-law, was it not perfectly normal for them to go out together, to enter a church and pray for a while? Nevertheless, it was with slight apprehension that she had scanned the few people scattered round the naves. They were women of the people, humble servants of God, almost entombed in their vast cloaks, whose hoods open out in the shape of a stoup for holy water. They merged more and more with the incipient darkness. Only the windows were still radiant. The rosettes formed a wheel. They were blue peacocks, rigid with pride. Immense silence. All that could be heard was the sputter of a few candles, the intermittent crack of the wood of the confessionals or the stalls, the vague respiration of sleeping objects. The blazing colours on the walls and columns faded. A veil of invisible black crepe descended over everything. There was a smell of musty incense, of mouldering glory, of the dust of centuries. The faces on the old pictures were dying, recalling the bones in the reliquaries.

Godelieve waited in a mixture of agitation and melancholy. She knelt on a chair, wrapped herself in the sign of the cross and looked through her prayer book for the marriage service. When she found it, she crossed herself once more and started to read the introit, her eyes fixed on the page, reading out the words with slow movements of her lips to avoid any distraction that would have been a sacrilege. Despite that, she had difficulty following the text. She felt uneasy and disturbed, standing up all the time and looking round, even to the farthest parts of the church, at the slightest noise echoing on the stone floors of the aisles.

Then she put her hands together and, her eyes on the altar, directed a fervent prayer at the Paschal Lamb, all in gold and bearing a cross, that is depicted on the swivel door of the tabernacle. 'O my Lord, tell me that it does not offend you and that you forgive me. I have suffered so much, Lord. And you have not forbidden us to love. He is the one I love, have always loved, the one to whom I have always been engaged. He is the one I have chosen before you, Lord, for my only and eternal husband. Even if he is not my husband in the eyes of men, he will be my husband before you. O my Lord, tell me that you forgive me, tell me that I have your blessing. Tell me that you will unite us, O my Lord, that you will marry us when you hear my vow and his . . .'

Abruptly she turned round. She could hear steps coming towards her. Someone was approaching through the accumulated darkness and it must be Joris. She could see him with her soul's eyes. She shivered and felt that she had gone very pale. Her blood, abandoning her face, surged into her heart in a hot, red flood. She felt a warmth in her breast, a brief touch like a caress of happiness, a rose suddenly opening, making it Maytime in her heart.

The human shadow grew, entered the ambulatory and was soon behind her, very quietly murmuring, 'Godelieve,' over her shoulder.

'Is that you, Joris?' she said, still a little anxious, a little uncertain of her happiness.

Then she pointed to a chair she had put next to hers and, without looking at him, without saying anything, opened her prayer book and went back to reading the marriage service.

Joris looked at her, captivated by the angelic mysticism with which she was carried away, transfiguring the impending sin. She was laying her soul bare before God, without remorse, with joy and certainty, as if she had seen Him giving His assent and His blessing from the depths of His mysterious paradise. For her it was not mere pretence, a way of deluding herself, of granting herself absolution. She was celebrating her true marriage. Perhaps she was right from the perspective of eternity. Joris was overcome with great joy. He was moved to see that she had taken care to be well dressed, had fastened on secret jewels, a luxurious display hidden beneath her long coat, but that she would doubtless reveal to him when they returned home.

He saw her, after a long time in prayer, take off her gloves. He watched, puzzled. What was she going to do? Next she brought a jewellery case out of her pocket and from it took two solid gold rings, two wedding rings. Reverently she placed one on her finger and, drawing Joris's hand towards her, slipped the other onto his. Then, keeping his hand in hers, in a chaste grip, as if a priest had enfolded it in his stole, she asked him, in a voice full of assured affection:

'You will always love me, won't you?'

Their rings touched, kissed, two links from a mystical chain that God had just blessed and which united them for ever in a love that was indissoluble – and lawful.

With all the actions and emotions of this exchange of rings, she had forgotten about her gloves, which she had just taken off. She looked for them as they were leaving. They had fallen on the floor. As Joris bent down to pick them up he noticed that their chairs had been standing on one of the funerary slabs with which St Saviour's is paved in many places. In that chapel there is a whole series of flat tombs in stone or brass, some with blackened effigies, the lord and his lady portrayed in the unmoving folds of their shrouds, with bunches of grapes and Christian symbols all round them.

Godelieve had seen it too. Beneath their feet was a grave-stone. On it the date of a long-ago death could be seen and, spaced out, incomplete, the letters of a name which was perishing in its turn on the slab, decomposing, returning to the void. Funereal emblems! How could she not have noticed when she had chosen those seats. Their love had been born above death.

The disturbing impression faded, however. Their happiness was such that even death could not cast a shadow over it, like the happiness of lovers who, during the village fairs on summer evenings, leave the dancing and go and lean against the grave-yard wall to take each others' hands and lips, to make love.

The affinity of love and death! It only made Joris and Godelieve's passion all the more solemn.

And that evening, in the moment of union, each felt they died a little in the other.

VII

How love immediately distances us from the world! Two of us together, as if on an island, an enchanted island, where nothing from the mainland concerns us any longer; we have each other and need no one else. We return to a primitive existence: no more ambition, no more art, no more interests, but a triumphant idleness in which our soul, emptied of everything else, can finally listen to itself.

Godelieve felt exquisitely happy. No remorse had yet emerged. She felt that being in love was like being in a state of grace; and the joy abounding within her recalled the time of her first communion when, on all the mornings that followed, she continued to feel a living God inside her. Now it was like her first communion of love.

Joris, for his part, felt full of the pleasurable freshness, sweetness of convalescence. His former life – the black days, Barbara's fits of anger, his bitterness at his failure to find happiness – had disappeared entirely, was no more than a hazy memory. It was as if that had all happened to another man, or in another life. He was amazed at his passion, in his former life, for ambitions that now seemed empty. What was the love he had harboured for the town but a cold, artificial passion which he used to veil his solitude. It was love for a tomb. And how dangerous to love death when life was there, simple and very beautiful. The only thing worth having was love. For a long time Joris had been unaware of that. He had found himself another reason for living and had spent years lost in a dream, that is in a lie. Now he realised that his dream of the beauty of Bruges was an illusion, and an unsatisfying one at that. Even if it were realised, it would not give him any real happiness and would leave him feeling he had wasted years, sacrificed his life. We must enjoy the moment, create immediate joys for ourselves, take our being of flesh and blood out into the sunshine, the wind, the flowers and not always set up a god inside ourselves.

Joris's days were idle and happy. His love was all he needed. Godelieve alone occupied his time. He abandoned the work that was already under way. Façades languished, half restored, having to wait on his pleasure to have their scaffolding removed, to throw off the sheets in which they were swathed and swaddled, and re-emerge, cured of the malady of being old. His projects for the future were neglected, even the restoration of the ancient building of the Academy, for which he had started on the plans, contemplating making it into a large-scale reconstruction with severe lines which would have been a new claim to fame for him.

Fame? That chimaera that dupes us. How can one shun life just for its posthumous promises?

Joris was happy just to let the days go by. And they did, swiftly and in enchantment. New lovers have much to occupy them. They have a very active inner life. And they create relations between themselves that are complex, subtle, delicate. They want to know everything about each other, to ask about each other every minute, to tell each other the essence of every thought which opens up inside them, the shadow of every cloud that passes. Each is living in two souls at once.

And they have so much to tell each other. All their life history, the history of their days and their nights going back to earliest childhood, what they have seen, felt, desired, dreamt, wept, loved – and also their daydreams and their nightmares, everything, without restriction, in detail, with every nuance, for they are jealous of even the most distant past and the tiniest secret. The blessed nakedness of love! The soul too removes its veils and reveals itself completely.

All that Joris found in Godelieve was gentleness after gentleness. An adorable creature, always yielding, agreeing, accompanying him, and with what clear intelligence!

Joris asked Godelieve, 'So you loved me from the very beginning?'

'Yes, straight away, from the first time you came to my father's house.'

'Why did you not say?'

'Why did you not see?'

They both felt it was their destiny not to come together immediately. Joris thought of the belfry, of the Bell of Lust that had tempted him to desire Barbara, of the whole mysterious conspiracy of the tower, from which he always came back down disoriented, stumbling and not seeing clearly among men.

As if speaking to himself he said, in melancholy tones, 'I have so often been blind in my life.'

Then he asked Godelieve, 'Why did you fall in love with me?'

'Because you seemed sad.'

Then she told him a story from her schooldays at boarding school, a childish love which had also come to her through pity. She had attended the Ursulines' convent school. There was a priest who took religious instruction. He was no longer young and not handsome, with his big nose and the bristly black beard on his cheeks. But there was a sadness about his eyes; he seemed to be carrying his heart within him, like a great tomb. The girls thought he was ugly and made fun of him. Godelieve, seeing him disliked by everyone, took his side in her soul, said prayers for him and, to compensate him, behaved in exemplary fashion during his lessons.

He was her father confessor and she often went to confession. He would pronounce absolution with tender words, sweet names: 'My dear friend, my dear little sister.' Days when she did not see him seemed empty and long. When he came into the classroom, she felt herself blush, then go pale. In the dormitory on winter evenings she would still be thinking of him and write his name on the icy windows so that it seemed to be emerging from lace.

Was that not already love?

During that time the annual retreat was held, with terrifying sermons on sin and hell. She had no doubt that she was the one God was concerned about, the one for whom He had sent the preacher with his images of fire and brimstone. For she was in a state of mortal sin, having slipped into the sacrilege of loving a priest.

Joris listened to the strange story, as innocent as a story from a saint's life. He saw Godelieve as a child, her honey-coloured hair in a plait down her back, with the air of a little victim, deluded by her own sweetness and need to console people. How had it all turned out?

'I was terrified,' she went on, 'and the very next day I went to kneel in the confessional of the man I was still in love with – for I loved him despite the anathemas of the retreat, despite God, even in that final minute when I had to accuse myself.

' "Father, I have a great sin on my conscience which I do not dare tell you."

' "Why?" he said. "You can confess everything to me."

' "No. It is you above all I would not dare to reveal it to."

' "Tell me. You must," he said. "Surely you do not want to make God sad at heart? Nor to make me sad?"

'At that I couldn't hold back any longer. There was such melancholy in his voice, as if a distillation of old sorrows had come back to him. Blushing violently, I spoke quickly as I admitted, "Father, I love too much."

' "But God has not forbidden us to love. Whom do you love too much? And how do you know that you love too much?"

'I didn't say anything. I didn't dare.

'Then he insisted, very cleverly, scolded me, became distressed himself; it was solely his sadness that made me weaken and start to change my mind. Abruptly, as if I were lifting a great weight from my heart which I no longer had the strength to bear, I whispered quickly, in a low voice, "You are the one I love too much."

'The priest did not smile, he remained silent for a moment. Then, as I watched him, full of apprehension, I saw his rough features soften in an expression of infinite woe. There was a distant look in his eyes, doubtless he was thinking of the past when he had known love and my childish naivety had summoned up its ghost. You try to forget, then a child's voice brings it all back . . .

'He quickly dismissed me, telling me to come to confession less often.

'You see,' Godelieve said in conclusion, 'there's nothing to be jealous of. That was my first love before you. And I fell in love with you because you seemed sad as well. But you are handsome and you will be a great man.'

Joris smiled, moved by the little story and by Godelieve's precocious vocation for consoling others. As far as he was concerned, she did more than console him, she took away all his sorrow, all his bitter memories, all his disillusionment. She gave him back his love of life, of the world. Now he hardly even regretted the misunderstanding of their hearts, which had sought each other for so long and suffered from being alone. They had found each other and the future stretched out before them. The past had disappeared completely. In their initial intoxication they had even forgotten that Barbara's absence would be brief, that she would return, come between them, casting over them a chill shadow, like that of a tall tower. Their happiness reached into infinity, it was as if they were living in eternity, an eternity where there would only be the two of them together.

This even led them to act imprudently in that provincial town where everything is noted, to take walks in isolated spots or late in the evening, which quickly gave rise to comment.

They suspected nothing.

In the evenings they liked to go to the Minnewater, that pleasant lake slumbering in the green outskirts, next to the Beguinage, the 'lake of love' whose waters are popularly believed to make people mad with love, a love that lasts until death. However, no sorceress had ever emptied her potions into it, its calm banks did not exude the infection of madness. When Joris and Godelieve got there, as night was falling, there was hardly a breeze blowing, just enough to make the poplars beside it stammer, but in laments without words. The only sounds to reach it were the echoes of prayers, the murmur of bells rebounding off gables and roofs.

Why should these waters make people mad with love? Make people love with an unchanging passion? Especially since all that is mirrored in them are the fickle reflections of the northern clouds, always on the move. Joris was so

155

overcome with joy that he stumbled along. Godelieve smiled at the pinpoint stars, at the waters, at the lilies that grew abundantly there and that she would have liked to take home with her.

They walked on, their arms almost round each other, enraptured by the peace of the scene and the night, without thinking that some passer-by might see them, suspect all and reveal their guilty love. They had no thought for Barbara, as if they were masters of themselves and their own destiny.

Was that the Minnewater working its spell, making them mad to the point of needless imprudence, so obsessed with their love they laughed at the whole world?

VIII

Joris had a dream of taking Godelieve up into the tower. All lovers like to show each other the places where they live. They need to know everything about each other. And the cherished presence will sanctify the surroundings.

Godelieve agreed to the plan joyfully, though not so much for the pleasure of seeing the mysterious belfry, nor even of hearing the carillon from closer to, of watching Joris sit down at the keys and bring into bloom the nostalgic flowers of sound which she had so far only known from the petals falling upon her and the town. It was above all because in that way she would enter a little more fully into Joris's life, would see the glass chamber, of which he so often spoke, which he called the most intimate chamber of his life and where he must have spent so much time thinking, regretting, hoping and, doubtless, suffering. Up there, in the enclosed air, there would be something of him which she did not yet know.

However, one anxiety tormented her: 'What if someone should see me?'

Joris persuaded her that it would be easy to enter the tower without being seen. Anyway, he argued, there would be nothing odd about her having the idea that she would like to see the bell-tower and accompanying him . . .

They climbed the tower together. Immediately Godelieve was filled with dread at the impenetrable darkness, the crypt-like chill. She had the feeling they were setting off to die together. At first, because of the tight turns of the spiral staircase, she bumped against the wall and almost stumbled. Joris placed her hand on the rope, a rough, thick cable serving as a banister, which she used to guide her. She pulled on it as if it were an anchor, hoping to find herself on terra firma soon, at the top, in the light.

The ascent took a long time. They crossed wide landings with empty rooms opening off them, the granaries of silence.

157

Then they had to set off again on a further climb through the gloom. Godelieve did not dare look, being afraid of falling, of the bats brushing against her – she could hear the muffled sound of their wings as they flew back and forth. She felt as if she were in a nightmare in which the colours curdle, the shapes and sounds match and distort. Joris talked to her, tried to reassure her, joked to keep her spirits up. Godelieve replied and went on like a sleepwalker. What frightened her most of all was that she could no longer see Joris, who merged into the shadows, and that she was no longer aware of herself, as if she had lost herself.

All that was left was their voices groping for each other in the dark.

Godelieve saw mysterious doors go by, as if lit by the flashes of a nocturnal thunderstorm, beams inspiring the fear and terror of a gibbet, overhanging bells, above all the Bell of Victory, alone in its large dormitory, a bronze gown almost touching the floor, the black habit of a damned monk.

They kept on climbing, captives of the stairs and the tower. It was like an uphill exercise yard, a vertical prison. Godelieve had never felt such fear, an attack of panic, of physical terror she could not keep down. When would deliverance come? Soon brightness appeared up above; there was more light around Joris's voice, ahead of Godelieve. Then she felt a great dawn break over her head. At the same time a strong wind blew, sweeping the dark away from her face.

They had reached the platform and were in the glass chamber, the windows of which opened onto a circular view of the town, the immense green landscape of Flanders, the North Sea gleaming in the distance. In one corner was the clavier of the carillon, the yellowing ivory of a keyboard waiting.

Immediately Godelieve was filled with amazement, with wonder. 'This is where you play?'

'Yes. You'll hear it soon.'

'I'm glad I came now,' she went on. 'That endless staircase is terrible, but it's beautiful up here, it's good to be here.'

She wanted to look at the horizon all round, but Joris drew her to him, kissed her.

'I'm so happy to see you here. Though in a way,' he added, 'you've already been here. You remember what you said at the beginning: "If only it had been God's will," those few words that decided everything? The next day was a day for the carillon. Climbing the tower I felt as if your words were coming up with me, climbing the stairs in front of me, running on ahead, coming back. After that I was never alone. The words, which were your voice, were up here, close to me.'

'Oh my darling!' Godelieve cried, flinging her arms round his neck.

Then she added, 'And it was here that you suffered as well?'

'Suffered so much. If you only knew,' Joris replied. 'My life was like the black ascent we've just made. But it always ended in the light. It's the tower that saved me.'

Then he told her how he had comforted himself, repeating, 'High above the world,' over and over to himself until he was carried away, as if he were escaping, leaving his sorrows behind, looking down on them from such a height that they were no longer visible and therefore no longer existed.

'See how small everything is down there.'

And he showed Godelieve the world spread out below, the town remote, the beautiful countryside forming tapestries. He pointed out the Minnewater, so dear to them from their evening walks. How narrow it looked, how straight! The lake was like a poor woman's mirror, a humble side-altar with its water lilies as votive offerings. What? That was it? So little space for love?

He also pointed out, almost opposite them, their old house on the Dijver, blackened and emblazoned behind the curtain of trees along the canal. It was tiny, casting a shortened shadow in front of it, thin and contorted like a piece of iron jewellery. However, the details could still be made out. They counted the windows, suddenly looking at each other in agitation, their eyes burning, lips ready. They had just stopped, both together, at the casement of the unforgettable room. Through that permanent communion of lovers they had both thought the same thing at the same moment. Immediately all their memories rose up to them from below. The panes of the nuptial chamber sparkled, transparent, willing accomplices in the passionate evocation of their first night, their first kisses.

They fell into each others' arms. It seemed to Godelieve that the town receded, grew even smaller, ceased to be, while they, together, entwined, rose higher, were no longer in the tower but merging under the caresses of the winds and the clouds, touching the sky . . .

But the time for the carillon had come. Joris sat down at the keys. Godelieve listened, disappointed at first. It was just a concert of shrill, strident voices that only sounded so sweet in the the town below because they were far away. It is distance that creates nostalgia. Up there the bells were singing out loud, fit to make themselves hoarse, a village choir, cantors giving the notes at random.

Yet Joris was doing his best, putting all his heart into his playing in honour of Godelieve. The basses came in with the old Flemish songs he played. Better than the sopranos of the little bells, which only took on angelic tones when heard from a distance, the big bells sang their noble dirges, with murmurs of organs and the forest, which moved Godelieve. She let herself be carried away by the vast hymn which Joris was creating for her, a stream of notes into which he seemed to pour his whole self.

The whole tower was singing of love.

The only ones who noticed this rejuvenated music, the renewed freshness of these flowers of sound floating down on the roofs and streets, were a few passers-by in the squares, a few townsfolk idling in their homes. What unexpected spring was blossoming up there? What was the matter with the old bells, what was making them sing faster, as if their black bronze was tinged with a feverish flush?

When Joris had finished he took Godelieve up the small staircase leading to the upper platform, a few more steps to climb . . . They were going higher . . . Then Godelieve saw the bells' dormitories, all the bells aligned with their inscriptions, their dates, their coats of arms cast in the metal. And the differing patina of age: the tones of etchings, the strange oxidations, the rust like a chiaroscuro by Rembrandt. The metal was still vibrating, still quivering from having sung. One large bell above all attracted Godelieve. It was taller than she was and hanging from massive beams. It was embellished with relief ornamentation. Godelieve wanted to go over to it, but Joris brusquely drew her away.

'No! Not over there!'

His voice was trembling with sudden emotion. It was the horrible bell, the Bell of Lust with all the ecstatic bodies and breasts picked like fruits, the vase full of sins, the ciborium held out by hell. Godelieve must not partake of that sacrament. Her eyes were too pure to contemplate that frozen orgy. And then the Bell of Lust was Barbara's bell. The sensual pleasures of its bronze dress were the sensual pleasures of Barbara's dress. It was the bell that had tempted him, had connived with Barbara and caused all their unhappiness. Godelieve must not go near it now.

He led her away, towards another bell, the one that sounded the hours, for he had heard the grinding of the rods that operated the clappers. A moment later the huge hammer rose, then came down on the sonorous metal. It was like a blow from a crozier striking the silence. The hour rang out, entire, episcopal.

Joris and Godelieve listened, suddenly serious. It was the passing of the hour, irrevocable, an hour they would never be able to forget, nor begin again, the most beautiful hour of their lives, the hour of the high point of their love, which had climbed to the top of the tower with them.

And when they found themselves hurrying down the stairs as they returned, already assailed by their fears for the future, they were well aware that they were coming back down from the summit of their love.

IX

Barbara returned after having been away for a month. Her health had hardly improved at all, nor her temper. The preparations for the journey home, the nervous exhaustion from travelling had, as usual, all upset her again. She was still irritable, bristly. Her face was pale. Joris recalled her too-red lips, now faded. A vision of a future black with threats and alarms opened up before him.

But Godelieve's love compensated him for everything. She had had the same impression of her sister when she returned and told Joris.

'What does it matter,' he replied, 'since I have you?'

Their happiness remained intact, nothing could darken it. They were still enraptured with each other, reflecting their love to one another as the sky and the waters do the moon. They bathed in its reciprocal light. Lovers have no idea it is so, but they exude brightness as they go. Sorrow is the rule, a dark livery worn by the mass of humanity. As soon as a couple are filled with joy they are so far outside the norm, they violate the rule so boldly, that they seem clothed in radiance, the radiance of a paradise from which they have come and to which they will return. Thus is happiness *visible*.

It was impossible that Barbara should not notice the change that had taken place in Joris and Godelieve. If they were happy at the same time, it was that they were happy together. She had observed certain signs, a greater intimacy between them. Beforehand they had hardly ever used the familiar *tu*; now Joris addressed Godelieve with it several times and corrected himself clumsily. At the same time Barbara received anonymous letters, a despicable habit but very common in the provincial world, where malicious gossip, envy and spite grow rank, like the grass between the flagstones. She was welcomed home; she was mocked for being accommodating enough to leave her sister alone with her husband; the time and place of their evening walks was cited and they were described as romantic and suspicious; she was even informed that one day they had gone into the bell-tower together.

Nothing goes unobserved in that strict town where people lack occupation. Malicious curiosity there has even invented what is known as a *busybody*, that is a double mirror fixed to the outside of the windowledge so that the streets can be monitored even from inside the houses, all the comings and goings watched, a kind of trap to catch all the exits and entrances, the encounters and gestures that do not realise they are being observed, the looks that prove everything.

Her suspicions thus aroused, Barbara was devastated, though also a little sceptical, despite the signs she had noticed herself. It was her self-esteem that was hurt. She had long since grown away from Joris, tired of him and of his kisses, but her pride rebelled, particularly at the idea of being betrayed and supplanted by her sister. She still refused to believe it and fell prey to indecision, accepting then rejecting it, finding it obvious then improbable. The two opposite poles. Swaying this way and that, like a boat to the opposite sides of a wave. And the worst was that there was no end to the vacillation.

Barbara was feeling her way, calculating the chances, examining the situation and analysing the two involved. Godelieve was all sweetness and light, true, but that manner often went with concealed subterfuges. Barbara felt a surge of bitterness and resentment towards her sister who, at the very least, had gone beyond the permitted bounds of familiarity, giving rise to her own suspicions and those that had prompted the anonymous letters.

Godelieve, all unsuspecting, was astonished at Barbara's fits of irritation, which were now directed at her as much as at Joris. Up to this point she had been spared and that was what had allowed her to intervene effectively, to make peace. Now she too was equally exposed to the changes of mood which swept through the house like a storm wind. But the two lovers were hardly affected, letting them wash over them; their eyes were on other things, their minds in accord as soon as the scenes began. They quickly fell silent, never responded, mutely exchanging soft words, from soul to soul.

With Barbara constantly on the lookout, they were rarely alone, but it only needed a moment for their hands, their lips to meet, for them to embrace behind a door, on the landing. Stolen moments of happiness! They plucked a joy, like a fruit, from each other as they passed. And that was enough to light up a whole day. Their immense happiness was condensed into a moment, just as a garden can be condensed into a bouquet. A sweet moment whose fragrance filled the solitude of their rooms. How intense is a love heightened by the frustration of waiting! Perhaps love, like happiness, is all the stronger for being intermittent.

Kept apart, Godelieve and Joris desired each other all the more. Several times they arranged things so that they went out at the same time and met outside. Barbara followed her sister, but at too great a distance and quickly lost her in the maze of the twisting, tangled streets of Bruges.

Joris and Godelieve also suffered from not being able to talk to each other, even though living in the same house. Now Barbara insisted on staying with them, not going to bed until the same time as they did, hardly leaving them alone together at all.

And they felt they had so much to say to each other.

'What if we wrote to each other?' Godelieve suggested one day.

She had always felt the need to write, to pour herself out onto paper, to become conscious of her own self by seeing it on the reality of that whiteness. Even as a child, when she was a boarder at the convent school, she had written letters to Jesus, harbouring a passion for the Man-God, whose statue dominated the chapel with its handsome face, hair parted down the middle, delicate hands pointing to a Sacred Heart burning with love in his breast. She wrote to him in the evening, in the study room, and then, once a week when they were allowed out into the town, surreptitiously dropped her missive into a letterbox in a envelope addressed to 'Monsieur Jésus'. She was convinced it would bring bring her good luck, help her to get what she was asking for and might even reach the addressee in heaven.

Now she passed on to Joris, ceaselessly, everything she could not say to him, everything which, from the very fact of living face to face with him, constantly rose up inside her and which she had to repress. In the evening she retired to her bedroom and wrote, sometimes late into the night. It was truly like being alone with him. She had won him back. She was talking to him on the paper. All she was doing was replying to what he was whispering in the darkness behind her shoulder. The act of writing itself is like an act of love. There is contact. There is exchange too. We no longer know whether the words come out of the ink onto the page, or whether they emerge from the page itself where they were sleeping, the ink merely giving them colour.

For her, everything she wrote out in her interminable letters was merely what she read in her soul. But who had written all that on her soul? Was it Joris's love? Or had he only made what had always been there visible?

The next day, after she had filled her long sheets, it took a great deal of cautious manoeuvring to be alone with Joris for a moment and give them to him. Joris replied. Godelieve wrote again, almost every day.

One evening Barbara, unable to sleep, got up and, walking round the house, noticed the light under Godelieve's door, so late at night! She went in to discover her writing – and immediately flustered by her sister's sudden appearance.

During the next few days Barbara remained baffled. You only wrote to someone who was absent. Godelieve couldn't be writing to Joris since she saw him and spoke to him all the time. People who are not, or no longer, in love can scarcely understand the refinements, the subtle, delicate pleasures of true lovers. The delight of tying invisible threads between them, so that they always feel attached by some part of their soul. The joy of communion in the sacred species of paper, which is transubstantiated, in which the beloved face shines through in a whiteness that resembles that of the host.

Barbara, hesitant, was doubly irritable in the face of her suspicions of a truth which by turns appeared, hid, crossed paths and finally reached a crossroads, clouding the future.

X

Since her sister's return, Godelieve had started to feel less happy. And not only because her presence interrupted their intimate life together, their permanent rapture, the unconstrained enjoyment of their love. Before, thanks to the blessings of their state and the gift lovers have for deluding themselves, they were able to believe themselves alone in the universe, forget reality and create a world in accordance with their dream. Now reality asserted itself once more. As if it were a crime, they had to hide the love they would have liked to pour forth, into the sea and into the air. The poor human heart is a bowl so shallow it overflows at the least happiness.

For a long time they excused themselves in their own eyes by blaming a destiny which had gone astray but which had since returned to the true path of their lives. This caused Godelieve no misgivings because Barbara had previously stolen Joris's love from her. She was the one who had been his first and eternal betrothed. Because of Barbara they, who were married in the eyes of God, had long been lost to each other. How could it be wrong for them to find each other again, to correct the error of a malicious Fate?

For a long time Godelieve had deluded herself with specious arguments, a casuistry of the heart, very personal and over-subtle. However, since Barbara's return she felt slightly guilty. How could she believe her love lawful if she did not dare reveal it to anyone? There was no point in being misled by words. Words summon up other words and they destroy each other. Yes, she was the first to love Joris. It was their will that had betrothed them, before Fate intervened; Fate alone had kept them apart. To say that would be to tell the truth, but one could also say that now she was the one who was bringing adultery to the conjugal home. And the adultery was aggravated by a hint of incest, since it was her sister's husband she loved, almost her brother . . .

How wretched a life, a heart can be! Soon Godelieve was suffering from what she saw, after all, as duplicity, a betrayal of trust, a forbidden love that dare not speak its name. She, usually so frank and open, was ashamed of the constant dissimulation. How could a love as noble as theirs, a love which had climbed as high as the tower, be happy to go in the shadow that made it look as if it did not exist?

In her evening letters she told Joris of her distress at the life she was forced to lead: lies, stratagems, deception with a smile, glib gestures, honeyed words. And having to watch herself all the time! What a disaster it would be, what an eruption of rage, if Barbara, with her dreadful, violent temper, should discover their secret. Their love, it seemed, was on a volcano; their love seemed to be waiting for the storm.

Godelieve wrote all this to Joris; she told him it in those brief exchanges they sometimes had when Barbara was dressing or occupied with some household task, leaving them alone for a moment.

'Let's go away together?' Joris said.

'Why?' Godelieve replied with a sad look. 'We can never get married.'

Being Catholic, she knew well that the Church would not agree to bless a second union. And with her pious, mystical nature, how could she live in that state? The present situation was different. God himself had blessed her marriage with Joris in the church where they had exchanged rings. In the eyes of God she had truly become *his wife*. They were not causing a public scandal. It was between God and them. And that was how it must stay. Their love must not be made public; it could never be acknowledged. Even if Joris were to obtain a divorce, the civil authorities would hesitate, would demand a dispensation because of the close relationship, the semi-incest. Society would be shocked, that was sure. They would have to leave, go far away into exile, and that would mean they would still feel they were in hiding, were denying themselves.

Godelieve was unhappy.

It was above all because of the town that she felt it would be dangerous, insane even, to think of leaving with Joris; away from it he would suffer so much. This was the natural setting for his life, for his dreams. He could not live away from Bruges. Godelieve certainly felt she was loved. But she also felt there was something that was loved more deeply. Joris's love for the town was far above his love for a woman. The two loves were as different as a house and a tower.

Godelieve realised that Joris, hardly had they left, would fall prey to incurable nostalgia. His longing for the town would follow him. All his ways would be darkened by the shadow of the ancient bell-towers. Bruges was his work, a work of art that would bring him fame and that he had to complete. To tear him away from it was an impossible hope.

But is it not events that are masters of our words and our decisions? Godelieve vacillated, discussing with herself and with Joris where their love might end. During those days there was a sudden, chilling alert which almost changed everything, brought it to a head. It was the perpetual fear, perhaps also the punishment, of illicit passions – the fear that the sin might be made flesh. Godelieve was terrified. Joris too, but he was regretful in equal measure. It was an irony of Fate, an extra, unnecessary cruelty. He had so much wanted to have children, in the early days of his marriage to Barbara, when he took her to the Museum to see the portrait of her patron saint by Memling and showed her the donors, kneeling among their numerous offspring shown as different-sized heads, squeezed together like votive offerings. Above all he had dreamt of having sons who would keep his name alive in Flanders, continuing the ancient family tree. But his home remained empty, barren of future. Now he visualised a situation where, if he had married Godelieve instead of Barbara, his happiness would have been complete with not only a love that was all sweetness, but the joy of progeny and the pride of his name living on.

Godelieve viewed the possibility like death. In the first place she would not survive until the end – the torment, the shame, the anguish would kill her. She recalled the ominous portent, the warning she should have seen in the gravestone where she and Joris had met, that evening in Saint Saviour's, the evening when she had become *his wife*. They had not noticed that their chairs were standing on effigies of the dead, that their feet were continuing the effacement of the names already worn down by the tread of centuries. It was only when Godelieve's gloves had fallen to the floor and they bent down to pick them up that their hands, bearing the new rings, their blind hands eager to rush into their misfortune, had truly touched death.

Now the portent was being fulfilled. Godelieve was still unsure; perhaps she was simply ill, had made a mistake and her sin was not bearing fruit inside her. She hoped, repented, prayed, went to bury herself for hours in churches, trusting in heaven alone to put an end to her torment. It was still possible she was mistaken. But every time she raised her eyes to the altars, a Virgin appeared to her bearing a child in her arms. It became an obsession, an inescapable allegory in which she saw herself soon carrying the fruit of her sin. Eventually she attached a superstition to these Madonnas. She told herself, 'If the first one I see when I go out today has her hands together, it will mean the oracle has replied in my favour and all my fears are groundless. If, on the other hand, the Madonna is carrying Jesus in her arms, it will mean the end of my hopes and confirmation that I am pregnant.'

Godelieve went to see the Virgin in its glass case at the corner of Zwarte-Leertouwersstraat, the one for which she had made a lace veil. Alas, she was carrying the infant Jesus. The same was true of the statue of the Virgin that dominates the console, with its foliage and rams' heads, on the façade of the Draper's Hall and of the Virgin by Michelangelo in Saint Saviour's. There were only a few statues of the Virgin Mary with empty arms to compensate for the accumulation of ill omens, but they all bore, beneath them, a reproachful inscription: 'I am the Immaculate Conception'. And the scroll on which it was written was undulating, like the flaming sword of the cherubim guarding the entrance to paradise.

Godelieve fled, conscious of her lost chastity, as distressed and frightened by the reproachful statues as by those of ill omen. What was the verdict of heaven going to be? Thus she spent days consulting the oracle of the Madonnas, in churches, at crossroads, on gables, letting her life depend on these chance encounters.

She multiplied her prayers, her propitiatory candles, made a vow to go to the next Procession of the Penitents in Veurne, started a novena, quickly went to confession because God cannot see those who are obscured by too dark a sin. That was the time of the Octave of the Holy Blood, the procession in May during which one single drop of the blood of Jesus Christ, brought back by the Crusaders, is borne round the town with great pomp, amid white choirs of the children taking first communion, rose petals, golden banners, monks of all the orders. For the whole week Godelieve exhausted herself in fasting, pain, penances, prayers. On the Sunday, when the little shrine, a jewelled bush, appeared in the bright sunshine of the street, Godelieve was seized with violent trembling, immense hope. The Holy Blood had passed. She felt the wound of her sex open once more . . .

After that everything was changed between her and Joris. God had taken her back. Did she not also belong to God? She had yielded to Joris's desire, out of pity and to make his heart less sad. It was time to stop saddening the heart of God. He had shown such mercy. He had saved her – and saved both of them with her – from what would have been a triple disaster, ruins piled up round a cradle. In return she must no longer trespass against God, must not fall back into sin. She had promised that to her confessor who, with his wise counsel and a new plan of life, had restored order to her soul.

Joris, for his part, continued to take her hands and her lips when they chanced to meet, on the stairs and in the corridors. Godelieve would slip out of his grasp, pushing him away gently but firmly. He stubbornly kept writing to her, his passion roused all the more by the feeling of distance while they were so close, moved to pathos by the anguish they had just shared, the sense that they had both died a little in what, perhaps, had never been. But she hardly ever replied now, at most she would occasionally slip him a short letter devoid of passion, encouraging his soul, calling herself his elder sister and his dead bride, talking of the future with the hope that they might come together again one day, if God willed, not in sin but in joy and lawful union.

XI

Autumn closed in. An autumn of dead leaves, an autumn of dead stones in a town in decline. It was the great week of the sadness of Bruges, the Octave of the Dead during which it wraps itself in mist and bells, sinking into even more inconsolable melancholy . . .

It is not only the dead who are commemorated. We also remember our personal griefs, dreams that died, hopes that faded, everything that existed inside us and died. Joris suffered from his sad love that was beginning to seem as if it was no longer. Day by day Godelieve was drawing further away from him.

Already affected by the terrible scare and influenced by her father confessor, whose advice she followed faithfully, she quickly resolved not to fall back into sin, which also brought danger with it. Oh, Joris struggled against God, but the struggle was brief. Still he missed her, longed for her, for her embrace which was so different from Barbara's. With Godelieve he felt she gave herself and took nothing. A gift to make him feel less sad. She brought balm, she brought oblivion. Being in her arms was like being in a sheltered cove, away from the restlessness of the open sea. And now she had taken it back, denying him first her lips, then her hands and, all the more, any meeting outside the house, which he could no longer hope for.

She hardly even wrote to him any more, only occasionally – and such calm letters! Joris realised she had been conquered by fear and by faith, was turning away from him without too much of a wrench and with calculated touches of gentleness. 'Let us purify ourselves,' she said to him. 'Our love will be all the greater for being chaste and strengthened by waiting.' She spoke to him of Saint Theresa and of their own union which had, after all, been a mystical marriage. And even her letters, short and purified of passion as they were, made her seem more distant, so that he loved her as one would love someone in their absence. And is not absence half way to death?

Godelieve was half dead to him. He mourned her during the Octave of the Dead when, high up in the belfry, in the grey air of a northern November, he felt more than ever that the whole town was in the grip of death. From up there it seemed empty, like a town seized with lethargy. The canals stretched out, inert, and the foliage, thinned out by the north wind as the willows prostrated themselves, moved on them as if on tombs. Despite the distance one could make out, all round the doors on the front of the churches, cards announcing obits, trentals, requiems, anniversary masses for the dead – death's notice board!

A thousand images of mourning came up from the town to the top of the bell-tower and Borluut observed them with rising sadness. His soul was in harmony with them. The greyness was in his soul as well, the dreary atmosphere of All Hallows. Joris felt alone. Godelieve's few words – which, so long ago, had gone with him into the tower, laughed as they climbed the stairs, settled and lived there for a long time – had died. A few tender words which were the voice of Godelieve and which, at one point, had become embodied in a bell and sung with the carillon.

In those days the carillon had been joyful and in listening to it Joris had been listening to his own heart. He had not even heard the other bells making their way through the sky above Bruges. Now – was it because of the more sonorous atmosphere at this season, because he had been made more sensitive by sorrow or because of the week devoted to the dead in which the sound of the parish bells was more insistent? – Borluut only heard the other bells. He was amazed that he had hardly noticed them before, up there in the tower. The carillon had rung out loud and clear, the whole tower vibrated under his fingers, so to speak, and the song that emanated from him returned to him.

During that week it was the bells of the churches that flooded his being. The carillon, the voice of past days but dominated now, drowned out by other sounds, kept on giving cheerful advice: 'Live! You must live!' But the tolling of the church bells proclaimed death and sent out funeral processions into the air. There was the knell of Saint Saviour's, trundling along like a hearse; the great bell of Our Lady's draping a catafalque of sound over the town; the little bells of the Beguinage wearing the white of mourning for a virgin; the bell of Saint Walburga's making its way in widow's weeds. Still others, farther off, came from the innumerable chapels and convents, like a flight of souls in torment swirling round in the wind, looking for the houses that had already forgotten them, assailing the bell-tower, going to kiss its gold clock face as if it were a communion plate.

Borluut himself was hovering amid death. The bells of the carillon fell in with it, their music too became funereal. The belfry sang of the end of love, mourned Godelieve in a flutter of slow, soft notes, as if the bell-tower were just another humble church and its bells were summoning parishioners to prayers of intercession for the dead.

Then their song expanded. The carillonneur, ashamed of his personal grief, fired the keys to expansive meditations – and the big bells joined in, sounding out the *requiem* of Bruges, soon dominating the tiny sounds of the other bells, absorbing all the obscure deaths into the death of the town, a fitter harmony to reach to the horizons.

XII

Joris had believed he would be able to win Godelieve back from her fear and from God. One day he realised his hopes were close to being dashed. As they were separating to go to bed and Barbara was a little in front of them, she furtively slipped an envelope into his hand. Overcome with joyful agitation, he hurried to his room, thinking he was about to read another letter after the long, disheartening silence, a letter full of tenderness, of new beginnings. The envelope contained nothing written at all, simply a ring, one of the two wedding rings they had exchanged that evening in the church, in an ecstasy of mutual love.

'Oh, that is cruel – and pointless,' thought Borluut, overcome, though more with discouragement than distress. He put it in a drawer without thinking, reflecting on this final trial, the clear sign this time. It was truly the end, the final link in a broken chain that no longer united them. In this Joris saw the hand of her father confessor, his advice to break completely with him, to remove the least occasion for sin, even – above all – the insidious little jewel that signified their pact.

However Barbara, her suspicions aroused, had not ceased her watchfulness. For weeks, for months, it was as if her every nerve were tensed, her whole being concentrated on finding certainty. Every evening she went to check the light under Godelieve's door and she had noticed that she was writing less. When her sister went out, she accompanied or followed her. As for Joris, she took advantage of his absences to search through his clothes, his drawers. She was almost convinced, but she needed evidence, evidence that would be undeniable, conclusive proof with which she could confront the guilty pair.

Joris, careless as ever, with the abstracted mind, the unfocused gaze of the man coming back from the bell-tower, had casually thrown Godelieve's ring into the drawer where he had already put his own. One day, as night was falling, Barbara found the two rings in the course of her investigations. They were in a corner, among some innocuous papers. At first she paid them scant attention. It was only when an inscription on the inside caught her eye that she looked more closely; there was the name of each of them – Godelieve and Joris – and a date.

It was the date above all that stood out. It coincided, as Barbara quickly realised, with that of her departure for the spa, the opportune moment when they were left alone together. Barbara's remaining doubts were swept away; she held the proof in her hands, the silent, sacred witness. The certainty sent her wild with fury, every nerve called to action, arrows quivering to be despatched.

Joris came back not long afterwards. It was dinner time and he went to the dining-room, where Godelieve was already waiting. Barbara was on the lookout, at the top of the stairs, breathing heavily, her head ringing, but content with the knowledge, as if relieved of all the suspicions, signs, clues, that elusive burden she had borne for months. Now it all came down to these two rings, and she held them so tight, in such a feverish grasp that at times she almost crushed them like two flowers.

When the guilty couple were together, she rushed down. Her entrance was like a thunderbolt: 'Miserable wretches!'

The cry was emitted by a voice that was completely changed, a panting voice, as if she had been running for a long time.

Immediately Godelieve foresaw a catastrophe. Joris watched, anxious to know just how much Barbara suspected.

Barbara repeated, 'Oh, you two miserable wretches!'

She swooped on Joris. 'I know everything!'

And she showed him the rings, clinking in the quivering jewel case of her palm, tiny, humble, appearing to ask pardon for having given them away.

And she laughed derisively, a madwoman's arpeggio of chilling laughter.

Then she turned to face Godelieve. 'As for you – off you go! Off you go! Leave my house!'

She was going to push her, use force; Joris stood between them.

At that her anger exploded with the fury of a raging sea that nothing could hold back, an onslaught of pebbles and wreckage, a spattering of foam that left Joris and Godelieve feeling wounded, sullied to the very depths of their being.

While she was heaping abuse on them she suddenly threw their two gold rings at them, like missiles. 'There you are! You can keep them, your rings!'

Her face seemed to be breaking up, like ice floes in a thaw. And she kept on repeating, like a hiccup, a refrain of despair: 'It's disgusting! Disgusting!'

Joris and Godelieve remained silent, not daring to utter a word to mollify her, to calm things down.

Provoked even more by their silence and furious that the rings had not hit either of them, Barbara, beside herself with fury, grabbed an old Delft vase from the sideboard and flung it with all the force she could muster at Joris's head. He fended it off, but the blue vase crashed into the mirror, which immediately cracked.

The vase fell onto the marble fireplace, smashing to pieces with a long, piercing noise which maddened Barbara even more. In that moment she saw herself in the mirror, her face appearing cut in two by a gash running from top to bottom.

She felt as if her head were splitting as well and, completely distraught, grasped other objects and threw them at the guilty pair standing there before her, aghast and pale, trying to stop her, to take cover, unable to get away since she was blocking the door, wild-eyed, foaming at the mouth, rabid, driven mad by the pain, by her pride, by the wound in the mirror which she thought she could feel on her face – widening, and all the more terrible for not bleeding – by the crash of all the things she was throwing at the walls and the windows, breaking crystal, vases, candlesticks, sending them flying across the room and falling to the floor in fragments, seized with a destructive furor, a frenzy to lay waste to everything around her, since there was nothing but ruins in her heart.

And when the carnage was over, weary and ashamed, she let out a long cry and left, sobbing along the corridors.

Joris and Godelieve were alone once more.

They did not say a word. Joris had the impression the whole world had collapsed around him. He felt as if he were in an empty space, in some depths where his fall had broken everything. As if he had fallen from the height of the bell-tower, from the height of their love, which had climbed as high as the tower. He was overcome with a disheartening feeling that something irreparable had happened. He saw himself as beyond life; and the drama he had just lived through appeared very distant, very old, as if it had happened in a former existence to a dead man who resembled him. Certainly the old love-story had come to a sorry end. It was the woman's fault for being afraid, for giving up too soon; and he had not been insistent enough. By denying themselves they had drawn the chastisement down on themselves.

Now it was like a dream, as if it had never been.

All at once he was pulled out of the chaos of his thoughts and brought back to reality by Godelieve who was standing there, holding out her hand, looking as if she was about to leave him.

'What are you going to do?' Joris asked.

'As you see,' Godelieve replied with the voice of one in mortal agony, 'I can't stay here.'

'Yes,' said Joris, 'let's leave.'

And, feeling alone in the silent disaster, he tried to cling onto her, to draw her to him, to hold her again in that moment when he felt his whole life slipping from him, when he had to think of making a new future for himself. Godelieve broke away, more afraid of what was about to happen than of what had happened. She withdrew to the other end of the room and said, in a faraway voice, as if in a dream, 'You must stay here, Joris. Your life is here, your work and your fame.'

Then she said, in a stronger voice, 'As for me, I'll go to the Beguinage in Diksmuide tomorrow.'

Joris knew it was irrevocable, the precipitate execution of a plan she had probably been considering for some time. It was less Barbara's discovery and the terrible scene which were separating them than the fact that their wills were already apart. It is not events that are the cause of things. They merely conform to ourselves, bringing out what is already there inside us. Here it was God who had started everything. He was the one who triumphed.

Godelieve had the strength to separate. 'Farewell, Joris,' she said, one last time. 'I will pray to God, *for us*.'

Her voice almost failed on the last words, which seemed to lose their colour, weaken, grow damp, as if touched by inward tears.

She went towards the door, her feet disturbing the debris, a landscape of ruins that crunched under her steps. In that moment she saw, as if in a flash, their meeting in Saint Saviour's, their nuptial evening, the exchange of rings over the tombstone. Truly their love, born on death, was bound to end in disaster.

Her mind was made up. She left, without looking back, irrevocably.

Joris, devastated, was alone, so alone he felt as if he were waking up among tombs. He thought of the two women as of two dead wives – and he their widower.

PART THREE

ACTION

I

High above the world! Joris clung on to the cry, saying it out loud, writing it on the blank air before him, so to speak. He repeated it to himself like an order, like an appeal for help with which he could save himself. It had always been his motto, the cry of joy to rally himself, the end of his sufferings, bursting from among them like water from among the rocks.

After the terrible scene and the departure of Godelieve, he was at a loss what to do.

The following days the house seemed dead to him. It had sunk into silence. All the comings and goings, the sound of steps and of voices had ceased. It was like a house where someone has died and one remains silent, afraid even to walk. The room where the final confrontation had taken place was left as it was: the floor strewn with debris, the mirror split by the wide wound which was continuing to deepen, slashing the pale glass with a mortal blow. No one had gone in there, it remained closed, the door locked and boarded up. It was truly the room of a dead person, at the door of which we tremble, but do not dare to enter.

Barbara did not leave her apartments, took her meals there, confined, solitary, shunning society, in a state of nervous exhaustion. The discovery of the proof, finally in her hands, her fit of anger, her wild excess, Godelieve's flight, leaving the next day, at dawn, without seeing her, all that had left her nerves twisted and tangled, like rigging in a storm.

Now her acute irritability was replaced by infinite lethargy. She was no longer prickly and irascible. She curled up in corners, shivering like a sick animal, her blood sluggish and cold. She wandered along the corridors, up and down the stairs, pallid, her face streaked with tears. Sometimes, when she happened to meet Joris in the course of her wanderings, her irritation would return momentarily, expressing itself in some violent, coarse word she threw at him like a stone. But her strength was gone, she only threw the one stone, as if night were falling and her thirst for vengeance too weary.

Joris, too, isolated himself, avoided her, no longer feeling anything more than indifference. Whether deliberately or through illness, she had caused him too much suffering. He even found it impossible to repress a feeling of resentment since, incapable of making him happy, she had wrecked his last, dear love which had been a balm to him, a new beginning. What consolation could he find now that he was alone again? How could he forget Godelieve, who had gone out of his life? She had loved him and yet she had left. It was irrevocable. At first he had made enquiries. No one knew where she had found refuge. Perhaps she had not entered the Beguinage in Diksmuide, as she had said, but had settled in some other town, from where she would call him soon. Was it possible that a love like theirs should end so quickly and for no reason? It was true that God had come between them. Since the scare that she might be pregnant, her confessor's advice, the sin laid bare, hell in prospect, Godelieve had suddenly turned away from him, recovered herself. But no doubt absence would be having its effect. It was impossible that the memory of their embrace in the tower would not follow her as she went. And memory can quickly turn into desire.

Joris waited, full of regret, hoping for news and, some day, a return of their love. But all that was over and done with, as he learnt from a friend of Godelieve's to whom she eventually wrote that she had become a Beguine.

High above the world! Joris drew strength from his cry, rejoiced in it. Twice he had been defeated, held back by love. It was the source of all his woes. First Barbara, then Godelieve. Each in her own way had made him suffer, and in making him suffer had reduced his strength, his drive in dealing with the world, his superiority over other men, his gift for creation and for art.

The astral force of love – a redoubtable power. Man is under the influence of woman as the sea is under that of the moon. Joris had suffered from no longer being his own master, from being subject to this capricious thing, constantly changing, evolving, smiling then disappearing behind dark clouds, in eclipses. A life in abeyance. Why not free himself, be his own master once more? Who knows, perhaps this suffering through women is the mark of the hero, atonement for all those who are sensitive, remarkable and strong, and too handsome; the price to pay for great dreams and great influence, as if, after all their victories over art and over men, this reminder of human misery were necessary, as if the victor had in his turn to be vanquished by woman?

Joris refused to be vanquished. He fought against the despair, the ache of regret at losing Godelieve. After all, she had betrayed him, quickly left him with no fault on his part, at the height of their passion, with a hint of desertion since she had abandoned him at a critical moment, in the uncertainty of defeat and ruins after Barbara had risen up, breathing fire, almost armed and stoning him.

Oh, the one was as bad as the other. Excessive weakness had harmed him as much as excessive violence. Neither was worth the hindrance, the obstacle to his future. He returned to higher things, to art, his earlier hopes, his noble ambitions. The love of woman was delusive and vain!

He went back to his love of the town. At least that love was not one that would deceive him, nor make him suffer. It lasted unto death. During those days Joris recalled van Hulle's death and the ecstatic cry that had revealed the fulfilment, in the hour of death, of the dream that had accompanied him faithfully through life: 'They have chimed!' To be worthy of his ideal he had to devote himself to it exclusively.

It was he who had betrayed his love for Bruges. Perhaps it would be possible, by doubling his efforts, to made good the interruption to his work? He returned to it with a will. He had better things to do than spend his time lamenting over the caprice of women or lost loves. He had to get back to his own destiny, to his vocation and his mission. He took up his projects again, his façades came back to life.

Thanks to him people again started repairing, renovating, resuscitating the old mansions, the ancient houses, everything that ennobles a town, brings a touch of dream to the streets, inserts faces from the past among the modern buildings. Once more Joris was carried away by his work, for the beauty of a town is a work of art that has to be realised, requiring harmony, a sense of the whole, an understanding of line and colour. Bruges would become such a town. And in return he, in the moment of death, would achieve satisfaction at its lasting beauty and, dispatched with it down the centuries, would, like van Hulle, be able to exclaim, 'Bruges is beautiful! Bruges is beautiful!'

Moreover it is not solely from the point of view of a self-contained work of art that the beauty of a town is important. The surroundings – colourful, melancholy or heroic – create inhabitants in their image. Joris had a discussion about this with Bartholomeus, one day when he had gone to see what progress he had made in his work, the great decorative paintings, still unfinished, the symphony in grey in which he was trying to encapsulate the beauty of Bruges.

He got carried away as he developed his idea: 'The aesthetic quality of towns is essential. If, as has been said, every landscape is a frame of mind, then it is even more true of a townscape. The way the inhabitants think and feel corresponds to the town they live in. An analogous phenomenon can be observed in certain women who, during their pregnancy, surround themselves with harmonious objects, calm statues, bright gardens, delicate curios, so that their child-to-be, under their influence, will be beautiful. In the same way one cannot imagine a genius coming from other than a magnificent town. Goethe was born in Frankfurt, a noble city where the Main flows between venerable palaces, between walls where the ancient heart of Germany lives on. Hoffmann explains Nuremberg – his soul performs acrobatics on the gables like a gnome on the decorated face of an old German clock. In France there is Rouen, with its rich accumulation of architectural monuments, its cathedral like an oasis of stone, which produced Corneille and then Flaubert, two pure geniuses shaking hands across the centuries. There is no doubt about it, beautiful towns make beautiful souls.'

Borluut was himself again, uplifted by vast and noble thoughts.

High above the world! Now he climbed the bell-tower as if he were climbing up into his dream, with a light step, relieved of all the vain afflictions love brings, petty private sorrows which had for too long hampered his ascent to higher goals. He went through a heroic period. The clock face on the tower glittered like a shield with which it defended itself against the night. And the carillon sang proud anthems. No longer a trickle of music that sounded like the tears of the man who had climbed the tower and was crying on the town; nor even a slither of music, like shovelfuls of earth cast into the grave of a dead past. It was a concert of deliverance, the free and virile song of a man who feels himself delivered, looks to the future, dominating his destiny as he dominates the town.

II

During that time Joris was tempted by the prospect of Action.
Until then he had kept away from public life, which did not
interest him. Politics were local, petty, sticking to platitudes
and to an ancient and artificial division of the populace into
two enemy camps which wrangled over influence and jobs.
Even the recent socialist upsurge did not excite him; before
long things reverted to the futile quarrel between Catholics
and liberals, the return of the old parties that had merely
changed their names. Ever since the Middle Ages there had
been a struggle in Flanders between the Catholic and the lay
factions, conflicts for supremacy between dogma and liberty.
Their antagonism even reached up into the air, symbolised by
the Spire and the Belfry, the religious tower and the civil
tower, the one where the Mystery was preserved in the consecrated host and the one where the charters and privileges
were kept in an ironbound chest – rivals, each risen to the
same height, casting the same shadow onto the town, which
thus belonged half to each. And they would go on until the
sun stood still, unshakeable, like the two principles they
embodied, with their bricks rising one on top of the other for
ever and ever, like individuals following one after another in
a nation.

Borluut remained aloof, indifferent and slightly disdainful.
But what if Action was about to be the sister of Dream
again? The joy of finally being able to act, to struggle, to
know passion, the intoxication of proclaiming a cause and
exerting influence over men. And all for an ideal. Not in order
to assert himself and his petty vanity, but to spread art and
beauty, to give time a bit of eternity. His dream was under
threat, the great dream of his life, his dream, for Bruges, of
a mysterious beauty which would be made up of hushed
sounds, still waters, empty streets, bells muffled in the air,
houses with shrouded windows. A town beautiful because

it was dead! And now people wanted to force it back to life . . .

It was the old Seaport of Bruges project, which had seemed a mere pipe dream at first when Farazyn described the plan during one of their Monday evenings at van Hulle's. It had gradually germinated and grown, thanks to obstinate efforts and daily propaganda. Farazyn had fashioned it into a weapon that brought success, an instrument that assured his name was known. His career at the bar had prospered, since the project brought him into contact with politicians and businessmen. Beyond that, it gave him the appearance of a public-spirited citizen. With his sonorous and loquacious style, always speaking the rough language of his Flemish ancestors, he lost no chance to evoke the Bruges of trade and commerce that he was going to bring back as soon as the canal was in operation, the new docks full of ships and the coffers of Bruges full of gold. The mirage was not unattractive, even though the inhabitants were sleepy and scorned exertion. They listened to the picture he painted of the future like a child listening to a story, finding it only mildly interesting and close to falling asleep.

Borluut had not seen Farazyn for a long time, not since the unfortunate day when his friend had come to dine with them and met with the refusal of his offer of marriage from Godelieve. Afterwards Farazyn was annoyed, even harbouring a grudge against Borluut, as if he had somehow been partly to blame for his failure. Since then Farazyn had avoided him, turning aside whenever they met. Subsequently Borluut heard he was making hostile remarks about him. Their close friendship had been poisoned by the Seaport of Bruges affair, which had immediately roused Borluut to violent indignation, as at a sacrilege, since he clearly saw that if the project was approved and the new port created, it would be the end of the town's beauty. They would pull down gates, precious houses and old districts, mark out boulevards, railway tracks, all the ugliness of commerce and modern life.

The period of resistance began. Since he had been elected Guildmaster, he possessed considerable influence in the Archers of Saint Sebastian. He went there more often, meeting the bowmen, the regulars, petits bourgeois who were easily manipulated and led quiet lives which did not dispose them to doubtful enterprises. He made them see how fanciful it was to imagine that a prosperity which had vanished could be re-established, how criminal it would be to ruin the authentic beauty of Bruges, which was just becoming famous throughout the world, for an uncertain end.

There was, moreover, a factor with affected them directly and determined their public opposition to the Seaport of Bruges project: their ancient premises themselves were threatened. According to the plans that had already been published, the new docks where the ship canal would terminate would be dug in that very district, where the picturesque ramparts stood, the two windmills, which gave that part a Dutch look, and the Guild premises, crowned by its 16th-century turret. Thus the glorious turret, pink and slender in the air like a virgin's body, would disappear along with the patron saint who had been watching over them for centuries and would now fall, assassinated by pickaxes. An act as barbarous as that of the soldiers massacring Ursula and her companions on the reliquary in St John's Hospital. And the centuries-old bricks, with all their scratches, would bleed from wounds that would be painful to see.

Borluut also tried to express his opposition through articles in newspapers. He had secured the support of one local paper in which he pursued a sustained, fiery campaign. But the results were meagre. The press has little effect on public opinion and even less on the powers-that-be.

Like other matters, this whole business of the Seaport of Bruges went on behind the scenes, in restricted discussions, meetings of officials, committee tactics. Engineers conspired with financiers and politicians. Farazyn was the moving spirit behind all these combinations. Everything went through him. An association was formed as a centre of propaganda, great care being taken to keep it above party politics. The president was one of the town aldermen; Farazyn was appointed secretary. A huge campaign of petitions was organised. The townsfolk, indifferent and timid into the bargain, all signed.

Finally, delegations were received by the various ministers, who gave their agreement and promised state support, part of the millions needed.

The whole of the the political machinery came into play, a formidable apparatus with hidden springs, endless drive-belts, irresistible flywheels.

Borluut felt it was going to snap up the beauty of Bruges and, under the pretext of hardly touching it, grind it down completely with its iron teeth.

Borluut intensified his efforts, seemed to be everywhere at once. His aggressive zeal even amazed himself a little. Where had he got these combative postures, these challenges he threw out, this constant sabre-rattling, like a call to arms, he who was a man of silence, of the past, of dreams? But was that not the point, was he not defending his Dream? And this time his dream was identified with Action, impassioned and frenzied action, no longer action against an enemy or adversaries, but action against the Crowd.

The Crowd appeared to be one, either through ignorance or indolence. He stood alone. Was that not the fight all superior men fought, one against all? They have to prevail against the unanimity of voices, which at first repudiate them. The beauty of Bruges, to which he had contributed, was also a work of art which had to be imposed. But by what means? What was the way to defeat a crowd? How could he, on his own, go from one to the other and open with his two hands all the eyes which were blind?

Scattered victories.

Borluut hoped the day would come when he could face the Crowd itself. Since he had written in the newspapers attacking the system of covert intrigues and a campaign conducted behind closed doors, the Seaport of Bruges Association had responded by appealing to all, by convening a public meeting at which they would report on the current state of the project, the plans adopted, the funding that was necessary, the support that had been promised.

Posters in Flemish were put up, indicating the purpose of the gathering and the names of the office-holders of the

Association. They also bore an unusual heading, as shocking as a blasphemous oath in the religious calm of the streets: 'Monster Meeting'. But the proposers of the scheme knew very well they were taking no risks, knowing the apathy of the townsfolk who, averse to any inconvenience, would hardly bother to read their brash summons, and would be wary of becoming involved in an affair and a meeting of which they knew nothing.

Farazyn had foreseen that Borluut at most would make use of the occasion. It was even he who had had the idea of the public meeting as a trap into which his enemy would fall. And indeed, Borluut did not hesitate. He was fired with bravado, the joy of finally doing battle, face to face with the Crowd and out in the open after too many skirmishes with an enemy behind cover or fortifications. Naive, he deluded himself into thinking the people of Bruges would attend en masse and that he would be able to convince them, get them to kneel before the beauty of Bruges he would evoke. Borluut spent the days leading up to it in a flurry of activity. He rallied his most faithful supporters among the Archers of Saint Sebastian, those who were most up in arms about a venture which threatened their ancient meeting place.

He was assuming all the members would accompany him there, would protest with him against the vandals, burying the project beneath a storm of laughter and boos. Was not mockery as good a weapon as indignation? That was why Borluut had got his friend Bartholomeus to make a caricature for him. It was done in secret, since the aldermen and town officials were supporters of the Seaport of Bruges project and the painter was dependent on them; they were the ones who had commissioned the paintings for the Gothic Chamber of the Town Hall which had so far been neither accepted nor paid for. However, he too was aquiver with indignation at the idea that they were going to change the town, with noise, demolitions and new buildings, all for the vile purpose of making money. He agreed and made a satirical sketch for Borluut, in the popular taste with simple lines, naive and strong, like a lament. It showed people with their houses on their backs, setting off to run towards the sea that could be seen in the background, fleeing as they approached, while their houses were scattering stone after stone behind them and the town was no more than a pile of rubble.

The coloured drawing was printed as a poster which was stuck up on the walls beside the Association's announcement of their meeting. It was a direct response, the struggle carried to the enemy's ground, without remission.

Borluut was alive with energy and in heroic mood. How he now despised all the pitiful little troubles to which he had attached such importance, the distress caused by Barbara, his regret at losing Godelieve, all the things that were trivial, transitory, petty and vain. He no longer had time to bother with himself, to suffer for trifles, to concern himself with his feelings. It was as if his life were being lived outside himself, carried along in his action, as in a great wind. There was an end to the pain of being free and being himself. He belonged to others, was becoming the Crowd . . .

On the morning of the long-awaited day, which was a day for the carillon, he climbed the belfry and put all his exhilaration into the bells, which rang out a battle hymn, the rebellion of the great old bells at being disturbed, the hubbub of the little bells at being threatened, a coalition of sound against those who wanted to bring back a port and fill the air with masts over which their peals would stumble.

Then came an anthem of hope; the ostinato theme of the melancholy of Bruges floated in the air, sending its grey music forth over the roofs, in harmony with the sky, the waters, the stones.

Finally the evening came. Borluut had counted on a large number of the Archers of Saint Sebastian attending; only two met him there. As soon as he entered the hall he realised that very few people had bothered to come. There were none of the ordinary folk, at most a few small shopkeepers who had been summoned and who were dependent on the Council. The Association of the Seaport of Bruges, on the other hand, was present, some thirty of its members, the leaders sitting round a table covered in green cloth in the sparse light of a few lamps.

The hall seemed icy, with its wooden benches, white-washed walls, expectant silence and dimly lit shadow with the unmoving faces of the few people present arranged as if in a picture. There was a sense of unease, a chill of catacombs in which words are afraid of themselves, fade away, die before they are spoken. The only sound was the rustle of papers, the documents and reports which Farazyn, sitting at the official table, kept looking through.

Borluut, too, had come prepared for a battle, but he had imagined it quite different. What was this funereal-looking assembly, where a few shadows came in, sat down and did not move any more, like ghosts that were starting to die over again? So this was the 'Monster Meeting' which had been announced with such commotion.

There was still only a scattering of people in the hall, even though the time fixed was already past. Just now and then a new arrival would enter, falter, intimidated by the scene, deaden his steps and go and sit down, without making a sound, at the end of an empty bench. Meagre alluvial deposits! The limited group of those present formed a silent, indistinct mass. None of them either wanted or dared to speak, but all were smoking and, because of the smoke, were only hazily visible in a grey gloom. Their short pipes had a metal cover to contain the fire, which could not be seen. Increasing darkness was added to increasing silence. The smoke was exhaled methodically, as if it were the mist coming out of the smokers themselves, the fog from brains empty of thoughts.

Were these the people Borluut had expected, wanted to fight against, dreamt of convincing, conquering? Instead of struggling against the Crowd, he would be fighting ghosts whose deployment would be directed by Farazyn alone, his enemy, whose eyes and irony he could already feel fixed on him.

This, then, was the contest for which he had devised his speech, a speech that was less technical than lyrical, written with an impressionable audience in mind, that he would have to move in order to carry them with him. In an atmosphere like this his speech would be as effective as the sun in the fog. Why had he not foreseen that this was how it was bound to be? Once again he realised too late that he had not seen clearly enough. He would have liked to leave, to give up, but he did not dare because of Farazyn who, from the platform, was sending him a challenging look.

The meeting was opened. The president of the Association gave a speech, then Farazyn read a long report; in passing he denounced those citizens who obstructed such an undertaking that was in the public interest and would bring prosperity. Then he adduced numerous documents, explanations, plans and figures, from which it emerged that the funds would soon be voted, so that in the very near future work could be started to realise the great enterprise of the Seaport of Bruges.

Farazyn sat down, smiling and looking pleased with himself. Some members of the Association, interested in the financial arrangements, applauded. The rest of his audience remained somnolent, their faces continued to be the faces of painted portraits. They looked as if their eyes were fixed on the centuries. Mechanically, moving their lips as little as possible, they blew out slow puffs of smoke into the lifeless air, a scattering of rising columns, each one contributing to the warp and weft of grey. It was impossible to say what they were thinking or whether they were thinking at all. The smoke was weaving an ever thicker veil between them and the speakers.

Once Farazyn had finished, the president seemed ready to close the meeting. Nevertheless he did enquire whether anyone had any observations to make. Borluut stood up to speak. He was under no illusion as to the futility of his speech in such an assembly, of this empty show which he had imagined would be a battle. But because of Farazyn, who was watching him, and since he had made the effort to come, he decided to go on to the bitter end.

He took out the text of his tirade, which he had written in advance, and started to read, trembling a little but unwavering in his conviction, which came across as spirited and profound. First of all he cast doubt on the projected results of the enterprise. It was not sufficient, he said, to dig a ship canal, as was proposed, to link Bruges artificially with the North Sea. Even supposing the canal worked well over the distance of ten miles, allowing unhindered passage to large ships, a town was not a port simply because it was joined to the sea. Having docks was one thing, but beyond that, and most important of all, it needed trading companies, warehouses, outlets, railway stations, banks; it needed a population that was young, active, rich, energetic, bold. To do business it needed to have businessmen, to bring in the Jews.

Bruges would never be able to do that. In that case being a port would be a sham, an empty luxury.

Borluut warmed to his subject: 'The goal that is being pursued here is a delusion. True, Bruges was a great port – but in the past. Can ports be resuscitated? Can one tame the sea, persuade it to return to habits it has abandoned? Can one renew routes across the waves that have been erased?'

As he spoke, Borluut sensed the discrepancy between his speech and his morose audience. He had come prepared for a struggle, contradiction, the gathering a true crowd, quivering, tense, drinking in sincere words like wine flowing from a fountain. He realised that everything he said immediately lost its strength, its flavour, in the pipe smoke, in the fog, which seemed to be the fog, rendered visible in the air, inside the skulls of those present, who resisted him with their indolence, their invincible, grey unanimity. So he was not getting through to them, was not communicating with them. He was even separated from them in physical terms since, because of the accumulation of smoke, he could hardly make them out; they were distant, hazy, like figures seen in a dream or in the depths of memory.

'What's the point?' he asked himself, but he continued to the end, so as not to capitulate before Farazyn who was exultant, regarding him with an expression that was ironic and also full of hatred. Does it not sometimes happen in life that our actions are solely for an enemy, so as to stand up to him, to confound him, to humiliate him by a finer effort or a more difficult victory? Without him we might perhaps give up.

Having an enemy stimulates us, gives us strength. In him we hope to defeat the universe and the malevolence of fate.

So eventually Borluut was speaking for Farazyn alone. After having demonstrated the absurdity of the project, he evoked, by contrast, the glory of being a dead town, a museum of art, all the things which were the better destiny of Bruges. Its fame as that kind of town was being established. Artists, archaeologists, princes were coming from all parts. Imagine the scorn of the outside world, how people would laugh when they heard it had abandoned such a noble dream, the notion of being a city of the ideal, something unique that is, in order to devote itself to the mean and common ambition of becoming a port. He contrasted it with Bartholomeus's project, though without mentioning the originator, of buying up all the paintings of the Flemish Primitives, which could then only be seen in Bruges – a much more useful way of spending the millions.

He concluded forcefully: 'In that way Bruges would become a place of pilgrimage for the elite of mankind. People would come, on a few special days but from all over the world, from the ends of the earth, as if to a sacred tomb, the tomb of art. Bruges would be the Queen of Death, while, with these commercial projects, it demeans itself and will soon merely be the Unfrocked Priest of Mourning.'

As he sat down, Farazyn, to spoil the effect of his peroration, closed it with an exclamation: 'An artist's arguments!'

An artist! Precisely the word that was needed there, a back-handed compliment, the height of derision! An artist! The definitive irony, sufficient to destroy a man in this provincial world.

Farazyn knew that well and his blow was well-aimed. Satisfied smiles appeared on the faces of the alderman who was chairing the meeting and the other promoters of the project. As for the audience, dry from their smoking, tired of long harangues, taciturn in the parallel rows of benches, not having understood much of all the statistics and elaborate sentences, impatient to get back to their snug homes, they waited.

No one had anything to add. After a minute's silence, during which the fluttering flames of the weak, smoking lamps could be heard, the meeting was closed.

Borluut left, mingling with the small gathering as it drifted away in silence. Hemmed in by the walls of the vestibule, it was a dark mass, something indeterminate, mechanical, a silent slippage which soon ceased.

Borluut wandered aimlessly, accompanied by the two Archers of Saint Sebastian, who remained faithful to him and did not speak. He quickly took his leave of them and plunged into the dark of nocturnal Bruges, alone and taking pleasure in being alone. He was escaping, as if from a nightmare, from a meeting with ghosts who were his enemies. It soon seemed as if it had never been. Then he came back to reality.

He went over the evening again, his futile speech, the pale silhouettes, the surly looks of Farazyn and the leaders of the Association. They were the only ones who seemed alive among all the self-effacement. They could have been a court in session. Borluut had the feeling he had just heard the beauty of Bruges condemned – to death! Everything had been decided in advance. All the publicity about open debate had been a sham. The decree had already been signed. Nothing would be stopped, they would have their Seaport of Bruges. Borluut could do nothing about it. He had achieved nothing, convinced no one. It had been as pointless as trying to convince the fog here, which was engulfing the nocturnal town, floating over the water, blurring the bridges. Oh, the Crowd! To do battle with the Crowd! Everything he had imagined, everything that had fired him with enthusiasm – vanished in the air with the smoke from flames he, more than anyone, had fanned himself. And his speech, so fiery and from which he had hoped so much, had ended like a puff of smoke among all the other smoke.

III

War had been declared between Borluut and the Town Council, most of whom, being involved in business and speculation, had an interest in the Seaport enterprise. Borluut had exposed them. Henceforward he was regarded as suspect, almost a traitor. Soon he was being called a public enemy who was harming the town's interests. His opponents' newspapers were not sparing in the insults and attacks they heaped on him and his friends. It was the start of a campaign of petty harassment, base and underhand.

The Society of the Archers of Saint Sebastian, of which he was Guildmaster, received an annual subsidy, enough to buy a few items of silverware as prizes for its competitions. The grant was cancelled, in order to get at Borluut, and also because the guild was seen as colluding with him in his opposition to the project.

But it was above all the painter, Bartholomeus, against whom the campaign was directed. He was known to be a close friend of Borluut; in addition he was suspected of being the author of the caricature about the Seaport project, the drawing which showed the inhabitants, with their homes on their backs, chasing after the sea.

He had just finished the series of large-scale paintings, which had been commissioned for the Gothic Chamber of the Town Hall. It was, perhaps, a good opportunity for reprisals.

Bartholomeus had been working on them for years and had refused to show anyone, even Borluut, the four panels of which the work consisted. In carrying it out he had borne in mind the place for which they were destined, keeping it in harmony with the style of the building, the colour of the walls and panelling, the curve of the ceiling, the sober light from the windows in the ceremonial hall. All that was left was to view them in their intended location.

Bartholomeus installed them and, despite his usual misgivings, his eternal dissatisfaction with himself, he was pleased, almost surprised, by the distancing effect produced now they were set in the frames, rather as if they were deep within a dream and outside time.

Borluut saw them and was filled with enthusiasm, was carried away. It was not so much painting as an apparition, as if the centuries-old walls had opened up and one could finally see *what the stones are dreaming.*

Bartholomeus had found a new manner of mural decoration in which things appeared through a mist, the way they must appear to a sleepwalker, the way they persist in memory. Human proportions no longer obtained. Everything was increased by one order of magnitude. The stones of the old canalside streets were wilting like a bed of flowers. Bells were making their way like little old women. The gestures of the figures were designed for eternity, they had the beauty of unnecessary gestures.

Borluut, as municipal architect, had supervised their installation. He then summoned the fine art committee who were to take delivery. He was a member himself, together with an alderman and several councillors.

They were disappointed, indeed, they were stunned and demanded explanations from Bartholomeus, who was there.

'What is the subject of your paintings?' the alderman asked.

The painter took them to the centre of the chamber, where the light was best, and then, after some hesitation, launched into an explanation, getting carried away, as if he had forgotten they were there.

'Look. They form a whole, a symphony on the grey town that is Bruges. That means a symphony in black and white: swans and Beguines on the one hand, bells and cloaks on the other; and all brought together by the circular landscape, which continues from one to the other and which is the orchestration.'

The members of the committee, disconcerted, gave each other grim looks, suspecting some irony on the part of the painter, who did not deign to explain things to them but was taking refuge in abstruse phrases, the clouds of his pride. They also quickly came to the conclusion that his paintings matched his gobbledygook. Should they uglify the Gothic Chamber, leave it open to ridicule with these incomprehensible paintings?

Wait and see. They could still be rejected. The paintings had not been paid for.

The examiners walked round, went to the other side, stationed themselves in front of the panel with the Beguinage. One councillor sniggered.

'But the Beguinage isn't like that at all.'

Bartholomeus decided there was no point in arguing.

Another remarked, 'There's no perspective.'

'Nor in Memling's paintings either,' Borluut retorted, hardly able to contain himself. At that very moment he had been in raptures at the delightful background which Bartholomeus had embedded with footpaths, as languid as wisps of smoke going up to the sky, as in the Flemish Primitives.

To tell the truth, the committee could not understand them at all. In addition they were hostile, stirred up by the alderman, who was the one who had chaired the 'monster meeting', and, because of the caricature ascribed to the painter, they were trying to strike a blow against him and, indirectly, Borluut.

The latter boldly accepted the challenge. Faced with the committee's reservations, their mindless criticisms, he declared his admiration.

'These are masterpieces! People will realise that later on. It is the fate of all new art to be disconcerting, even disliked. Bruges now has one more treasure and a great painter whose name will live on.'

The alderman and the councillors protested at being treated to a lesson like schoolboys. They had their own opinion, which was just as valid and perhaps more accurate.

'M. Bartholomeus is your friend. We are impartial,' one of them said in angry tones.

The meeting was threatening to turn into an argument.

The alderman, more wily and prudent, broke off, declaring that he and his colleagues would report to the Council, at which they all withdrew.

Some days later Bartholomeus received an official letter notifying him that the town, on the recommendation of the committee, would only be able to accept the decorative paintings for the Town Hall if certain modifications and changes were made, a detailed note of which would be forwarded to him at a later date.

It was the expected, cowardly blow. Bartholomeus replied immediately that he would not touch his paintings, which had matured over a long period and were in their definitive state. He added that no conditions had been attached to the commission, which he considered binding.

The worst thing was that payment had not yet been made. Borluut, indignant, denounced the malicious and ignorant machination in one of the newspapers. He threatened the Council with a court case which the artist was bound to win. Bartholomeus, for his part, was above all concerned about the fate of his pictures. He would willingly have foregone payment, but he insisted it was essential they remain in the Gothic Chamber of the Town Hall, bound as they were to that famous building, incorporated in it, so to speak, like images in a brain. Was it not the dream of Bruges itself that he had painted and should that dream not be perpetuated in the communal hall?

He was thinking above all of his fame, of the future. Would people come to see his work in the succeeding centuries, just as they went through the gardens with their box hedges and along the white corridors of the Hospital to contemplate the Memlings? Oh, the pride he felt at the thought of lasting, of conquering death and oblivion, of being the bread and wine of art that the elite of the future would receive in communion! That was the aspiration of Bartholomeus, the priest of an art-religion.

During that time Borluut published a moving portrait of his friend: an unselfish, noble figure who ought to be the honour and glory, the throne and sceptre, the living beacon of the town.

But these threats and these eulogies only served to fan the flames. Borluut's support did more harm than good, because of the animosity he had aroused in opposing the Seaport project. The paintings were on the point of being officially removed but the Council intervened, made uneasy by all the commotion the affair had aroused and not daring to take responsibility for the case. They conferred with the artist, looking for some way of reconciling the differences.

Wearying of the conflict, the two sides agreed to accept the arbitration of a commission composed exclusively of painters, of which each would choose half. In order to ensure complete impartiality, they also agreed to have it chaired by a well-known French artist who exhibited frequently in Flanders.

This is what happened: when the painters gathered to view Bartholomeus's pictures there was a unanimous outburst of enthusiasm, an exclamation of surprise and admiration for a work of such perfect unity and clear symbolism which attested to a skill and confidence in his handling of his art, a sense of line and a feeling for the harmony of tone which were truly breathtaking. They were, they felt, in the presence of a master who was an honour to Flemish art and to the town of Bruges.

A report to that effect was drawn up and submitted.

Borluut was exultant and trumpeted his jubilation. The campaign had been successful after all! The truth had prevailed. He heaped irony on those who had not seen it, exposed their ignorance as well as their baseness. Borluut took keen pleasure in these struggles. He enjoyed being involved in action. He felt he was living in the fire and smoke of battle.

Though victorious, the fight for Bartholomeus had been nothing more than a skirmish, after the other fight, the one of the meeting, which had been a disaster, which seemed like a defeat to an invisible enemy, through the night and rain. The war would continue, the war against the Seaport of Bruges, the war for art and the ideal, for the beauty of the town. This beauty of Bruges, still incomplete, was his work, his own large-scale picture in stone, which he had to defend, as Bartholomeus had his – and against the same enemies.

Action! Action! The intoxication of being alone and victorious! Perhaps he could still triumph. But how many obstacles there were, how many attacks! Borluut realised this and reflected, not without a touch of melancholy, that great men only impose their authority *despite* everyone else.

IV

Action had fired Borluut to a heroic fervour. He was soon condemned to silence, to a life of stagnation, to the mournful meditations of defeat.

Impetuous and disorganised as he was, it had not occurred to him that he was dependent on the town and the councillors against whom he had campaigned to oppose the Seaport project and, later, to defend his friend Bartholomeus.

He was made to pay for his double audacity. Not long afterwards he received a letter from the Council informing him that, following his hostile attitude towards the authority by whom he was employed, he was dismissed from his post as town architect.

It was a terrible blow for Borluut, a punishment without appeal, without release. How brief it had been, the intoxicating thrill of Action! It hadn't taken them long to cut him down; now he was dead. They had hit him where he was most vulnerable. He should have foreseen it and held back. But could one stand aside and let one's dream be destroyed? He had only let himself become involved in Action because in this case it coincided with the Dream. More than himself, it was his Dream that had been vanquished, the dream of the beauty of Bruges. He had been its faithful guardian, its indefatigable artisan. How many projects were suspended. And so many others still to be undertaken which, at a stroke, were jeopardised, sacrificed, lost. Indeed, he had only just submitted his plan for the restoration of the Academy, which would have formed a worthy companion piece to the Gruuthuse Palace. There were many façades still waiting for him to have time for them, waiting for him to come with his meticulous hands, the hands of a physician, an obstetrician, to examine them and deliver them of the sculpture of an angel, a gargoyle, a child's face. No one else had – nor would have now – his cautious art of restoring without renewing, of contenting himself with shoring up, repointing, exposing intact details, finding the original bark of the stones underneath all the parasitic growths.

Now all his work would be destroyed. They would name some mason as his replacement.

That was what distressed him, not the financial loss, since he had a private income, nor the honour it brought. He had always viewed the world from a higher perspective and his only regret in his loss of favour was the imminent ruin of all he had worked for, the encroachment of bad taste, of a fake archaism which would have nothing better to do than to destroy the harmony of greys and pinks which he had created throughout the town.

The beauty of Bruges was a work to which he had devoted himself exclusively, subordinating everything to it, sacrificing his time, his thoughts, his affections, his desire to leave, to flee when his life at home had become intolerable. It was his creation, which he had hoped to harmonise and complete and crown with the final sculpted garlands which remained to be brought into bloom – and now they had decided to take it away from him. There was nothing he could do about it. But it was as distressing as the abduction of a little girl, carried off at the moment when one was about to deck her out in her most beautiful dress.

Barbara was extremely vexed at Joris's dismissal, heaping bitter reproaches on him, harping on again about his usual thoughtlessness and blindness. A new and constant grievance. She even claimed it was a dishonour and that she was tainted by it as well. She would have to put up with ironic remarks, wounding allusions to it. Distressed by the affair, she went through a period in which she was in a permanent state of excitation: she did not calm down at all but went on and on at Joris, determined to provoke a scene. She poured abuse on him, interminable reproaches. At the same time she brought up the business of Godelieve again, the cowardly betrayal. Along with all this, her health deteriorated: she had nervous fits, falling flat on the floor, her face lifeless, her lips taut, closed and resembling a scar, while her legs were kicking up and down, her arms flapping. She looked as if she were fighting against someone who was trying to crucify her on a horizontal cross.

The fits would finish with mournful cries and strangled appeals, which filled the house until she eventually dissolved in floods of tears and laments. She called on death, a recitative declaring her tiredness of life.

She was back at her worst: suddenly running over to a window, frantically opening it and threatening to throw herself out; or rushing out of the house, striding up and down the streets, along the canals, looking at herself in the water from up on the bridges, as if attracted by the image of herself she saw, cured and calm, showing her what she could be, what she was going to be . . .

Joris, suspecting she was tempted to commit suicide, would hurry after her. He was trembling, initially out of fear of the scandal because of his old Flemish name, a heritage which weighed on him and which would have suffered, as if from a stain of its own, from the blood that was spilt on him; then out of fear of the sharp pangs of remorse which he foresaw would haunt him daily if Barbara killed herself. He had a heart which *lived backwards*. It was true that she had caused him much suffering, but he knew that if he lost her, he would go back, to mourn her, to the distant past, to the days when he had loved her, to the days of the too-red lips.

He refused to allow himself to think, even for a moment, that it would be a relief for him. Each time the thought came, he dismissed it in horror, as if it were the idea for a crime, as if he were thinking of pushing Barbara out of the window or into the water himself.

Anyway, what would he do if he were suddenly free? He would only be even more alone. Life had been good with Godelieve's love, but she too had abandoned him.

'If only it had been God's will!' The old words started going though his mind again, coming back from the farthest bounds of his memory, soaring, weeping. Where was Godelieve at that moment? What was she doing? What was she thinking? Why had she left him? Now that he had been dismissed by the town he could have gone away with her, left everything and started a new life elsewhere.

He had only put up with Barbara's fits of anger, a house that was either dreary or in tumult, an existence of anguish and grief, because of his love for his work, because he was bound to it, would not have been able to live anywhere else, would have sensed, in another town, its towers reaching out to him; because he felt incapable of leaving Bruges. Now it was Bruges that was leaving him.

Alas, now that they would have been released, free to part, Godelieve was no longer there.

'If only it had been God's will!' Joris felt his sorrow at the loss of Godelieve return. He went to the bell-tower to seek the elegiac words which, in those days now gone, had climbed the stairs ahead of him and come back down to meet him, out of breath from having run up the stairs and from being in love.

Fortunately he had not been dismissed from his post as municipal carillonneur as well. The reason was not some remaining scrap of goodwill or recognition of services rendered but because the public competition and his choice by the people, more than his investiture by the councillors, seemed to make that function a position from which he could not be removed.

So Borluut had kept his refuge. No longer did he climb up to it as if climbing into his dream, into the tower of his pride. Once more the belfry was his place of departure, of escape from himself, of ascent, of a journey into the past and his memories. He no longer had the courage to look down from the glassed-in bays onto the town, now in the grip of others. He isolated himself, plunged into intimate memories, relived the time when Godelieve had been there . . . This was where she had sat down; she had laughed, had run her fingers over the keyboard. There he had embraced her – a moment of heaven, an altar, which still seemed fragrant with the smell of her fair skin.

O Godelieve! She was the only light in his sombre life, the bright little bell in which he had represented her then and which rose above the dark flood of the other bells. Once more, now that his days were darkening for good, the little bell alone rose above and brightened, for a while, the great waters of his sadness. He knew it well, knew which key he had to touch to make it ring out.

It was Godelieve's soul returning. Joris became obsessed with his loss of her, with a new desire to see her again, to win her back, perhaps. He had no idea how he had come to start thinking of her again, imagining her, speaking her name without knowing why, that sweet name of litanies, the name of which *God* was the root and in which it seemed that the name of God was beautified.

He thought he had almost forgotten her.

Once more she haunted him, even appearing in his dreams. There are these mysterious returns, feelings reawakened, the heart's anniversaries. Perhaps some instinct had alerted him? What if Godelieve were unhappy, poorly adjusted to the Beguinage, and were thinking of leaving the order? In that case she would be coming back and the thought had only occurred to him because she was already on her way.

V

Joris had not forgotten the vow Godelieve had made to go on pilgrimage to the Procession of the Penitents in Veurne if her great fear of a possible pregnancy should turn out to be unfounded. Since her prayer had been granted, it was almost certain she would go. Joris could bear it no longer, he wanted to leave, to see her again, even if only from a distance, even if she were dead for him in her Beguine's veil and dress. No matter! To see her, to be seen! The past could be reawakened, their eyes meet again, their lives be restored to them and take wing together in a flight without end.

The religious procession takes place every year on the last Sunday in July, as it has done since the beginning, since 1650 when the Capuchins instituted it. Together with one of his comrades, a soldier from Lorraine called Mannaert, who was garrisoned at Veurne, stole a consecrated host. He then burnt it in the hope of using the ashes to help him open all sorts of locks and to make him invulnerable in battle. But there was no protection against the blows from God. He was arrested and burnt alive with his accomplice as a punishment for his sacrilege, which was compounded by his mysterious operations, which the judges saw as works of satanism and magic.

In expiation the Capuchins established this Procession of Penitence. A sodality was set up to organise it and it has been held every year since then.

Nothing has changed over the years. There is the same ceremonial, the same composition of scenes and groups, the same hoods with the same holes framing the eyes of successive generations, the same text, a poem in harsh, throaty Flemish verses, declaimed in the streets and filling people's mouths from century to century. Borluut had never seen this extraordinary procession in which the ancient ways of Flanders attest their continued vigour.

It was the evening before the Procession that he went to the little dead town on the western edge of the land. He had come above all because of Godelieve, as if he were staking his life, his future, on one last chance, but the town captured his attention, distracted him from himself for a while.

Everything was unified in a harmony of melancholy. Even the sign of the hotel where he was staying was 'The Noble Rose', a royal sign looking back nostalgically to inns of the past. His open window framed a centuries-old townscape: the nave, without a bell-tower but rising high with flying buttresses, of Saint Walburga's, and the belfry, octagonal but tapering to a slim campanile. Between the two buildings innumerable crows were wheeling, a dense flock, close to each other, almost touching. They kept flying from the belfry to the church and from the church to the belfry, alighting for a moment, then flying off again, a quivering mass, like leaves in the wind. It was a ceaseless ebb and flow, a black wave in the gold of the evening, constantly changing shape, curving in a scroll, sculpting itself in darkness. There was something inexorable, something fateful about this coming-and-going, like a flock of unworthy thoughts surrounding the church and the bell-tower, trying to enter but never being allowed in.

Joris fell into a daydream, seeing himself in the allegory and what he ought to have been.

In his belfry in Bruges he had opened the window to the black swarm, to evil desires, to voluptuous thoughts. All the crows which, here, were flying round the towers, he bore within him: a commotion of wings, hoarse cries of remorse, the eternal to-and-fro of uncertainty. What a lesson was falling to him, at that moment, from the church and from the belfry, where the cawing of the crows was all outside.

Joris went out, wandered round the town and came to Saint Walburga's by a little esplanade, a sort of quincunx planted with a few old trees, as silent and melancholy as a Beguines' enclosure. The area was grey, with the dampness of a perpetual autumn, as if it were always November there. The leaves seemed scarcely able to cling on to the branches, ready to fall, pale from the shade the high church cast on them. The dilapidated bulk of the church rose up before him: there were blocked doors, blind passages, brickwork entrances sealed with barbarous padlocks which had not been opened for centuries and which led to who knows what crypt or oubliettes.

Greenish glass filled the tall, ogival windows. They were like stretches of water that nothing can make ripple, tremble any more. The musty air had a smell of mildew. The outer walls were covered in large pink and green stains, poisonous tattoos, a polychrome decoration of decay and rain. In the past there had perhaps been a graveyard in the grass. Now it was the marbling of decomposition which lingered on, the chemistry of death which had passed into the stones.

Hovering over all was the weariness of being alive.

Borluut went into the church by now almost drowned in darkness. The same smell of mildew had taken a deep hold. Black-faced statues of the Virgin were wasting away on the altars. They looked as if they had lived and been embalmed in ancient times. That explained the smell of mummies in the naves.

A few candles were burning, making the shadow bleed, here and there, in the chapels, which were closed off by barriers and cluttered up with tinselly decorations, statues, escutcheons and other props for the procession.

Suddenly he saw, in one of the side aisles, the crosses for the penitents to carry. There were hundreds of them, propped against the walls in batches arranged according to size and weight. Some were made of rough wood, as if hewn with an axe, and painted in coarse ochre; others were smaller, black and smooth. The largest were as tall and heavy as a tree; Borluut tried in vain to lift them. Yet on the morrow penitents would come from all over Flanders who would think them less heavy than their sins and would be able to carry them along the streets, barefoot and sweating under their hoods. Each one would choose a cross that matched their sin.

Borluut thought of Godelieve. He could already see her

exhausting herself with a burden which was deliberately too heavy, a double burden, since she would intend to carry *their* sin, the sin of love which belongs to two people.

Which of these crosses would she choose?

Joris was trembling, daunted by all the stacks of crosses in the gloom, upright or lying flat. For them it was the evening rest, the vigil before the drama of the procession. It was as if a graveyard had been on the march – and ended up here. They were like all the different-sized crosses of a graveyard: having left the dead, who are the living of yesterday, to be for a while with the living who are the dead of tomorrow. For that evening alone they were free of the crowd and could rest.

Overcome with this flood of funereal thoughts, Borluut fled, looking for noise, people, different images. He came to the Square, embellished with several fine pieces of architecture, almost a corner of Bruges, on a smaller scale and more modest, but picturesque nevertheless with the façade of an ancient lord's castle and the Town Hall with its open-work peristyle and its slim colonnades. Opposite is the old bell-tower of a church, all the more moving for being unfinished. What beauty there is in interrupted towers, which continue in dream and which we all complete within ourselves!

Unfortunately a fair had been set up in the middle, booths, painted sheets, merry-go-rounds covered in glass beads and glitter with the braying of organs and brass. An absurd anomaly, permitted by the authorities, to mix this funfair with the procession, the clown's pranks with the sacred drama of the Passion. Should the penitents not appear in emptiness and silence? Here once more Borluut took offence at the lack of taste of the modern world, which has no sense of harmony. He told himself he would go to watch the procession elsewhere, in some distant, silent street, where a few tufts of grass growing between the cobbles would be kind to Godlieve's bare feet.

At four o'clock on Sunday afternoon the procession set off. The slow peals of the bells rang out from the belfries of the parish churches. A murmur of voices rose from the town, like the sound of a lock-gate opening somewhere.

Borluut was waiting at an out-of-the-way crossroads. There were only a few people there, thinly scattered and quiet.

He was filled with great agitation, a nervous apprehension which made it impossible for him to stay in one place, from time to time gripping his heart and making it stand still, like a mysterious beast captive inside him.

The moment was coming which had to come. Everything comes so quickly, apart from happiness. He was going to see Godelieve again, but doubtless very much changed, very different with the cornet hiding her hair, another woman almost.

Even supposing he managed to see her and that she saw that he was there, what could he do to take her back, to drag her away from the voluptuous pleasure of penitence, to disengage her from the cross, which also has its arms open?

Joris had no great hopes. He told himself that he had come simply to convince himself that what was past was past.

A joyous cry rent the air; the crowd stirred. The procession appeared.

Heralds in mediaeval costume, doublet and hood, were blowing shrill trumpets. But immediately after them angels appeared, a soothing vision in gowns of pink and blue and iridescent wings; then girls in artless head-dresses carrying escutcheons, placards, emblems. Scenes from the Old Testament followed: Abraham offering up Isaac, Moses in the desert, the eight prophets, the three punishments of David – War, Plague, Famine – followed by his Repentance.

The penitents who had undertaken these roles played them conscientiously and fervently. They were not professionals, but members of the Sodality, men of faith and zeal who, for the forgiveness of their sins and to glorify the Church, agreed to take part in the age-old procession. Their costumes were coarse and gaudy. False beards bristled on faces already fierce and fiery from the crude make-up.

The great originality of the procession of Veurne lies in the fact that the characters do not just walk past, they speak. It is not merely a parade of people in costumes, of *tableaux vivants*, a silent mystery play, it is the authentic divine drama acted out, true-to-life rather than theatrical, with realistic gestures and vehement, sincere declamation. The prophets pass, genuinely foretelling the future; the angels have truly asexual voices which, singing or calling out, flutter and ripple like banderoles.

The illusion was complete.

When the shepherds and magi appeared they were all truly on their way to the manger. With conviction they conversed in loud voices, called out to each other, engaged in discussion, debate, following the age-old text, versified by some canon years ago, which they recite from memory.

The air was filled with the hubbub of their voices, the hoarse dirge of Flemish alexandrines, all the more guttural for coming from the voices of ordinary folk.

It was in the scene of Jesus with the doctors in the Temple that the declamation became sonorous and convincing. The twelve doctors, old men with grey beards and supercilious expressions, were carried away, gesticulating and shouting. Each one had a different, specific character. The third doctor seemed uneasy, conciliatory too. He declared:

> *The prayers of Judah never will be answered,*
> *Until the coming of Him who is to come.*

The tenth doctor was the proud one:

> *Who will see the things I cannot see?*
> *Who, apart from me, is there who seeks?*

Other opinions made themselves heard. The lines rolled out, clashed, voices mingled. It was the sound of a highly-charged debate which it would not take much to turn into an argument. They were all declaiming their lines with convulsive gestures and impassioned tones. All at once Jesus spoke, a gentle child dressed in a linen tunic, his hair as golden as the corn in Flanders:

God gave you ears to hear and yet you hear not.
What is the truth his prophet's words impart?
The praise of God will cure the sore at heart.

And the clear voice continued to flow for a long time. The doctors replied, denied, argued, declared their knowledge innate and infallible. Jesus carried on. Even once he had passed, his clear voice could still be heard alongside the doctors', a thin tributary to the river of their deep basses.

At intervals between these groups, Stations of the Cross were carried past or pulled on carts, carved and painted wooden statues, by an unschooled hand, of the Stable or some other episode from the life of Christ. Crude works of art! They were daubed in garish colours, the red could have been real blood. They looked as if the crowd itself had fashioned them with a naive but miracle-working faith, as if they had been hewn from the tree of the Cross.

Joris watched and listened to the strange procession. It created such an extraordinary regression it abolished all sense of the present and its modern identity, making it contemporary with the great centuries of faith.

Moved and taken out of himself, he gave himself up to the voices and gestures, especially when the group appeared representing Christ's Entry into Jerusalem, a triumphal, diaphanous host, the daughters of Bethphage in muslin veils, caressing the air with their palm leaves, chanting hosannas. The branches rained down in that ethereal spring. Everything was green and white. It was like a garden on the move. The Apostles were in two lines, proclaiming Christ and thanking the crowd in ringing voices. Then he came, mounted on the legendary she-ass, amid the children and virgins. A pure countenance in a halo of light! Where had they found him, this visionary summoned to the role who, for himself, had become Jesus, as he had for everyone around? Was it a man of the people who had this delicate beauty, pensive and emaciated?

It was as if a light burned within him, like a night-light. He had two fingers raised in the gesture of blessing and did not change his posture during the whole of the procession, which lasted two hours. The people around Joris, who knew him well, said that it was a vow he had made. He was a pious man from the town whose face, because of his holiness, always had that otherworldly radiance.

The other events of the passion – the Last Supper and the Garden of Gethsemane – were represented by stations carved in wood which came at intervals, accompanied by a ceaseless throng of penitents, angels and clerics, all declaiming, prophesying, blowing horns, announcing the next scene . . .

Women passed, their arms bare, their dresses low-cut, like courtesans, each holding huge jewels in their hands. An inscription held up by one of the penitents, said, 'Women carrying the jewels of Mary Magdalene.'

Joris was much affected by the disturbing concept, which had something of a lament and of a popular print. Indeed, all the symbols and emblems there were powerful, suggestive ways of putting things in a nutshell, allegories attesting to the Flemish sense of understanding the life of objects.

Christ bearing the Cross, which was the essential scene of the procession, was also preceded by emblems announcing it: angels and penitents passed carrying the lamp, Pilate's basin of water, St Veronica's handkerchief, a sponge, a water-clock, the torn veil of the temple, a hammer, three nails, a crown of thorns. It was, in advance, all the trappings of the Passion, the instruments of torture, the symbols, all the more deeply moving for appearing on their own, as if they signified merely the ornament of a destiny, what determines it and what remains of it.

Soon a violent tumult erupted. The trumpets rang out louder, mingled with cries of impatience and anger. Roman soldiers in scarlet cloaks came prancing along on horseback. There was a flash of lightning which was Longinus's spear. Jews followed, with pikes and other weapons; then the executioners with ladders and torches. The tumultuous procession became congested, furious curses were heard. The whole throng started to speak. Anger suffused the text, sparking off debates and savage onomatopoeia, a pandemonium of voices and instruments. Christ passed by, bent under the weight of his heavy cross. He fell. The cries of rage increased, the actors in the grip of a fury that seemed real. Some rushed up and jostled Christ, forcing him to take up his cross again, aided by Simon of Cyrene, and continue on his way to Calvary. The Man-God was pale, truly sweating in mortal fear.

The one who was playing Christ bearing the cross was not the same as the one who had taken the role of Christ entering Jerusalem, but he resembled him, though slightly less thin and not as young. It was another moving feature to see this Christ with, basically, the same face, but changed and grown old in such a short time. He was weakening, starting to stumble for his third fall. The uproar started again, completely uncontrolled this time. The Roman soldiers and the Jews were seized with a wild fury. It was as if the storm itself were blowing the trumpets. Wooden rattles joined in, grating as if they were crushing bones. The hunting horns were in full cry. Megaphones blared out mournful appeals. Vinegar to wet the sponge dripped out of the trumpets.

At that moment the executioners intervened, treating Jesus harshly.

Women of the people lining the pavement started to cry.

Joris, too, had been moved by the raw violence, the honesty of the performance. It had almost made him forget Godelieve, forget that he had only made the pilgrimage there in order to see her again, if only for a moment, in the procession where the penitents following Christ were also carrying crosses.

Now they came, spectres in mourning, humbling themselves, ghosts, their eyes the only points of brightness. It was harrowing: a long cortège of shadows. This time silence had come flooding in. Not a sound, not a cry. A silence all the more sinister for being black. There is the white silence of the Beguines' workrooms; it is sweet. Here was a black silence that strikes terror to the heart, slipping past like water, as full of pitfalls as the night. At first all that could be made out was a tangle of crosses, all the raised arms of the crosses of a graveyard. All with their dead.

Hundreds of penitents were walking in the procession, all barefoot on the hard cobbles, the only reminder of their humanity beneath their homespun robes which rendered them all similar and anonymous. Yet their eyes shone, burned in the holes of their hoods. They were the will-o'-the-wisps of this morass of sin. Only a few faces were exposed to public gaze, those of penitents belonging to religious orders, because it was impossible to put on the robe and hood over their monk's habit or nun's cornet, which they must never take off. Moreover their penitence would be all the more edifying and expiatory for being public.

Fervently Joris searched, scrutinised, scoured the confused and, because of the robes and the crosses, almost uniform throng. Like bees gathering pollen, his eyes flew, fluttered over all the faces that were not concealed. He did not have enough eyes and it seemed then as if his eyes had given birth, multiplied, becoming the innumerable eyes of a crowd in order to be able to see everything at once and to find Godelieve. Was there no longer a current flowing between them that would enable them to recognise, sense each other at a distance, attract each other?

All at once Joris started to tremble. Yes! Godelieve was there. But how changed, very pale, no longer herself. She was walking in the last rows, a little behind the others because of a penitent who required a large empty space round his ostentatious pilgrimage, bearing an enormous cross beneath which he was faltering, dragging it along like the sails of a windmill.

Godelieve was following him, as exhausted as he was under the cross she had chosen, smaller but still too heavy for her. Was that the punishment for the double sin, the weight her sin would have had if it had borne fruit?

Seeing her again, Joris was reminded of her vow, of the motive for her vow. Godelieve was walking, barefoot like the rest, resolute though bowed, as if she intended to continue walking like that until she came to her tomb, for which she was already carrying the cross. How she was changed! Was it the Beguine's habit, the severe coif tight round her hair, which could not be seen? Joris felt the tears come to his eyes when he remembered those honey-coloured tresses. Was it the melancholy of a life into which she had thrown herself in the immediate aftermath of a catastrophe, perhaps without vocation?

Hope sprang up inside him. He moved forward, craned his neck. A few steps more and he would hold out his arms, risk everything, push through the rows, enter the cortège of ghosts to take her back, to drag her by force from the cross on which she was crucifying herself.

Godelieve saw him. Immediately she turned away. It was as if she had seen the devil himself. Her face fell, her eyes closed. She remained like that, her eyelids down, like a corpse. She was already past. Her pale face had gleamed for a moment, like the moon on the sea, then a wave of humanity had swept on, blotting it out; others followed. Joris continued to look for her beyond the backwash. He clung on to his hope. She had recognised him. Now she would be thinking, remembering perhaps, prey to renewed temptation, feeling in her flesh their old embraces, their smouldering kisses, their unforgettable love. It could all begin again. He would go away with her, somewhere, anywhere, to the ends of the earth.

He called out to her, 'Godelieve! Godelieve!' as if to exorcise her, release her from her possession by God, cast the spell of his own love over her, as if her name were a sacramental word, an all-powerful magic formula.

Trembling, he rushed off to find her again, at another point in the town, for the procession had a long itinerary, extending the ambulant play over two hours, declaiming the same text, repeating the same scenes. He caught up with the procession. Everything passed once more: the Prophets, Abraham, the idyll of the manger, the painted Stations of the Cross, appearing to come to life with the jolts of the men carrying them, the Disputation with the Doctors, the Entry into Jerusalem, Christ Bearing the Cross. A confused vision, a nightmare of shouts and smoke. Joris could not see any details. He waited for Godelieve.

She appeared, more weary and more pale, her eyes still closed, afraid of seeing him again, not wanting to see him again. Now she was holding her cross in front of her, clasping it to her. She had barricaded her body behind it.

At the same moment an angel preceding the banner of the Sodality started to chant, in a voice worthy of the Last Judgment:

> *Too long, o man, your sinful ways have lasted.*
> *Time flies, alas, your time on earth below.*
> *Take heed, o man, and pray and save your soul.*

It was like an annunciation from beyond the world, a song poured out from the very edge of eternity, a warning that death was on its way. Joris heard it and felt his miserable love wither inside him, die inside him . . .

At that moment a heavenly sight burst upon him, making him feel ashamed. It was the religious procession, which follows the penitents and which he had not seen the first time. White muslin fluttered, the enchantment of dawn after the storm and the night-dark hoods. Virgins, members of various orders, altar boys robed in red, priests, clerics in gold dalmatics that blazed like stained-glass windows. Carried along on the air were snowstorms of roses, garlands of hymns with the scales of the sopranos, the plainchant of the deacons, deciphered from their antiphonies. And the canopy appeared, surrounded by torchbearers and thurifers swirling their silver censers in a jingle of chains. As one, all the bystanders fell to their knees, brought together in the faith by the blue ribbons of the incense.

Joris was carried away. He knelt as well, prayed, worshipped, becoming part of the crowd's acquiescence. For a while he lost himself in the ancient faith of Flanders and forgot Godelieve.

But in the evening, when he went back to his room in the hotel to get ready to leave, he felt alone and weary unto death. Memories of the Procession of Penitents came to mind. His destiny was fixed irrevocably. He had not succeeded in establishing contact with Godelieve. There would be no consolation. He did not even have a handkerchief such as Saint Veronica's. His career was ruined. He was about to return to his joyless home, where he would live out the rest of his days between his regret for Godelieve and his horror of Barbara. At that moment, framed in the open window, he saw again the innumerable crows ceaselessly flying from the church to the belfry, from the belfry to the church, a swarm tossed to and fro, an ebb and flow of wings, a black wave breaking on itself, turning in the air, constantly starting again. Was it not an image of his future? Black thoughts wheeling back and forth between two joys that were closed to him.

VI

In the belfry Borluut found a refuge, a dream world where he could forget. Once more, every time he climbed up there he had the feeling he was leaving behind his troubles, himself and the world. It was a spell that never failed to work. Hardly had he started to climb the spiral staircase, than he suddenly felt at peace. In the impenetrable gloom he could no longer see his wounded soul. The wind blew in from the open sea, came down to meet him, to greet him, sweeping across his face, waking him to a new existence in which everything else disappeared like a nightmare.

He withdrew to the tower every day now, spending long hours there, even when it was not required by the carillon. It became his true abode, his place of voluntary exile. How fortunate he was that they had not also removed him from his position as carillonneur. It would be the death of him to have to spend all his time among people. He was so different from them. He had become too much accustomed to seeing things from a higher vantage point than them, as they must be viewed from eternity. What had he been thinking to try and bring about a reign of beauty? His town had banished him, in a sense, for trying to impose his ideal on it and for not thinking in the same way as it did. Now he was alone.

In his solitary refuge he felt a kind of intoxication, a darkly voluptuous pleasure. Was not the belfry solitary as well, rising above the dwellings below? The belfry was taller than they were, had risen higher in the conquest of the air. Climbing it, Borluut was also raising himself up, becoming the belfry himself, surrounding himself with it like a suit of armour that fitted him. Oh, the solitary joys of a pride that towers above the world below and looks into the far distance.

Autumn returned, autumn which is the season of mist in Flanders. Borluut rejoiced in it. It increased his isolation in the tower, new curtains thickening round him and hiding the world, which was starting to become abhorrent to him. The only thing that, in the distance, still attracted him, communicated with him, was nature, eternal in its monotony of plains, trees and sky. He no longer wanted to see the town, spread round the foot of the tower. He had suffered too much there. Moreover he no longer recognised it, already disfigured by structures that did not belong, modern intrusions and the sin of vanity increasing inside it.

Bruges had been taken over by others. Like Godelieve, it had left him.

Thank goodness for the late-autumn fog which at the moment was spreading its blanket over all these loves that were now a thing of the past. Borluut shut himself away in double isolation. To the prison of stone was added the prison of mist.

All that held him captive now was the wide horizon.

Everything was unified in a renunciation of self, a soft, resigned fusion. The flocks of sheep, frequent in the countryside around, appeared as nothing more than a little additional vapour, which had gathered at one point and was going to disperse. Even the sun became anaemic, turned the colour of pewter and disappeared amid diaphanous banks of tulle. The town as well, enveloped in a layer of mist, receded, losing solidity and colour, and ceased to be. All that was left of it were a few drifts of smoke from the invisible roofs which, docile tributaries of the mist, soon gave up.

Borluut was part of this collective effacement. The autumn mists and the smoke pervaded him, too, as he watched their silent motions from the belfry above. Everything blurred inside him, misted over, erased itself.

In the pale flatlands some windmills were just visible, black crosses looking as if they were exorcising the mist, which avoided them, drew back, afraid. Borluut often sent his eyes travelling from mill to mill, counting the crosses. They reminded him of the crosses in the Procession of the Penitents. Were they not the same ones, now dispersed? They were scattered over the land, taking him as far as Veurne, which could be just made out, away to the west, close to the sea ever shimmering on the line of the horizon.

Borluut sought out Veurne. He sought out Diksmuide as well and Godelieve's face returned, piercing the mist . . .

However autumn was coming to a close. The windmills too paled, were absorbed into the mist. There were no more crosses to remind him, and no more memories.

Borluut would spend hours listless and drawn in on himself, with no regrets and no hope, alone in the glass chamber of the belfry. The soul reflected in the season! On the carillon he only played wan melodies. Muted tunes, white notes the colour of the mist itself, colourless sounds, as if the bells were made of cotton wool and were shedding a slow downdrift of flakes and carded wool, a scattering of down from the pillow of the child he never had.

VII

What Borluut had foreseen happened. It was his guiding hand alone that had maintained the unity and discipline of his vision. He had been on his way to accomplishing the miracle of creating a harmony of beauty for a whole town. As soon as he had been dismissed, the sacrilege commenced. The man who was named as his replacement was an obscure and ignorant architect who quickly became a willing tool of the aldermen's every whim.

Borluut felt his dream was over. It was the end of the beauty of Bruges as he had conceived it, as a harmonious whole. Every day the dissonance increased, the profanation, the vandalism, the anachronisms.

The town had given up.

The fashion for restoration had become general, but not at all in the way in which Borluut had started it. After having neglected the old façades and allowing them to deteriorate, people were now going too far in the opposite direction, reviving, repairing, modifying, decorating and renovating them. In fact, what they were doing was reconstructing them. They were new buildings, parodies of the past, facsimiles of old architecture like the copies of ancient buildings in concrete and painted canvas you see in exhibitions. Neatness and tidiness were the order of the day. People wanted their brickwork nice and pink, and nice and new, light-oak window frames, crisp, clear carving. Out went the blurred faces – the heads of angels, monks, demons – which hardly break the surface, having withdrawn a little into the walls over the centuries. Out, too, went the black dust, the severe patina or ornamentation of bricks that had been allowed to mature. People wanted houses that were 'as good as new'. A barbarous craze, like that of having old pictures scraped clean, repainted and revarnished.

At the same time some architectural curiosities disappeared, their owners believing the sites could be put to more profitable use; picturesque districts were altered. The face of a town can change so quickly. Demolition, reconstruction, watercourses filled in, tramways laid. Oh, the horror of the noise, the whistles, steam and jolts defiling the nobility of silence!

A collective profanation! The brutal utilitarianism of the modern age! No doubt in Bruges, too, they would straighten the streets, shorten the connections. And it would be even worse if the Seaport project were realised. It had already been decided, according to the plan submitted, that the Ostend Gate would disappear, the tower and rooms that were such an ornament to the town, a delightful buckle fastening the belt of the ramparts. It was to be sacrificed to widen the road leading to the new docks.

As long ago as 1862 and 1863 they had already knocked down St Catherine's Tower then the Byre Tower, survivors of the nine towers which had originally stood guard on the threshold, proclaiming the rule of art. Now it was the end.

'The town of the past, the town I had made, is in its death throes,' Borluut said to himself. 'Its splendid walls are going to fall. I alone preserve, I alone carry in my heart everything that was Bruges. Soon I will be all that is left of the town here below.'

Borluut lamented the fate of Bruges as he lamented his own.

There were other torments that were sapping his strength. Barbara continued to be irritable, sometimes responding vehemently. He hardly saw her, only at meals. She now lived completely apart. She had retired to a different floor of the house, the second storey, which she had appropriated for herself in order to be alone and free. Sometimes she went out on a whim, wandered round for hours on end, only returning when it was dark. At others she shut herself away and plunged into long periods of nervous exhaustion which would end in fits of tears and shrill sobs.

Joris could do nothing to help, feeling himself so far away from her. Anyway, she had completely withdrawn from him. Since she had discovered his unfaithfulness she had not lain with him. She felt a kind of fear of him, a physical revulsion. It seemed to her that if she gave herself to him now, she would be the one committing adultery, as if Joris belonged more to Godelieve than to her. All carnal relations between them had ceased.

Borluut resigned himself to his life as a quasi-widower, to a return to celibacy with no way out. Why had he not done something to remedy the situation? He went over the reasons: for a long time, despite the outbursts, the quarrels, the scenes, he could not prevent himself from feeling bound to Barbara, to the body he still desired, to her too-red lips; later, after all the squabbles, all the insults, which wearied him and released him from her, he could have left her, but Barbara, with her rabid Catholicism, would never have consented to a divorce (and he would not have found any *legal* grounds); later still, when he was in love with Godelieve, that would have been the time to make a clean break, to abandon his home and set one up elsewhere; but then it had been the town that had held him back, his commitment to the beauty of Bruges, his poem in stone, which was still awaiting completion; his regret at leaving it unfinished would have followed him everywhere with the persistence of remorse; finally, when he had fallen from favour and was free in that respect, ready to go anywhere, he had been unable to win back Godelieve, who already belonged to God and to eternity.

Thus everything had conspired against him. He had never had control over events, over his own destiny. And now there seemed to be no point in leaving Barbara. Where would he go if not to even greater solitude? He felt incapable of making any kind of fresh start. He was weary. His life was a failure, with no hope of remedy.

Here at least he still had the belfry which provided an inalienable refuge. More than ever he found himself climbing the grisaille stairs to the glass chamber, to the granaries of silence, the dormitories of the bells, the bells that never dozed off, confidants he could trust, friends who would comfort him.

Only the Bell of Lust aroused him once again. He had almost forgotten it. It was lying in wait for him. His long period of continence left him open to its onslaught. The temptation of the breasts he saw once more, tips thrusting out, hardened in the metal as if in eternal desire! And the buttocks too, tensed, arching under the kisses. He became obsessed with the flesh to the point of madness. He scrutinised the bronze for the precise details of the lechery. He took part in it. He was living amid a frozen orgy. He recalled the thrill when the obscene bell had revealed to him his carnal love for Barbara. How he had dreamt of her body, still unknown, as he looked up the bell as he would have looked up her dress. A bell full of sensual pleasures and which was Barbara's dress. It had shattered his life, Barbara's cold dress, as hard as the bronze, only giving the appearance of passion, a frozen simulation of pleasures which came to nothing. Oh, the evil spell cast by the Bell of Lust! At least Joris had been on his guard the second time. He was afraid of it when he was in love with Godelieve.

He had even stopped her approaching it, on the day when she had climbed the bell-tower with him . . .

Since his love-life was non-existent, he became the lover of all the women on the bell. It was to him that they were giving themselves. He was living in a whirl of lips and breasts. As he bent down for a closer look, his face touched the icy bronze, giving him a burning sensation, as if he had kissed skin that was on fire. He embraced every sin.

When he came back down from the tower, he would spend a long time wandering round the town, late at night, feverish with a desire for bare flesh. The obscene scenes of the bell followed him, taking shape in enlarged, living images. He would stay out late strolling along dubious alleys, towards the working-class districts, on the lookout for some unexpected encounter, a lighted window, perhaps, which some woman, unhappy in love, might open – all the things we do at twenty, tormented by the sap rising in our veins.

VIII

By isolating himself, by constantly taking refuge in the bell-tower, Borluut came to relish death alone.

From the top of the belfry the town appeared more dead, that is, more beautiful. The people disappeared from the streets, the noises died away before they reached him. The Market Square stretched out, grey and bare. The canals were at rest, their waters not going anywhere; they were bereft of boats, redundant, apparently living on after their own death.

The houses along the canals were closed up, as if there had been a death in each one.

A funereal impression, the whole town in harmony! Borluut was exultant. That was how he had wanted Bruges to be. He had only devoted himself to restoring, perpetuating all these old stones because it gave him the sense, the joy of carving his own tomb.

He had only sought and secured the carillon the better to celebrate and proclaim the death of the town to the four horizons. Even now, when he played, running his hands over the keyboard, it made him feel as if he were gathering flowers, tearing them, with great effort, from resistant stems, persevering all the same, bringing in his harvest, pillaging the flower-beds of the bells and then pouring baskets of petals, bouquets of sound, garlands of iron, over the town in its coffin.

Was that not the way it ought to be? The beauty of Bruges lay in being dead. From the top of the belfry it appeared completely dead to Borluut. He did not want to go back down ever again. His love for the town was greater, was endless. From now on it was a kind of frenzy, his final sensual pleasure. Constantly climbing high above the world, he started to enjoy death. There is danger in rising too high, into the unbreathable air of the summits. Disdain for the world, for life itself brings its own punishment. It was doubtless for that reason, and because of a clear warning from his instinct, that he had felt he was taking the key to his tomb when he had been handed the key to the tower.

Henceforth, when he returned from the bell-tower he had the impression he was leaving death. How tiresome to come back to the world, to life! And the ugliness of human faces! The hostility of the people he encountered! Stupidity and vice openly flaunted!

More and more the carillonneur wandered about aimlessly. He did not know where to go, no longer having anything to do, incapable of coming to any decision, of exercising his will. He found the life he had resumed tedious, like Lazarus brought back from the dead and still benumbed by the shroud. His steps faltered. He stumbled over the cobbles as if he were making his way across the humps and bumps of a graveyard. The fact was that coming down from the bell-tower *he continued to walk in death*.

IX

All of a sudden the town decked itself with flags. Telegrams had come from the capital announcing that parliament had finally passed the Seaport of Bruges project. They were no longer simply hoping, expecting possible delays – the millions they needed had been voted, the work of destruction could begin.

Immediately the streets were filled with jubilation, a Sunday, holiday mood, a feeling of joy spread by the crowd, unaware that they were happy because the reign of beauty was about to come to an end.

There had to be public rejoicing, an impressive demonstration to thank the government. At once a notice signed by the burgomaster and the aldermen was posted summoning all the societies of the town to form a huge procession that evening, with music and torches; at the same time the people were asked to put out their flags and Chinese lanterns.

They were to assemble in the Market Square at eight o'clock.

Borluut was informed that he would be on duty from the same time. The Victory Bell, which was hung on a lower floor of the tower, would ring the whole time, would not cease its heroic gallop through the air. The carillon, too, was to let its peal ring out, a whole concert that would last as long as the procession.

At first Borluut was indignant and upset. He had been utterly defeated, all his efforts, his long campaign, had had no effect whatsoever; in the parliament, with its narrow outlook, there was no one to speak up for art. Electoral interest had prevailed and that was that. And then Bruges had renounced its fame as a dead town. He was devastated, and now they were demanding songs of joy from him, his participation in the blind jubilation of the populace. He thought of refusing, of resigning on the spot rather than climb up to the belfry and exhaust himself at the keyboard for hours on end, making his noble bells sing out at the tops of their voices in joyous peals when his soul, like theirs, was in mourning.

But he feared the reproaches he would hear from Barbara and dreaded the days to come when he would feel at a loss without the refuge of the bell-tower, the dormitories of the bells, where he could go to let his sorrows sleep awhile.

Towards eight he went to the belfry. It was the first time he had climbed up in the evening. The caretaker of the Draper's Hall gave him a lantern and he started to go up the stairs. The sensation was even stranger than during the day. In the daylight he was so used to it that he climbed almost unconsciously, drawn on, as if in a calm whirlwind, by the twisting staircase. Now, with the black of night superimposed on the obscurity of the tower, it was pitch-dark. He could no longer sense, far above, the bleaching of the gloom by air coming in through an arrow-slit or a gap in the masonry. Borluut stumbled and had to hold on to the smooth rope, which serves as a banister, hanging, slightly slack, around the pillar, like a snake round a tree trunk. The light from the lantern splashed over the walls, making it look as if there were patches of blood here and there. Beasts fled before it; they had always lived in the gloom and took the glare for a flash of lightning which had pierced the tower, pierced their eyes. It had all the ambiguity of chiaroscuro. Borluut saw his shadow preceding him and then, immediately after, following, moving, climbing the walls, squashing itself over the concave ceiling. His shadow had gone crazy. Was he keeping up his steady ascent?

Reality returned. As he approached the platform the noise of the crowd in the square below, like the murmur of water, came streaming down the stairs as if they were a sluice. He recalled that he had heard the same murmuring before, the day of the contest, they day when he had been victorious. On that day his soul had imposed itself on the crowd. He had made it understand art, melancholy, the past, the heroic.

He had transubstantiated it! He had lived inside it. Now it was going to live inside him, impose its soul on him in its turn, that is its ignorance, its triviality, its cruelty.

The Market Square was already packed. The procession was being organised, was about to move off. A confusion of bands, bouquets, banners and torches. All the societies – the choirs, the sports clubs, the political bodies, the Seaport-of-Bruges Association – set off, one after the other, all wearing some badge, a cocade or an armband, some emblem to identify the group. Elaborate invention abounded. The members of the Circle of St Christopher were wearing luminous hats, each representing a letter to create a celebratory chronogram. Those of the gymnastic societies strutted along in jerseys as unsightly as swimming costumes and carried canes, ridiculous weapons, which they brandished as they marched in step. They were followed by the cycling club, their machines decorated with paper lanterns and some made to look like boats as an allegory of the future shipping and prosperity of the port. A parade of all the vulgarity, the limited imagination of the crowd.

The carillonneur at the top of the tower was cut to the heart. What was happening to the dead town? The graveyard was being desecrated by a carnival. What had the noble swans to say to that? Borluut imagined there was not a single one of them left on the leaden waters of the canals. Doubtless they had fled, sought refuge in the outskirts, so as not to know, to preserve a little silence, to cry amid the water lilies.

Suddenly Borluut, leaning out to have one last look, to drink his fill of the desolation, was shocked by an even more unseemly sight, causing him a distress that was more personal. He saw the company of the Archers of Saint Sebastian, represented by a fairly large number of its members, shaming its venerable banner, the medals and insignia worn by the King of the Shoot, all its history, in these ridiculous saturnalia. And yet for a long time the Guild had opposed the Seaport-of-Bruges project. What is more, Borluut was still the Guildmaster; it would have been courteous of them to show more consideration and not disavow him in public.

In its turn the old guild was giving up, denying its past and the town, supporting the vile ideal. For Borluut it was the final blow. Henceforward he would be completely alone.

He no longer wanted to see or hear anything of the vulgar display that was going on at ground level.

He threw himself into his task, plunging his hands into the keys, as if into the sea. He played. The Victory Bell was already sounding. It was leading the way, pitching and tossing in the air. The whole flotilla of the notes of the carillon followed, dispersed, flew in the wind and the stars.

The carillonneur played frenetically so that nothing of the scenes in the street would reach him, calling on all the bells, from the biggest which, usually, only came in to punctuate a melody, as the windmills punctuate the plain, to the smallest, tiniest, childlike bells whose sparrow-like twittering created a cloud of noise, a strident chorus in which no individual bell could be heard. A huge orchestra, a final unison. The belfry was vibrating, creaking, as if all the bells, having decided to leave their joists, their monotonous dormitories, and go elsewhere, were already tumbling down the staircase. The carillonneur was carried away. He hit the keys with his hands and feet, hung onto the iron rods that raise the clappers, working himself up into a frenzy as he made the bells ring, as if he were in the midst of a battle between his sounds and the noise from below.

Exhausted, he had to rest for a few moments between two pieces. The cries were heard once more, the murmur as of water, the demented shrillness of the fanfares. The procession continued on its noisy way, trailing its glitter, its stupidity, its gaudy snake, its funereal fancy-dress frolics through the gloomy maze of the streets.

It went on for several hours. The carillonneur, resigned, kept on playing, mocking the irony of fate which forced him to make the bells sing, to sprinkle the town with joyful airs, while his dream had died that very day. He thought of actors who, sometimes, have to amuse the audience on the day their child has died.

Later, when he returned home, Borluut was confronted with a dramatic scene. The servants, still agitated and trembling, were going to and fro like madwomen. The hall was covered in stones, debris and broken glass. They told him that, after the procession, some groups had continued to walk round the town. They had heard them approaching, singing Flemish songs, worked up and a little drunk already. Then, as they passed the house, one of them started up a racket, shouts and shrill whistles, insults and curses. Loud voices cried, 'Down with Borluut!' There were many of them and they were organised. There was no doubt that it had been premeditated, that they were obeying orders. Amid their shouts a tinkling crash was heard, the sharp sound of all the windows breaking and falling to the ground, splintering. A volley of stones had been thrown, flying though the windows and into all the rooms, breaking ornaments and mirrors, scattering debris over the whole of the house.

Borluut looked around, aghast. It was as if there had been a war. The house looked as if it was in ruins.

His immediate suspicion was that it was an act of vengeance by Farazyn, who, since Godelieve's refusal, and especially since his opposition to the Seaport project, of which Farazyn had been the prime mover, had been unremitting in the hatred with which he had pursued him. It would have been easy, this time, to stir up some of the common people against him by representing him as a public enemy, as an undesirable who had almost wrecked the project, the glorious vote in favour of which they were celebrating that day.

Barbara appeared at the top of the stairs, simmering with fury. In order to avoid a scene in front of the servants, Joris went into one of the ground-floor rooms. The floor was covered in stones and shards of glass. They had even thrown in some excrement. Barbara came in, livid. Her too-red lips looked like a wound, as if she had been struck in the face by a stone and was bleeding. She was dishevelled, her hair flopping against her back like angry waves.

'Look what's happened to us now. It's all your fault. You behaved like a madman.'

Joris realised what a state she was in, her nerves jangling, a paroxysm of rage imminent. He managed to contain himself and tried to get to the door and escape. Barbara, exasperated even more by his calm, which was nothing but indifference and disdain, threw herself at him, seized him by the arms and shouted into his face, 'I've had enough! I'll kill you!'

Joris had already heard the horrible threat once before. Beside himself, he freed himself from her grasp and pushed her away roughly. It drove her wild and she started to scream. All the old insults reappeared, raining down on him as if she wanted to stone him with words after the crowd had stoned him in effigy.

Joris went to his bedroom. Everywhere was the same devastation, projectiles had been thrown in through every window. He remembered he had looked on a similar scene before, recalling the room where the old quarrel had taken place, the room in which Barbara, when she discovered Godelieve's treachery, had also broken the mirror and the furniture, the room no one had entered since and which had remained in the same state, like the room of someone who has died . . . Now all the rooms were like that one. It was contagious, perhaps, the ills of the one calling them down on the others. Now every one was a dead person's room. They were all dead. The whole house was dead.

Borluut wished he was dead too.

He seemed to have been shown *the order of things*. Immediately he felt it was settled, irrevocably.

Death itself had beckoned him, had hunted him out in his own home. The stones, the murderous stones, had searched him out. After all, had not the crowd condemned him to death? He valiantly accepted their verdict. And above all let there be no delay! He was ready, he would give himself up the very next day, at dawn. He did not want to see his home by the light of day again, desecrated as it was, like a ruin, all its mirrors broken, repeating the ill omen from one room to another. Nor did he want to meet Barbara again, who, out of spite or because of her ruined nerves, had gone too far this time in offering physical violence amid the worst insults and threats.

At that moment he heard her above his head, on the upper floor, pushing trunks around, emptying wardrobes, once more preparing – or pretending to prepare – to leave, as she did after every scene. He listened to the sounds coming through the ceiling and began to pace up and down the room, getting carried away as he talked out loud to himself:

'I'm the one who'll leave first, and on a journey from which there's no return. I'm tired, tired of it all. I've had enough. Tomorrow will be another horrible day: more scenes with Barbara; or she'll run off, without any idea of where she's going, like a lost sheep; and the mess everywhere, the stones, the revolting filth; and the petty annoyances, the formalities with the police, with the law; and, all around, the cruel laughter of the town when the news gets out. No, I cannot face that day, not at any price! I'll be dead first.'

Reasoning thus with himself, Joris had calmed down. He was even astonished that he had made up his mind so quickly and so clearly. Doubtless it was something that had been building up inside him for a long time. During the last few weeks he had acquired too much of a taste for death when he went up the bell-tower. It was like an initiation, a presentiment, the shadow of the goal he was approaching already falling across him. Now he was going to reach it. What peace suddenly spread inside him once he had made up his mind! Once chosen, a destiny takes possession of us in advance. We already are what we will be.

Joris had entered upon the serenity of death. He went back over his life. He recalled far-off times, episodes from childhood, his mother's caresses, a few details, the things that flash before our eyes in the moment of death, things which sum up our life. He also thought of Godelieve, the faint pink flush of a unique dawn; again he relived the sweetness of the beginning, their secret marriage in the church.

The church! He suddenly saw God again. God appeared to him, spoke to him, was his witness, almost his judge. Joris defended himself. He believed in God. But in a sublime God, not in the God of simple folk, the God who forbids them to kill themselves because they would do it without discernment, but in God the *All-intelligent* who would understand. He worshipped him, he humbled himself before him, rediscovered the faded prayers, a slightly jumbled mosaic that he put together again.

Again he thought of Godelieve. It was time to destroy her letters, the last memento, relics he had preserved, a packet of consolation he had kept until now. He reread them, conjuring up the past with the aftertaste of their kisses, the ghostly fragrance of dried flowers, the bitter residue of tears – all the sadness contained in old letters where the ink is fading and seems to be returning to nothingness. Then he tore them up and burnt them.

There was nothing left tying him to the world, to life.

Now, since he was going to die, no scandal. An invisible death that would be like a disappearance. If his body could not be found! Would the belfry not be the best place? He now understood perfectly why, when he had been handed the key after the contest, he had felt he was taking the key to his tomb. His soul *knew* already. It had trembled at the sign which created the inevitable. There could be no doubt that from that moment on his destiny had been brought to a standstill. The bell-tower became a premature tomb where he was to busy himself for a few days before the long sleep.

That, then, was where he would die. And a clean death . . . no blood, no firearm, no knife. A rope does the job silently and is more certain. Joris went to fetch one and examined it coldly, testing its strength, then put it in his pocket in order to avoid any hesitation or a renewed debate with himself in the morning, at dawn.

Thus settled, he waited for day to break, at peace and strong, already feeling a little avenged, satisfied at his bequest of remorse to Barbara, to the town; happy above all to be dying in the bell-tower which, in the future, would cast a more sombre shadow, truly the shadow of a tomb, a gesture of reproach, over the grey square.

X

Dawn broke, hesitated, then spread over the sky, greenish and
sad. As soon as it was light, Borluut left the house, furtively, so
as to be neither heard nor held up, but steadfast in his intention. The bell-tower immediately rose up before him, the
implacable tower that can be seen from the end of every street.
The belfry was waiting; it was calling. Borluut did not look for
an escape. He even took the most direct route. He went along
beside a canal, across a bridge. Bruges was asleep. All was
empty, drab, silent, still shivering from the rainy night. How
melancholy a bare city is, at dawn! It makes one think of an
epidemic, when everyone has fled. It makes one think of
death.

Borluut kept going. He was not interested in anything any
more, not even in the Town, for which he had had such an
enduring love. He walked through it, already indifferent, as
one is to a country one is leaving for good. He did not look at
anything, neither the façades, nor the towers, nor the reflections in the water, nor the old roofs, monochrome in the dull
morning light.

Is it not strange how quickly one can become detached
from everything? How empty life appears when one is close
to death!

When he reached the bell-tower he entered with the dawn,
and just as pale. The staircase was trembling. The light was
descending to meet the man who was going up, it was like the
meeting, the final struggle of darkness and light. Borluut
climbed. With each step he seemed to be leaving life a little
more, starting a little more to die. He was not thinking of
anything any longer, neither of Barbara, nor the town, nor
himself. The only thing in his mind was the 'act'.

However, climbing the stairs seemed to take a long time. It
was icy cold. The musty smell of the walls grew worse. It was
like being in a graveyard. Noises could be heard, bats, birds

flapping blindly against the ceiling. Also the damp slither of animals that only come out at night quickly scuttling back into some dark hole. A proliferation of hidden life was crawling, flying, clustering round Borluut, as if he already *smelt of death*.

Fear coursed across his skin, as real as a touch. His flesh trembled, while his spirit remained resolute and calm. Instinct awoke, protested, but tended to dither, not casting doubt on the events or the decisive reasons. Its skill lies in questioning the act alone, whether to carry it out or not carry it out, but solely on physical grounds. A clever ploy of instinct, which causes a person to hesitate before throwing themselves into the canal because they don't like the idea of the cold water and which, in Borluut's case, suggested the horrors of the viscous trails of creatures going to feast on the corpse.

Borluut shuddered. It was his moment of weakness, his sweat of agony on the Mount of Olives. He halted, struck with anguish. But the stairs kept turning quickly, showing no mercy, offering no respite, pulling him up into their short spirals. Borluut went on, still determined but weakening in the flesh. A little further on he stumbled. Despite being accustomed to the steps, he had to hold on to the rope that serves as a banister, hung round the pillar of the stairs like a snake round a tree. The Serpent of Temptation! The rope was a further temptation, implying that he had hesitated. Had he not chosen it as the instrument of his death? Now, resuming his hold of the rope, it was as if he had resumed his intention, abandoned for a moment and quickly grasped again. His grip weakened, his hands drew away, rejecting the dreadful contact . . . But the stairs plunged on in a rapid vortex; the darkness thickened. He had no choice but to hold onto the support. The rope reappeared, asserted itself . . .

Borluut recovered, climbed towards the act. It was no longer the rope that was helping him; it seemed as if he were pulling the rope, carrying it to the top.

He reached the glass chamber, glancing vaguely at the keys, motionless as if they were dead, and at the tiny clock fixed to the wall, making the noise of its humble, regular life in time with the huge clock-face outside. Had he been anything in the tower other than that little beat of a human pulse? He hardly looked. His eyes were already elsewhere.

He had just had a sudden inspiration, at last finding the details of the 'act', which he had not wanted to envisage in advance, counting on the last minute. It came when he thought of the bells, the great bells he wanted to see again, to call by their names in their dormitories, caress with a farewell hand, the bells that had been his grave friends, the trusty tombs of his sorrows, a sure source of consolation.

What if one of them were now to be the tomb of his body? Yes! He would choose one of the huge bells; they have a ring inside, right at the top, to which the clapper is attached. That was where he would tie the rope, a very short piece so that he would disappear completely in the dark abyss where no one would find him for a long time, perhaps never. What joy to end deep inside one of the bells he loved so much!

Which one would he choose? The great bells were on the top floor, on the platform reached by the final few stairs, only thirteen. As he was about to start his climb he thought of the unlucky number; this time he did not hesitate, but resolutely set out on the number that guards death. He was in a hurry. The great bells appeared, towering over him, eternally restless. An incessant quivering filled the room with reverberation. Borluut saw the Bell of Lust again. He looked on it as his examination of conscience. It had been the sin of the bells and the sin of his life. Listening to it had made him lose his way. He had yielded to the temptation of the flesh, fallen into the trap that is woman. He had loved bodies instead of loving the town alone. Having betrayed his ideal meant he would not see its fulfilment in the moment of death. He recalled van Hulle's ecstatic end: 'They have chimed!' He would not see the beauty of Bruges made reality since he had not devoted himself to it exclusively. It was the fault of the obscene bell, which continued to obsess him. At that very moment it was calling out to him. It was trying to tempt him once more, and to the worst sin: the rope was like a lover, with it even death became a sensual delight, so let him die within its bronze dress, mingling with the ancient orgy . . .

Horrified, Borluut turned away.

A little farther along the venerable bell that rings out the hours presented itself, immense, dark, a silent abyss which would swallow him up entirely. He sensed that that was his goal and hastened his preparations, calm, thinking of God, meticulous and swift, his own executioner.

And he went under the bell like the flame under the candle-snuffer.

On that day and all the following days the carillon sounded, the hymns and the hours started up again, played by a mechanism, the aerial concert took flight, wreathing its garland of melancholy round noble souls, the ancient gables, the white necks of the swans, without anyone in the ungrateful town sensing that henceforward there was – a soul in the bells.

Recommended Reading

If you enjoyed reading *The Bells of Bruges* and would like to read another book by Georges Rodenbach we have published *Bruges-la-Morte* and in 2009 we will publish a collection of his short stories.

There are other books on our list which should appeal to you if you like the books by Georges Rodenbach:

Là-Bas – J.-K. Huysmans
Parisian Sketches – J.-K. Huysmans
Marthe – J.-K. Huysmans
The Cathedral – J.-K. Huysmans
En Route – J.-K. Huysmans
The Oblate – J.-K. Huysmans
Lucio's Confession – Mario de Sa-Carneiro
The Golem – Gustav Meyrink
The Prussian Bride –Yuri Buida
Paris Noir – Jacques Yonnet

These can be bought from your local bookshop or online from amazon.co.uk or direct from Dedalus. Please write to **Cash Sales, Dedalus Limited, 24–26, St Judith's Lane, Sawtry, Cambs, PE28 5XE**. For further details of the Dedalus list please go to our website www.dedalusbooks.com or write to us for a catalogue

Bruges-la-Morte – Georges Rodenbach

'Dedalus should be treasured: a small independent publisher that regularly produces works of European genius at which the behemoths wouldn't sniff. If the corporations did care to look at this new work, they would find, on the surface, a precursor to W G Sebald, a Symbolist vision of the city that lays the way for Aragon and Joyce, and a macabre story of obsessive love and transfiguring horror that is midway between Robert Browning and Tod Browning. Bruges, "an amalgam of greyish drowsiness", is the setting and spur; Hugues is a widower who finds a dancer nearly identical to his lost love. "Nearly" is here the operative word. This is a little masterpiece, from a brave publisher.'
Stuart Kelly in Scotland on Sunday

'A widower of five years, Hugues wanders Bruges in mourning. Heavy with a spectral misery, Rodenbach's symbolist novel, first published in France in 1892, is a compelling albeit flawed work. As Alan Hollinghurst remarks in his introduction, it is a novel "by turns crude and subtle", but although not a classic, it is also significantly more than a curiosity. There is an opiatic quality to the writing which at its best hovers on poetry's border. Hugues's relationship with the dancer who closely resembles his dead wife provides the plot, but the book's real heart lies in the descriptions of Bruges itself, and its "amalgam of greyish drowsiness".'
Chris Power in The Times

'In this Symbolist work, mirrors and metaphors take on a special significance. Rodenbach makes a case for the "indefinable power" of resemblance, appealing to the two contradictory needs of human nature: habit and novelty'. Metaphor – like translation, it might be said – endows old worlds with new life. Resemblance is revealed to be a life, however, just as words are lies, merely metaphors for the concepts they represent. The only assured resemblance Rodenbach can foresee is death, and accordingly the fear of death pervades the novel, deepened by the many reflecting surfaces.
Daniel Starza-Smith in The Times Literary Supplement

£6.99   ISBN 978 1 903517 23 9   166p   B. Format

Là-Bas – J.-K.Huysmans

'As with most of Huysmans' books, the pleasure in reading is not necessarily from its overarching plot-line, but in set pieces, such as the extraordinary sequences in which Gilles de Rais wanders through a wood that suddenly metamorphoses into a series of copulating organic forms, the justly famous word-painting of Matthias Grunewald's Crucifixion altar-piece, or the brutally erotic scenes, crackling with sexual tension, between Durtal and Madame Chantelouve. If it is about any-thing, *Là-Bas* is about Good and Evil. This enlightening new translation will be especially useful to students of literature.'
      Beryl Bainbridge in The Spectator

'The protagonist, Durtal, is investigating the life of Gilles de Rais, mass-murderer and unlikely – or not so unlikely – companion-in-arms of Joan of Arc. Long meditation on the nature of art, guilt, the satanic and the divine take him to a black mass. This superb new translation by Brendan King vividly recalls the allusive, proto-expressionist vigour of the original; images snarl and spring at the reader.'
      Murrough O'Brien in The Independent on Sunday

'The classic tale of satanism and sexual obsession in nineteenth-century Paris, in an attractive new edition. Strong meat for diseased imaginations.'
      Time Out

'Sex, satanism and alchemy are the themes of this cult curio, which understandably caused shock waves in the Parisian literary world when it was first published in 1891. Its antihero Durtal, is researching a book on the 15th-century child murderer Gilles de Rais. Soon enough, his studies lead him to all sorts of unspeakable deeds and occults rituals. This Gothic shocker is not for the faint-hearted.'
      Jerome Boyd Maunsell in The Times

£8.99   ISBN 978 1 873982 74 7   294p   B. Format

Parisian Sketches – J.-K. Huysmans

'No one, not even Toulouse-Lautrec, was so tireless a tracker of Paris's genius loci as Huysmans. Like many of his radical contemporaries, he was obsessed by the idea of beauty within the ugliness of back-street Paris, by the thought that the distortions of depravity presented a truer picture of our spiritual nature than conventional religion or revolutionary excess. The excellent introduction to these cameos show how Huysmans saw his art as complementary to the painter's.'
Murrough O'Brien in The Independent on Sunday

'First published in the 1880s, this collection of atmospheric journalism reveals the great decadent ("nature is only interesting when sick and distressed") moving from a broadly naturalistic, almost Dickensian style; as in a 1879 account of the Folies Bergere; to the heightened subjectivity of " Nightmare", inspired by Odilon Redon: "blurred infusoria, vague flagellates, bizarre protoplasms". An enthusiastic flaneur (if that's not too much of a contradiction). Huysmans created evocative prose-pictures of Parisian life; a visit to the barber, a gloomy railway café, a chestnut-seller; that merit comparison with the pictures of Caillebotte, Degas and Atget.'
Christopher Hirst in the Independent

'There's a vicious little piece about the Poplar Inn by the blighted river Bievre, which Huysmans conned himself would be a theatre-set-like homely hostelry with tart local wine, and was of course a mouldering dump dispensing big-brewery donkey-piss. Huysmans was a genuine flaneur – no posing and no lounging, he was up and out every day filling notebooks with info we wouldn't otherwise now know about, such as the varied erotic odours of the female armpit before the invention of antiperspirant.'
VR in the Guardian

£6.99   ISBN 978 1 903517 47 5   196p   B. Format

Marthe – J.-K. Huysmans

'Huysmans was part of Zola's coterie of naturalist writers driven by a desire to break from the dominance of romantic fiction. Certainly this tale set in a brothel, his debut novel banned at publication in his native France in 1876, would be fertile ground for such a venture. The translation, its first in 50 years, is wonderfully bawdy and a fine tribute to a great work.'
The Herald

'Originally published in 1876, this is a translation of the pioneering French classic. *Marthe* became Huysmans' landmark novel, culminating a Parisian demimonde setting with the portrayal of a would-be-actress, turned prostitute. Unique in its day as one of the earliest to deal with the theme of sex in exchange for money. Prepare to be led into some of the lowest dens and dives in the whole of Paris to be told the tale of Marthe and her brief relationship, ultimately doomed from the start.'
Buzz Magazine

'Flitting from brothel to theatre to kept mistress, with the threat of utter destitution never lifting. Marthe's sad existence crushes her natural spirits into apathy. Brendan King's slangy translation does bring out the vivid, earthy language of the 19th-century demi-monde.'
Scotland on Sunday

'It is a tragic novel, and sorrowful in part, as one would expect of a prostitute's tale in the nineteenth century and includes infant mortality, starvation, and poverty. However, Huysmans's beautiful portrayal of Marthe, a young woman of the night, is both sympathetic, and incredibly modern. The wonderful way in which he writes eclipses the traditional boudoir scenes of the era. One can almost touch the wallpaper, smell the musk of body sweat and alcohol, and lives the lives of those complex and very colourful characters.'
Jan Birks in The Erotic Review

£6.99   ISBN 978 1 903517 47 5   149p   B. Format

Paris Noir – Jacques Yonnet

'Concentrating on the seedy area around Rue Mouffetard, Yonnet reveals the dark side of the City of Light in the 1940s in this "secret history of a city".The street life of the Left Bank ticks on much as normal during the Occupation, though Léopoldie the tart stops turning tricks because "the green German uniform does not suit her complexion". Keep-on-Dancin', the killer with a fondness for history, rules the roost. Though describing himself as "sceptical, disillusioned, cynical", Yonnet casually dispatches a traitor in the Resistance. This is film noir in book form.'

Christopher Hirst in The Independent

'Yonnet evokes a wonderful and frightening world that lurks in the dark interstices of the City of Light: beggars, whores and poets, people who are quick to draw a knife or cast a spell, and are completely foreign to notions of 'responsible' drinking and sexual behaviour. The Old Man Who Appears After Midnight, Tricksy-Pierrot, the Watchmaker of Backward-Running Time and many others haunt a warren of streets and stews where supernatural events are frequent: a vicious one-eyed ginger tom is reincarnated as a murderous lover; a gypsy curse putrefies a hostile hostelry.

What makes Yonnet's memoir so special is the way the real and fantastic meet. The secrets of Paris play a role in the struggle against the Germans and their collaborators. Thus, the occultist spiv Keep-on-Dancin' initiates Yonnet to a "psychic circuit" that enables him to unmask a Gestapo informer in "the room where only the truth can be told".

Yonnet portrays Paris as a character in her own right: the city is "edgy", the Seine "sulks". The geography determines the behaviour of its inhabitants, and will live on after their deaths. Certain névralgique points in the city incite Parisians to raise barricades, be it during revolutions or the Liberation of 1944. But, like François Villon and Charles Baudelaire, Yonnet conveys the fragility of things.'

Gavin Bond in Scotland on Sunday

£9.99   ISBN 978 1 903517 48 2   280p   B. Format

The Prussian Bride – Yuri Buida

'The Kaliningrad region is in an odd geographical and historical situation. The region itself is only recently Russian – it was once East Prussia and its Russian inhabitants replaced the indigenous German population after the Second World War. Yuri Buida's magnificent collection of stories about his home town reflects these anomalies and presents a powerful and hilarious meditation on dislocated identities. Everything here is transformed, but only to give a greater force to the depiction of human suffering and joys. The whole effect is of a people's imagination confined by historical and geographical forces bursting forth in Rabelaisian splendour, without losing the stoicism that enabled them to endure the hardships of Communism. The stories show an ironic awareness of the power and dangers of self-deception, while seeing it as the only way of living a coherent life.

Buida's earlier novel, *Zero Train* (2001), was also powerful, but the theme of history's power to fragment ordinary lives works better in short-story format than in a continuous narrative. As we read through the stories in *The Prussian Bride*, we get a Brueghel-like picture of a community held together by ragged threads. The families in these stories are disjointed, cobbled together from casually adopted orphans and catatonic or otherwise absent wives and husbands. As in *Zero Train*, there is a sustained engagement with the absurd fantasies of self-empowerment that men construct to cope with their political impotence, but there is also more obvious engagement here with a range of women's characters, some suffering silently, others taking control of life and their appetites.

The form of the stories is wonderfully varied, and the different registers are brilliantly captured by the translator, Oliver Ready. Perhaps the most effective are the longer ones such as "Rita Schmidt Whoever". Yet here, as in some of the more lyrical miniature stories, it is the casual references to the town's life, often fuelled by a delighted cloacal fascination, that gives the collection its particular character.'

Tom MacFaul in The Times Literary Supplement

£9.99   ISBN 978 1 903517 06 2   363p   B. Format

The Golem – Gustav Meyrink

'A superbly atmospheric story set in the old Prague ghetto featuring the Golem, a kind of rabbinical Frankenstein monster, which manifests every 33 years in a room without a door. Stranger still, it seems to have the same face as the narrator. Made into a film in 1920, this extraordinary book combines the uncanny psychology of doppelganger stories with expressionism and more than a little melodrama; Meyrink's old Prague, like Dickens's London is one of the great creation of city writing, an eerie, claustrophobic and fantastical underworld where anything can happen.'

    Phil Baker in The Sunday Times

'This is a fever of a book. An hallucination, a wild writer's improvisation on an old Jewish fairy tale. The Golem reveals its secrets in the lives of murderers and thieves, not seers. Its sufferings are not devilish torments, but bitter sex games played in the shadows of Ghetto corridors. There is no sweetness in the low-life, no salvation in a condemned man's understanding. There is not a letter of sentimentality in *The Golem*. For an esoteric classic Meyrink's novel is short on mysticism and long on materialism. It does for Prague what Joyce did for Dublin and Bely for St.Petersburg.'

    Phil Smith in Venue

'The book is profoundly unsettling, shifting from dream to wakefulness. Pernath, the amnesiac, is searching for the key to his past, looking for the door to his memories. The ghetto is a winding cityscape populated by extraordinary characters, many of which have their own secrets which Pernath attempts to untangle. The novel reminds of the London of Dickens's darker novels, as well as Kafka.'

    Sarah Singleton in The Third Alternative

£6.99   **ISBN 978 1 873982 91 4**   262p   **B.Format**